ALSO BY BATTLES & BROWNE

THE ALEXANDRA POE THRILLERS

POE

ALSO BY ROBERT GREGORY BROWNE

THE TRIAL JUNKIES THRILLERS

TRIAL JUNKIES
TRIAL JUNKIES 2: NEGLIGENCE

STANDALONES

KISS HER GOODBYE
WHISPER IN THE DARK
KILL HER AGAIN
DOWN AMONG THE DEAD MEN
THE PARADISE PROPHECY

ALSO BY BRETT BATTLES

THE JONATHAN QUINN THRILLERS

THE CLEANER
THE DECEIVED
SHADOW OF BETRAYAL (US)/THE UNWANTED (UK)
THE SILENCED
BECOMING QUINN
THE DESTROYED
THE COLLECTED
THE ENRAGED

THE LOGAN HARPER THRILLERS

LITTLE GIRL GONE
EVERY PRECIOUS THING

THE PROJECT EDEN THRILLERS

SICK
EXIT NINE
PALE HORSE
ASHES
EDEN RISING

STANDALONES

THE PULL OF GRAVITY
NO RETURN

THE TROUBLE FAMILY CHRONICLES
(For Younger Readers)

HERE COMES MR. TROUBLE

TAKEDOWN

An Alexandra Poe Thriller

BRETT BATTLES

and

ROBERT GREGORY BROWNE

BRAUN HAUS MEDIA

TAKEDOWN

ONE

THEY CHOSE A Wednesday in March for their day of atonement.

Malina had told him that people rarely called in sick on Wednesdays, and the early morning commuter lines into Times Square were bound to be elbow to asshole—standing room only.

"When the blast is triggered," she said, "we'll send a message to the world it'll never forget."

Ivan didn't argue. He had only agreed to do this because he was in love with Malina. He didn't hate America the way she did, and he hadn't really cared when Kosovo declared its independence five years ago—he was barely thirteen at the time. But Malina was passionate about her beliefs, and that passion translated into a dynamic, all-encompassing charisma that Ivan found hard to resist.

The night before, she had said, "We should be proud, Ivan. What we're about to do will change everything. Everything."

Ivan wasn't so sure, but who was he to challenge her? He had never been much of a thinker, and when he tried, he too often found himself unable to articulate the confused thoughts he did have. Better simply to shut up and listen and try to follow along as Malina lectured him on the dangerous tyranny of the US government and the willful ignorance of its arrogant, self-centered citizens.

Ivan had once tried to point out that *they* were citizens as well, both born to naturalized parents less than twenty years ago, but that didn't matter to Malina.

"Where and when you were born isn't important," she told him.

They may have looked and acted like most young Americans, but they were Serbian by blood, and would forever be linked to a part of the world Ivan had never visited.

And never wanted to, when it came right down to it.

Malina, on the other hand, had been to Serbia twice now. Had gone to Belgrade to visit her uncle Radovan for two summers in a row, and returned to New York full of ideas and plans and that irrepressible passion Ivan found so captivating.

Radovan was a radical Serbian nationalist who believed a conspiracy between the United States and Germany had been instrumental in tearing their country apart, and his desire for retribution was no less potent now than it was in 1999.

Ivan had never heard Malina say it, but he suspected it was her uncle's idea to bomb the subway train. She and Radovan were in regular contact, and it was Radovan who had told her whom to trust and what parts to buy and how to assemble the bomb, which looked nothing like that crude pressure-cooker device those two fools in Boston had built.

There was talk of cell phones and arming switches and a lot of technical terms that flew right past Ivan's ever-stymied intellect, but he didn't suppose the mechanics of the thing mattered all that much. What counted was what it could *do*.

And he knew it would not be pretty.

Part of him didn't relish the idea of hurting so many people, but Malina had gone to great lengths to assure him that those who would die this morning were far from innocent. Their own complacency, their stubborn unwillingness to see, their continued apathy toward a government that manipulated and controlled and spied and murdered, made them just as culpable as the highest placed government official.

"Their hands," she told him, "are stained with the very same blood. The blood of the Serbian families that were slaughtered by NATO bombs."

Ivan sometimes wondered how much of this was Malina speaking and how much was Radovan.

But it probably didn't matter. Her mind was made up and he wasn't about to try to stop her.

"The only way to awaken these people from their self-induced stupor," she continued, "is to show them exactly how it feels to watch your loved ones die."

They drove to one of the smaller rail yards in the city, the ribbons of track and rows of dormant subway trains illuminated by a few tall lampposts and an anemic wash of moonlight.

Shortly past three a.m., Malina pulled her dilapidated Ford van to a curb at the far side of the lot, grabbed her backpack, and reached behind her for the aluminum suitcase she had assembled just prior to the drive.

"Let *me*," Ivan said, then quickly climbed out and rolled the side door open.

"Careful," she told him as he stretched an arm toward the case. "Be very careful."

He knew by the almost imperceptible tremor in her voice that she was nervous. He himself didn't feel nervous so much as pumped full of adrenaline, his hands and body unable to keep still, needing to move. But he froze at her command, willed himself to be calm, then took hold of the suitcase handle and carefully lifted it out.

Moments later they were walking along the perimeter of the yard, looking for the hole in the chain-link fence that Malina had made two days earlier. Ivan kept the suitcase at his side, doing his best to curb the natural instinct to let his arm swing, the nerves he had dismissed only seconds ago now a mild but incessant buzz in the pit of his stomach.

"Where is it?" he asked, suddenly wishing he hadn't volunteered to carry this thing.

"Almost there," Malina said, illuminating the fence with her miniature flashlight as they moved. She had used a pair of wire cutters from Ivan's garage to clip the links, readying the fence to be bent back for easy access to the yard.

When they came to the seventh fence post, nearly a block from where she had parked the van, she slowed and softly counted, stopping when she got to ten.

"Here," she said. "It should be here."

Studying the fence in the beam of her flashlight, she reached out, grabbed hold of one of the links, and pulled. A small section of the fence split apart, groaning faintly as she bent it back, creating a gap just large enough for Ivan to squeeze through. When she gestured him forward, he looked in at the tracks and the silent train cars and the squat cement building that housed the maintenance shop, and briefly considered telling her he had changed his mind.

What they were about to do was madness.

But the thought disappeared as quickly as it came, lost to whatever demon had made him want so desperately to please this woman.

"Hurry," she said with a hint of agitation. "Before someone sees us."

Though the yard seemed quiet—only a single security guard and a handful of repair personnel on duty at this early hour (or so Malina had been told)—Ivan heeded her command and carefully held the aluminum case in front of him as he ducked his head and stepped through the gap.

Malina followed and returned the fence to its original condition. When she was done, she pointed toward the subway trains in the distance.

Five rows, side by side.

"Choose," she said.

"Me?"

"They'll all be operational in less than three hours. Any one will do."

Being offered such a responsibility didn't sit well with Ivan. It forced him to think about the people who would occupy that train, each with a life that—barring the presence of a beautiful Serbian-American anarchist—was not all that different from his own. How many husbands and wives would sleep alone tonight? How many children would wake up tomorrow without a father or a mother? All because of the choice he'd made.

"Ivan?"

He pointed to the middle row.

"That one," he said, and started forward, wanting to get this done and be gone. He would struggle with his conscience later. Let Malina soothe him in bed.

She was very good at soothing him.

They moved together through the darkness, Malina's flashlight lighting the ground in front of them. The last thing Ivan wanted was to stumble with this suitcase in his hands.

Malina checked her watch and said, "We have to hurry. The guard will be making his rounds soon."

Ivan frowned. "How do you know all this?"

"You think we're working alone? We have friends, Ivan. All over the world. Always remember that."

"Yes, but..."

"Just hurry up. We need to get inside the train before the guard comes."

But as they stepped over a set of tracks and headed into the narrow passageway between two parked trains, the silhouette of a man appeared several yards in front of them.

"You!" he shouted. "Stop right there. Who *are* you?"

A beam of light cut through the darkness and lit up their faces. Ivan jerked to a halt, but, to his surprise, Malina did not. Instead, in a single, flowing motion, she took a step forward, slipped her backpack from her shoulder, and produced a pistol from inside, firing two shots in quick succession, the sound dulled by the attached silencer.

Ivan heard a groan as the guard's flashlight fell to the ground. Malina sprang forward, stepping over to where the man now lay. Without hesitation, she fired another shot into his head.

Oh, Jesus. She just killed him in cold blood.

Malina turned to Ivan and shone her miniature flashlight at him. "It had to be done," she said. "I couldn't let him radio for help."

Ivan stood there, unable to move, his legs trembling. Killing a train full of anonymous people from a remote location was a notion he could view in the abstract, but killing a man up close and in person was something else altogether.

The buzz in his stomach began to rise toward his chest and throat, carrying with it the chicken chow mein he and Malina had eaten for dinner. She must have sensed his dismay, because she moved toward him, her light still in his face.

"Pull it together, Ivan. Can you do that for me?"

He knew she had the gun in her other hand and wondered if she would use it on *him*. Swallowing bile, he nodded, vigorously, but couldn't make himself speak.

"You need to pull it together, all right? Put the suitcase down, very carefully, and help me move him inside." She gestured to the line of subway cars on their right.

Ivan nodded a second time, stooped down, and carefully set the suitcase on the ground. She gestured again and he joined her and took his first good look at the guard. The guy couldn't have been much older than they were. He had died with surprise on his face and dark round holes in his chest and forehead.

Ivan had never seen a dead man before, and the chow mein once again threatened to choke him.

"Are you good?" Malina asked. "I can't do this alone."

Ivan nodded a third time.

Malina studied him for a moment as if waiting for him to change his mind. When she seemed satisfied he wouldn't, she moved to the nearest subway car in his chosen row, and pried the doors open with a crowbar from her backpack.

"Grab his feet," she said as she returned to Ivan and the dead man.

Ivan didn't resist. What was the point? Still trembling, he grabbed hold of the guard's ankles as Malina took the man by the armpits. She counted *one-two-three* and they hefted the body, carried it through the open doorway into the sub-way car, and laid it on the floor.

"Get the case," she said.

The moment he returned with it, she took it from him and laid it flat on one of the plastic chairs in the middle of the car. Handing him her flashlight, she told him to shine it on the case, then popped the latches and swung the lid open, revealing the pipes full of explosives and the wires and the cell phone mounted to a small board in the center of it all.

The phone had been modified and given to her by one of her uncle's contacts—a burner, she'd called it. But a very special one.

"You call the number," she had explained the first time she'd shown him her creation. "The phone vibrates, the wires connect, and *boom*."

"You can call it from any phone?"

"Yes, from any phone. Anywhere."

Now, she flipped a small lever that looked like a miniature light switch mounted near the phone, then closed the lid, locked the case, and placed it on the floor under the seat.

She gestured to the body of the guard. "They're bound to start wondering about him at some point. We'll have to hide him somewhere in the yard and hope they—"

The ring of a cell phone cut her off.

Ivan flinched, thinking the sound had come from the suitcase, but then realized it was Malina's personal phone. She pulled it from her back pocket, looking as relieved as he felt. When she saw the name on the screen, she smiled and pressed a button, putting it on speakerphone so Ivan could hear.

"Uncle Radovan," she said. "I was hoping you'd call. We had some unexpected trouble, but we've just delivered the package and it's ready to go."

"That is good to know," a voice said, but it was clearly not the one Malina had been expecting. The accent sounded German.

"Who is this?" she demanded.

"People call me Valac."

"Who?"

"I am a friend of your Uncle's. Unfortunately, it seems he is very much in need of a lesson in proper business etiquette."

Malina looked alarmed. "What does that mean? What

have you done to him?"

"It means you pay your debts on time or you will be assessed a surtax. A very significant surtax. Something he is about to learn the hard way."

"I don't understand. What do my uncle's debts have to do with me? Have you done something to him?"

"I'm sorry," the voice said. "Do you mind if I call you back?"

"I—"

The line went dead and Malina remained crouched there, looking both exasperated and dumbfounded.

Ivan was about to ask her what was going on when her expression shifted, as if she had just thought of the solution to a very difficult puzzle, but found no comfort in the answer at all.

"Oh my God," she said. She jumped to her feet and shouted, her voice filled with panic, "Run, Ivan. Run! *Run!*"

But before either of them could take a single step, another cell phone rang—this one muffled by the aluminum case it was stored in.

Then the world around them exploded, tearing Ivan Kovac and the love of his short life into a thousand tiny pieces.

TWO

WHEN SHE WAS young, Alexandra Poe had often dreamed of working in a hospital, but *this* wasn't exactly what she'd had in mind.

The scrubs she wore were half a size too small and her shoes squeaked. And as she worked her way through the corridor, she felt uncomfortable and conspicuous, certain she wasn't blending in as well as they had hoped she would.

Fortunately, despite its age and current state of disrepair, Yardim Hastanesi was one of the busiest hospitals in all of Istanbul. Alex tried to convince herself that anyone watching —Yusuf Solak's bodyguards, for example—would see her as nothing more than another woman in hospital green.

Pretending to read the chart in her hands, she made her way to the elevator at the far end of the corridor. The uniformed guard who waited outside its open doors had undoubtedly been paid off by Solak. He was checking the credentials of anyone who attempted to board.

Alex kept her eyes on the chart and acted as if she hadn't noticed him, but he stopped her just short of stepping inside.

She smiled politely, hoping to disarm him a bit, but he was all business. He snapped his fingers and gestured to the ID card clipped to the lanyard around her neck.

She removed it and handed it to him.

As he studied it, he said in guttural Turkish, "Where are you headed?"

The words came out so quickly that Alex barely understood them.

In the months since she had associated herself with Stonewell International, she had spent her spare time taking crash courses in a multitude of languages. Her instructors had been surprised to discover she was something of a savant. What took most people weeks to learn took Alex only a matter of days, including conversational Turkish, which she had come very close to mastering—although not quite as close as she liked to believe.

"Where are you headed?" the guard repeated impatiently. "Which floor?"

She caught it this time and said, "The radiology lab on four." Istanbul was a melting pot and the small imperfections in her accent didn't seem to faze him. She pointed to the ID. "See? I'm an X-ray technician."

He studied the card again, then handed it back to her without expression and let her pass.

Alex heaved an inward sigh of relief and got on board, where two nurses, a doctor, and three civilians were waiting, none of them happy about the delay.

One of the nurses muttered something unintelligible and hit a button on the panel.

Friendly place.

The doors closed and Alex leaned past her, bypassed the button for the fourth floor and pressed six instead. The elevator car groaned and lurched into motion, a lumbering beast that wasn't any happier than its occupants. Alex waited patiently as the numbers above the door ticked off their progress.

The car stopped at floors two and five before finally landing on six.

When the doors rolled open, she was the only passenger left, which was just as well considering how crowded it was up here. Several patients lay on gurneys in the hallway, waiting for someone to attend to them. The hospital staffers chatting nearby seemed about as interested in these poor people as weary morgue attendants in a room full of corpses.

"I'm on the target's floor," she said quietly. The pen clipped to her breast pocket had an extremely sensitive microphone built into it.

"Good," Cooper said in her ear. "What's your ETA?"

"Half a minute, give or take. Deuce, are you in position?"

"Ready whenever you are, kid."

Alex threaded her way past the gurneys, giving one of the patients a reassuring pat, and moved down the corridor, headed in the direction of Room 633.

Yusuf Solak's room.

After grabbing a stray wheelchair, she pushed it in front of her as she rounded a corner and found herself in a much less crowded hallway—empty except for two casually dressed but very dangerous-looking men, who immediately eyed her with suspicion.

Solak's bodyguards. Both were JİT, Turkish Gendarmerie Intelligence, doing a bit of moonlighting on Solak's dime. Alex knew from the intel that there should be two more men inside the room, and another half dozen in various parts of the building, including the stairwell where Deuce was poised and ready to strike.

She pushed the wheelchair toward the bodyguards, offering a smile. One of them came forward and raised a hand, commanding her to "Halt."

When she did, he unceremoniously grabbed her by the elbow, shoved her against the nearest wall, and ran his hands along her sides and up and down her legs, coming perilously close to a molestation charge. She half expected him to order her to drop trou, but she was spared the indignity as he turned her around and decided instead to concentrate on her bra.

When he was done pawing her breasts, he took hold of her arm again and shoved her back toward the wheelchair.

"She's clean," he said to his partner. "Let her through."

The partner nodded and stepped aside, offering her a crude grin as he gestured toward the open doorway to Room 633. She could feel his gaze on her as she passed, no doubt studying her ass, and she hoped he stuck around long enough to let her wipe away that grin with a well-placed fist.

She was greeted at the doorway by another bodyguard, this one smaller than his colleagues but no less dangerous. "Who are *you*?" he said.

No trouble with comprehension this time.

"Enise," she told him. "From radiology. Mr. Karga is due for an X-ray."

As a security precaution, Solak had been admitted under the name Nazim Karga, his occupation listed as importer-exporter. What the hospital didn't know was that "Mr. Karga" exported terror, in many different forms. The network he commanded was responsible for a number of attacks on US and European targets, and had ties to the Taliban and several Islamist splinter groups in Iran, placing him on a number of wanted lists around the world.

As a result, Stonewell International, which specialized in fugitive retrieval, had been commissioned by the Department of Homeland Security to do a little exporting of its own. And because Alex was female and half Persian, allowing her to easily infiltrate the facility, she and her team had been tasked with grabbing Solak from his hospital bed and putting him on the next available transport out of the country.

Despite mixed feelings about her association with Stonewell, Alex had no misgivings whatsoever about the target. Slugs like Solak set her teeth on edge, and she was all too happy to be part of this acquisition.

The guy in the doorway frowned at her. "We weren't told about any X-rays."

"It's right here on the chart." Alex showed it to him.

He took it from her and flipped impatiently through the pages that had been expertly forged by Stonewell's Photoshop whizzes.

"This is indecipherable," he said. "What are all these numbers and abbreviations?"

"Things I spent many years in school to learn." She pointed to a line on the top page. "There it is, right there. AP and lateral CSRX, two o'clock." She checked her watch. "And if we don't hurry, he'll be late."

"Who ordered this?"

She pointed again. "That's there, too. Doctor Hasan."

Hasan was one of three doctors who had been caring for

Solak since his heart bypass a week earlier, and as far as Alex knew, he hadn't ordered a damn thing. But it would take the guards a while to figure this out, and all she needed was to get inside Solak's room. Once Deuce did his thing, the rest should fall into place.

That was the theory, at least.

The bodyguard sighed impatiently, handed back the chart, then gestured Alex through the doorway.

Bingo.

Another bodyguard seated in a chair near a curtained-off bed rose to his feet as the smaller one pointed at Alex. "Watch her."

Alex stood there looking as submissive as possible as he pulled a phone from his pocket and dialed. Glancing at the bed curtain, she could feel the adrenaline starting to pump through her veins.

Her target was only feet away.

She said, "Is it all right to prep the patient while you call?"

She had raised her voice a bit, to make sure Cooper and Deuce could hear her. It was their signal to begin phase two of the operation—distract and snatch.

"Stay still," the second man said and took a step toward her. He looked as though he wanted to smack her around a little just for the fun of it, but before he could turn that thought into action, the piercing scream of a fire alarm blasted through the hallway, courtesy of Cooper.

The two men exchanged startled looks, the first lowering his phone as the second one planted a hand on Alex's chest, and shoved her into a nearby chair. "Don't move."

"But we can't stay here," she said, feigning concern. "We need to evacuate."

"Don't move or I'll hurt you."

Alex tried to look appropriately terrified and stayed put.

Right on schedule, the radio on the smaller man's hip squawked. "Intruder on three. Northwest stairwell."

Deuce.

The two bodyguards exchanged another glance as the

smaller one ripped the walkie free from his belt and hit the call button. "How many?"

"Just one. Big guy. He took out Terzi on two and he's headed this way."

The smaller one turned to the guard eyeballing Alex and shouted over the blare of the fire alarm. "Go. Now. Take Burakgazi and Yilmaz with you."

"What about her?"

"She's a woman. Leave her to me. Now go!"

The second one nodded and darted into the hall. Alex heard him shouting instructions to the other two men, as the one who'd stayed behind shot forward and grabbed her by the throat.

"You think we're stupid? You think we weren't expecting this?"

One can dream, Alex thought, then jammed the edge of the chart into his forearm, knocking his hand free.

As he stumbled back, she jumped to her feet, grabbed him by the collar, then kneed him in the balls and shoved him into the nearest wall. He reached for the gun on his hip as he fell to the floor, but before he could raise it, Alex kicked the weapon from his hand and moved in. She swung a right hook into his jaw and snapped his head to the side, knocking him out cold.

With no time to waste, Alex wheeled around and grabbed the bed curtain, wondering why Solak hadn't uttered a word of alarm during any of this. Could he be that far gone? But as soon as she pulled the curtain aside, she got her answer.

The bed was empty.

Shit.

She checked the bathroom and found it empty, too, but wasn't surprised. The twerp on the floor was right. They *weren't* stupid. This room was a decoy. They had Solak stashed somewhere else, maybe even another floor, and *that* was where the other three bodyguards were headed.

Chastising herself for her own stupidity, Alex darted into the hallway. The three men had a head start, but couldn't have gotten too far.

"Deuce, Cooper, do you read me?"

They both answered in the affirmative, then Cooper said, "I heard the tussle. You okay?"

"Fine, except they pulled a bait and switch. Solak's not here. We're gonna have to improvise."

"So what else is new?" Deuce said. "Tell me what I'm looking for."

"Three hostiles. Maybe more. They should be headed in Solak's direction."

"I'm on the fifth-floor landing. No sign of activity in here."

"Nothing on the CCTV cams, either," Cooper said, "but there're a couple dead feeds on your floor, Alex. They must've cut 'em. They're probably still around there somewhere."

"Roger," she said. "I'm checking it out now."

The fire alarm continued to ring as Alex rounded a corner to find the main corridor flooded with staff and patients in the middle of a full-scale evac. In hospitals this size, building-wide evacuations were unwieldy and impractical, so the alarms were often localized, affecting only the floors closest to the potential threat. Unfortunately, that didn't help Alex. What they'd hoped would be a distraction was now an obstacle, and an already crowded hallway was twice as packed now, a sea of bodies in motion, all wanting to get the hell out of there.

She quickly scanned the crowd and saw nothing out of the ordinary—an orderly helping a child in a walker, a nurse pushing an elderly gray-haired woman in a wheelchair, several staffers rolling gurneys carrying patients still attached to IV drips. There was a sense of organized urgency as they all worked their way down the corridor.

Then Alex spotted him, the bodyguard who had leered at her, disappearing down an intersecting hallway at the far end. Picking up her pace, she threaded her way through the crowd, which was akin to traveling the I-695 beltway during rush hour back home.

But as she neared the nurse and the old woman in the wheelchair, something out of the ordinary registered at the periphery of her vision—a bulge in the nurse's scrubs at the small of her back. Either she was hiding a tail or that bulge was a holster and gun.

Alex fell back slightly, nearly bumped into a moving gurney, and stared intently at the old woman in the wheelchair.

The gray hair was a wig.

Son of a bitch. Solak.

"Deuce," she said quietly, hoping she could be heard over the sound of the alarm, "you'd better get your ass up to six. I've spotted the target."

"I'm right behind you. And speaking of asses, did anybody mention those scrubs you're wearing look a little small?"

Alex grimaced. "Thanks for reminding me. The target's in the wheelchair about two meters ahead, dressed like an old woman, and the nurse pushing him is sporting an SOB holster and weapon."

"Naughty nurses with guns. Be still my heart."

"One of the hostiles is running point around the corner," Alex continued, "but I don't have a position on the others, so watch your back."

The crowd had nearly stopped moving now, slowed by a bottleneck at the end of the hall.

"Roger that," Deuce said. "We've got a pathology lab to our right, and if the BPs are more reliable than our intel, there should be a small freight elevator at the rear of the lab. Cooper, can you be ready to party in two?"

"I'll be there," Cooper told him.

"Okay, Alex, I've got your flank. Make your move and make it smooth."

"Roger," she said, then weaved past another gurney and a tight group of patients and positioned herself directly behind the nurse pushing the wheelchair, almost close enough to spoon. After a quick look around, she reached forward, slipped her hand under the nurse's scrub top, and lo and behold, discovered the woman wasn't hiding a tail.

Alex grabbed the grip of the weapon. "I don't think you're supposed to be carrying this in here."

As the nurse started to react, Alex ripped the weapon free and jammed her heel into the back of the woman's left knee. The joint buckled and the nurse went down with a grunt. Alex sidestepped the fall and yanked the wig off Solak's head, shoving the nose of the pistol—a SIG Pro SP—into his upper back. "Get up."

Someone nearby screamed and heads swiveled in their direction. Grabbing hold of Solak's hospital gown, Alex yanked him to his feet, knowing that if the other bodyguards hadn't already been closing in, they would be now. She shoved him toward a door about three meters to her right, marked PATHOLOGY AND LABORATORY MEDICINE.

She felt a sudden rush of movement behind her as a hand grabbed for her shoulder. But before it could fully connect, its owner grunted and hit the floor.

"Go! Go!" Deuce said, taking his place beside her.

They slammed through the door, pushing Solak in front of them, and worked their way through a maze of tables and microscopes and machines and racks of test tubes filled with blood. Alex scanned the lab and spotted a set of elevator doors down a short hallway at the rear of the room.

"At least something's going right," she murmured, nudging Solak in that direction.

Behind them, two more bodyguards burst into the lab—Alex's friends from the hall outside Solak's room. She heard the sharp cough of a suppressor and glass shattered nearby. Deuce whipped around and raised his own weapon, returning fire.

One of the bodyguards went down as the other—the grinner—dove for safety behind a lab table, and then came up firing on the other side.

Bullets whizzed past Alex's head as she shoved Solak to the floor, then crouched and spun, squeezing off two quick rounds. The SIG wasn't silenced and the shots echoed loudly. One went stray, but the other hit its mark, the slug ripping through the grinner's shoulder in a burst of blood. He grunted in pain and slammed backward into a rack of test tubes, and they toppled over and shattered around him, splattering a dozen or more blood specimens across the linoleum.

Alex grabbed a handful of Solak's gown and yanked him to his feet. "Hurry it up."

As they shoved him toward the elevator again, Solak spoke for the first time. In English, no less. "You realize this will all come to nothing. You risk your life for what?"

"A chance to put you on a plane to nowhere," Alex said.

"You're American, yes? Private contractors?"

Neither Alex nor Deuce responded. Reaching the elevator, Alex pressed the down button, hoping this one was faster than the beast she rode in earlier.

"Why else would you be here?" Solak went on. "It is obvious you haven't yet received word."

Deuce frowned. "About what?"

"I have negotiated terms with your government just this morning. I am no longer a wanted man. Not by the United States, at least."

Deuce snorted. "Nice try, dipshit. At least you get points for creativity."

"You doubt me," he said. "And that is understandable. But be warned that if you harm me, there will be reprisals."

"Too bad you didn't warn that busload of kids you killed in London," Alex told him and looked at Deuce. "Are you buying this bullshit?"

"I've never been a big fan of fairytales," Deuce said as the elevator doors slid open.

Alex shoved Solak a little harder than she needed to and he stumbled forward, hitting the elevator wall. "Oops. My bad."

They stepped inside and the doors closed behind them. Once the elevator lurched into motion, Deuce said, "Cooper, we've got the package ready for delivery. Are you in position?"

There was a long pause.

"Shane?"

Still no answer.

Alex and Deuce exchanged a look, and as the elevator came to the ground floor, they braced themselves, weapons ready.

The doors slid open to reveal a loading dock, and the ambulance Cooper had been driving parked haphazardly in one of the bays. Cooper stood outside the vehicle, looking glum, surrounded by a phalanx of men in suits and dark glasses—none of them Turks—several of them pointing weapons directly at Alex and Deuce.

Americans. No doubt about it.

"Step out of the elevator and release your prisoner," one of them said. "And put your weapons on the ground."

Alex frowned. "What the hell is this?"

"Just do as they say," Cooper told her. "The op's been burned. They're letting Solak go."

Alex couldn't believe what she was hearing. "*What?*"

"Step out of the elevator," the American repeated, "and put your weapons on the ground."

Then Solak smiled and said, "Not a fairytale after all."

Alex barely spoke a word on the plane ride home. She felt used and abused and didn't like being taken advantage of.

A phone call from McElroy, the op coordinator at Stonewell International, had confirmed that Solak had indeed cut a deal with the US government and was no longer on their hit list. The reasons were classified, but McElroy guessed Solak was more valuable to the intelligence community as an ally than an enemy.

McElroy had apologized for the confusion, and explained that the DHS had somehow forgotten to inform Stonewell of the change until the operation was well under way.

"Screw them," Alex said. "And screw you, too. Deuce and I almost got our heads shot off because of their incompetence."

"It happens," McElroy told her. "We'll try to do better next time."

"Next time? Don't count on it. I'm done."

"But you've only just started, Alex, and you've already proven to be a valuable asset to the organization."

"Lucky me," she said, and hung up on him.

Now, as the Stonewell jet carried them home, she thought about the slippery nature of politics and shifting allegiances and how she didn't much like it. One minute you're hunting a man down and the next you're in bed with him. But what could possibly justify cozying up to a guy who had been responsible for the deaths of so many innocent people? Alex didn't care what kind of cards he was holding, Solak should not be a free man. The fact that he *was* free royally pissed her off.

"You okay?"

She turned with a start, unaware Cooper had taken the seat next to her. They had served together in Baghdad but hadn't kept in contact after her discharge, in large part because she had blamed him for a mission that had gone south and gotten people killed. But the blame was misplaced, and she had finally come to terms with what had happened.

Shane had been instrumental in helping Stonewell recruit her. In fact, he was part of the reason she had agreed to sign on.

"Alex?"

She tried a smile, but lacked the conviction. "I'm fine. Just trying to figure out what the hell I'm doing here."

"Same as the rest of us. Making the world a better place."

"Do you really believe that?"

"It's on the company brochure, isn't it?"

She laughed in spite of herself, some of her anger easing. "I wish I could be as nonchalant as you."

He shrugged. "I'm good at hiding my rage. The right amount of alcohol and regular vacations and you'll get good at it, too."

"I don't really drink and vacations aren't my thing."

"Not true," he said. "What about the trip you're taking to the Keys?"

She shook her head. "Strictly business. I've got some real estate I want to get rid of. I can use the extra money to help take care of Danny."

Danny was her older brother. He had Down Syndrome and lived at a special-needs home outside of Baltimore. Alex had always felt bad about placing him there, but with their parents gone and the nature of her work, she had done what she'd needed to do.

"When do you leave?" Cooper asked.

"Couple days. I want to visit with Danny a little. Why?"

He shrugged again and seemed to hesitate. "I don't know. I thought you might want company."

Alex was surprised. In all the months they'd been working together, this was the first time Cooper had made such a suggestion, and she didn't know what to think of it.

She shook her head again. "It's just a quick trip. A day or two. I'm gonna meet with the buyer's agent, pack the place up, and head home."

"You don't need any help?"

"No. But I appreciate the offer."

He gave her a wan smile, nodded, then patted her hand and got to his feet. "Trust me, you'll get used to dealing with the political bullshit. I'd tell you we're all just pieces on a chess board, but that's a cliché." He paused. "It's probably closer to checkers anyway."

"I didn't mean to chase you off," she said.

"No worries. You look as if you could use some sleep, and I wouldn't mind catching a few Zs myself. If you need me, I'll be in coach."

Then he turned and worked his way down the aisle.

THREE

THE MEETING WITH Mr. Gray took place where it always did.

Gray had chosen it the first time he and McElroy did business, over five years ago, and neither had found a suitable reason to make a change. Besides, McElroy had always liked the Museum of Natural History and often came here when he was in town. He was particularly enamored of the Ancient Egyptian exhibit, with its alabaster vases and ornate coffins and mummified corpses representing a belief that the road to eternal life was just beyond death's doorway.

McElroy himself didn't believe in eternal life. He had decided long ago this was as good as it got and he might as well make the best of all he'd been blessed with.

As always, Mr. Gray was waiting for him in the Hall of Paleobiology. McElroy wasn't sure why Gray had chosen this particular exhibit, because the man never seemed to show much interest in the fossilized dinosaur skeletons or the collection of amphibians and reptiles. It was, McElroy assumed, simply a place to meet that was out of earshot of anyone who might take an interest in what they had to say.

Mr. Gray stood in front of the Tyrannosaurus rex and was carefully cleaning his glasses with a handkerchief as McElroy approached. "I heard about what happened in Istanbul. Pretty nasty business, that."

McElroy nodded. "You might explain to me why the US government is so anxious to cozy up to a known terrorist."

Gray shrugged. "I wasn't in the loop on that op, but one man's terrorist is another man's freedom fighter. Besides, since when have you cared about who we choose to do business with, as long as you collect your incentive?"

"That's just it," McElroy said. "Stonewell put up quite a bit of money for the operation."

"And I'm sure you'll be adequately reimbursed. But I didn't ask you here to talk about your budget concerns. I have an acquisition for you. One that should make up for this unfortunate business in Turkey."

"Oh? What is it?"

Mr. Gray tucked away the handkerchief, slipped his glasses on, and smiled. "Shall we walk?"

As they moved slowly through the hall, pretending to be interested in the various exhibits, Gray said, "You remember the rail yard bombing in New York six months ago?"

McElroy nodded. "I heard it was a couple of meth heads who had some kind of grudge against the MTA and decided to go DIY."

"There was nothing DIY about it."

"Oh?"

"The device was assembled by someone who was very well trained."

"So they weren't meth heads after all?"

Gray gave him a tight smile. "We felt it prudent to let the public believe that it was the work of a couple of disgruntled morons." He paused. "The truth is that one of the bombers was a young woman by the name of Malina Zupan."

"Doesn't ring a bell," McElroy said. "Croatian?"

Gray shook his head. "Serbian American. Her parents immigrated here from Belgrade before she was born. But she's been on the watch list for a while now. Her uncle is a radical Serbian nationalist whose wife and daughter were killed in a hospital strike during Operation Noble Anvil in ninety-nine. He's held a grudge against the US ever since."

"Can't say I blame him."

"Maybe so, but he's dangerous and unfriendly and Malina visited him in Belgrade two summers in a row. So, after the mishap in the rail yard, we naturally thought it might be a good idea to visit him ourselves."

"And?"

"His procurement wasn't particularly difficult, but it did take us a while to get him to talk. It turns out that what we thought was an accidental detonation wasn't an accident at all."

"You mean they *meant* it to go off when no one was around?"

"Oh, it wasn't set off by Malina or her partner in crime or even her uncle, but it *was* triggered intentionally."

McElroy frowned. "I'm not sure I understand."

They reached the end of a hall and stepped through a doorway into a dark, narrow room lined on either side with lighted glass tanks. Inside the tanks was a collection of reptiles that brought to mind several members of Congress McElroy had known over the years.

As they moved up to a tank containing an iguana, Gray said, "The bomb was set off in order to convey a message. Not to the public or the government, but to Malina's uncle himself. He loved his niece very much."

"Okay, so what was the message?"

"It seems that Mr. Zupan owed a significant amount of money to someone, and when he didn't pay up, that someone wanted to teach him a lesson. This man coerced Zupan into giving up the number of the cell phone detonator, and called it while Malina and her partner were less than a foot away from the bomb. His timing was impeccable."

"That's pretty cold," McElroy said. "Who is this guy?"

"Someone who's been on the Stonewell acquisition list for nearly two decades now."

McElroy smiled. "If you give me a minute, I could probably narrow that down to half a dozen people."

"This one is German."

The smiled faded. "Valac?"

"The one and only."

Reinhard Beck, aka Valac, was a former member of Germany's Red Army Faction who split off in the mid-nineties and formed his own terror network, the Black Hat Battalion. Beck's nickname was taken from a book called *The Lesser Key of Solomon*, which claimed the demon Valac was one of the rulers of the Kingdom of Hell. McElroy had always felt the name was appropriate, and apparently Beck did as well.

Valac had been a fugitive since 1994, after he was accused of the brutal and very bloody assassination of a German businessman and his two young sons while they were vacationing in France. Valac had since been linked to a number of terrorist attacks, both directly and behind the scenes, and had been a fixture on the FBI's and CIA's Most Wanted lists through three administrations.

Whoever was lucky enough to catch the man could name his reward, which was why Stonewell International and at least five other top-flight security firms had long considered Valac a priority. Unfortunately, he was very good at evading capture. The best ID the intelligence services had on the guy was a murky black and white surveillance photo from an Italian bank robbery fifteen years ago.

Just the mention of his name set McElroy's heart pounding. If Gray was offering him a chance at grabbing the guy... "You know where he is?"

"Let's just say we know where he *will* be in the next couple days, if he isn't there already."

"Where?"

Gray raised a brow. "Your impatience is unbecoming, Jason. You need to learn to temper that. Pretend you don't care, like the rest of us do."

"And you need to learn to get to the point. Where's Valac?"

"Somewhere private and isolated," Gray said. "But I can't tell you until you ask me how I know."

It was a game Gray had always played. He took great pride whenever his people uncovered a juicy bit of intel, and he enjoyed sharing the details.

As usual, McElroy played along. "Okay, so how do you know?"

Gray offered him another smile, this one more generous than the last as they moved on to the next glass case—a desert sand snake.

"Malina's uncle had a contact number that he used to get

in touch with Valac. It went through a third party, of course, but our friends in the NSA were able to sift through the go-between's calls and find the ones that directly coincided with Zudan's attempts to reach Valac. This in turn led them to yet another individual, and when they tapped *his* phone, they soon found themselves listening to a call from Reinhardt Beck himself and were able to piggyback his private line."

"I'm impressed," McElroy said.

"You should be. Unfortunately, Valac is smart enough to change phones frequently, so it didn't last long. But before he discarded this one, they managed to record an exchange that turned the simple acquisition of a fugitive into something slightly more intriguing."

"Meaning what?"

"I'll need to give you some background," Gray said. "Are you sure you have the patience for it?"

McElroy eyed him dully. "I'm listening."

"Three weeks ago we suffered a loss in the field. A young scientist we had high hopes for was captured while vacationing in Switzerland and tortured by an ex-patriot and newly minted French citizen named Frederic Favreau. Yet another American gone rogue."

"I didn't hear about this."

"You wouldn't have. Unfortunately, what Favreau managed to extract from the man were some highly sensitive codes that only a handful of people are privy to. Codes that, if obtained by the wrong party, could prove quite deadly."

That sounded ominous, but McElroy had enough sense to not ask what they were for.

"Favreau, however, isn't our biggest concern," Gray went on. "He's an opportunist, not a terrorist. A crude, low-level rodent, operating far above his weight class, and he'd much rather sell the codes to someone who can make use of them. Someone who will pay the appropriate price, of course."

"Like Valac."

Gray nodded. "One of the calls the NSA listened in on was an exchange between the two men. They were arranging a meet on a private island just north of Cuba."

McElroy's heart kicked up. "The Bahamas?"

"Geographically, yes. Politically, not so much."

"You're talking about St. Cajetan..."

"That's the one, yes."

St. Cajetan had been purchased from the Commonwealth, but it was completely sovereign, with its own laws and security force, and had become quite the hot spot for the rich and famous. The *very* rich and famous.

"Okay," McElroy said, "so you know where they're meeting. Why come to Stonewell with this?"

"Believe me, we considered sending in our own strike team, but this is a highly sensitive situation, so we'd like to keep it as far off the books as possible. And, frankly, Stonewell has never let us down. You're discreet and highly efficient."

McElroy knew when someone was blowing smoke up his ass, but he let it go. If Gray wanted to hand him a once-in-a-lifetime acquisition, he wasn't about to argue.

"So what's the priority here? The codes or Valac?"

"Oh, the codes, most definitely. Preferably before Valac takes possession. But once they're secure, he's all yours, along with all the benefits that might bring."

In other words, the name-your-own-price reward McElroy desperately wanted. "When is this meeting supposed to take place?"

"As far as we know, the actual day and time haven't been set," Gray said, "but Favreau *has* booked a flight for the day after tomorrow."

Now it was McElroy's turn to grin. "I'll assemble a team right away."

"Excellent. I have only one request in that regard."

"Which is?"

"It's our understanding that one of your assets is already in that vicinity, and we'd like very much to see her involved."

McElroy frowned. "Which asset is that?"

"The one you sent to Turkey. Alexandra Poe. She's on her

way to Key Largo to sell off some family real estate, which puts her within spitting distance of St. Cajetan."

McElroy was surprised. "You know about her?"

"Considering who her father is, you can't for a minute think that we don't. We've had her under telephone and e-mail surveillance off and on for over ten years. And I must say, I thought it was brilliant of you to recruit her into your organization."

McElroy shrugged. "She's a natural. We wanted to exploit that."

"Don't try to con me, Jason. With that little excursion she took into Slavne prison last year, she proved she's more than capable. But we both know that your real interest in her has more to do with finding her father than any skills she might possess."

"At first, maybe, but she's turned out to be a valuable member of the team."

"Indeed," Gray said. "Which is why I'd like her to be part of this operation. Favreau has a weakness for beautiful women, especially the exotic ones. She's just his type."

"She's also got a mind of her own, and she isn't too happy about how things went down in Turkey. I might have trouble convincing her to join your cause."

"I assume you want this acquisition?"

"You know I do."

Gray lifted his shoulders. "Then you'll do everything in your power to make it happen."

FOUR

ALEX WAS THIRTY minutes from her destination when her phone rang.

Third time in the last hour.

She didn't bother to check the screen. She knew it was McElroy again, and had no more interest in speaking to him now than she had the first two times he called. He could wait until she was good and ready for him.

Which might be never.

It had been at least three years since she last made the drive from Miami International to Key Largo. Three years that felt like thirty. And as she watched the road roll beneath her, and looked at the marsh and the mangroves and the glassy surface of the ocean, the memories tumbling through her mind went even farther back, to a childhood that had not yet been ripped apart by the twin cruelties of death and abandonment.

Christ. That sounded dire, didn't it?

The truth was, despite her occasional treks into the land of self-pity, Alex had turned out just fine, thank you. As much as she had missed having a mother and father around, she hadn't allowed herself to fall prey to the lesser path of drinking or drugs or involvement with some loser who thought the fastest way to a woman's heart was a blistering insult or a well-placed fist.

She had never been interested in such nonsense. She'd had a brother to care for. One who required time and attention from a sister who understood the value of self-discipline and focus.

But in their childhood years, before their mother had been taken from them, Alex had been a carefree spirit who had loved making this drive with her family. She remembered squirming on the backseat with Danny, both giddy with anticipation, looking forward to the fun they'd have at the Shimmy Shack.

That was the name their father had given to the beach house. He had come up with it after a balmy night on the back patio, drinking a beer and staring out at the bay as their mother tried to teach the kids to dance to Little Anthony's "Shimmy, Shimmy, Ko-Ko-Bop." Alex and Danny had found the record in the storage room, along with several more discs and an ancient but still functioning turntable, remnants from the days when Grandpa Eddie and Grandma Ginny had lived there.

The ritual was repeated up until the month before their mother's death. Then the first blow of the one-two punch that defined Alex's abrupt entry into adulthood had landed like a hammer to the temple.

And everything changed.

A few years later, when her father disappeared under a cloud of scandal, accused of things she knew he couldn't have done, Alex had been surprised to learn he had signed the house over to her and Danny. The Shimmy Shack was now theirs. And shortly after her dad left, a Key Largo property manager had contacted her to ask where to send the checks he regularly collected from vacation renters.

Dad's way of making sure they'd never go without money.

At the time, Alex hadn't really cared about any of that. She had simply wanted to know why he left and where he had gone. Two questions she still didn't have answers to.

But as time wore on, she had become accustomed to the extra income, happy to have it to pay for Danny's assisted care at Ryan's House. She had placed him there when she went into the service and had instructed the management company to forward the checks to Mrs. Thornton, the home's founder and principal caretaker.

Unfortunately, when the economy tanked, the rental checks began to dwindle. And after the management company closed its doors, Alex had never gotten around to hiring another one. So the Shimmy Shack had spent the last few years rotting in the Florida humidity as Alex tried to eke out a living on the bounties she and Deuce managed to collect. The money from Stonewell was an unexpected bonus, but she knew she couldn't rely on it forever. She had no desire to.

So, despite the memories, when the opportunity arose, she decided to sell.

Key Largo was the first and longest of the Florida keys, made famous by an old Humphrey Bogart movie that Alex had seen only once as a teenager. She hadn't particularly liked the film, mainly because it had been shot in black and white, and the Key Largo she knew seemed to exist in a perpetual state of living color. Everything was brighter down here, with its pastel greens and blues at full saturation. Even the cement dividers along the highway were painted turquoise, as if to announce to travelers that the town they were about to enter was something special.

Baltimore, where Alex made her home, was a big and unwieldy and often dangerous waterfront city, while Key Largo was about as laid back as you could get without dozing off in your lounge chair. It moved at a lazy pace and smelled of the sea, and those who visited were often reluctant to leave.

With the town of Homestead in her rearview mirror, Alex drove along what the locals called the Stretch, the last bit of highway before you hit Largo proper, and felt the tension inside her begin to seep away, as if someone had released a pressure valve. She thought of her childhood again and wondered if she was making a terrible mistake.

Had she decided to sell the house too quickly?

Should she call the agent who had contacted her and tell him she'd changed her mind?

Just as she was thinking this, her phone rang and she groaned, assuming it was McElroy still trying to ruin her day. But when she glanced at the screen, she was surprised to see the name THOMAS GÉRARD, the agent she was scheduled to meet at the Shimmy Shack.

Talk about timing.

Gérard was the one who had convinced her to sell. A few days before she left for Turkey, he had e-mailed her with his pitch, assuring her that his client was willing to pay above market price for a chance to own property there. The neighbors in the area had told him they hadn't seen anyone around her place for quite some time, and if she had no real use for it, why not bid it adieu and collect a hefty payoff?

She thought he was being a bit presumptuous at first, but after letting the idea percolate, she decided he was right. Sometimes it was better to move on.

Looking out at the bay again, she saw the boats bobbing in Gilbert's Marina. The phone kept screaming at her to pick it up, so she pulled it from its cradle and put it to her ear.

"Hey, Thomas. Sorry I'm late. I stopped at a fruit stand along the way."

The fruit stand was a place called Robert Is Here, and sold the best strawberry key lime milkshake Alex had ever had. It had always been a scheduled stop when she was traveling with the family, so she'd made sure to include it this time, too.

"Not to worry," Gérard said in a voice that held the tiniest hint of a French accent. "I'm calling to apologize myself. I have to speak to one of my clients before I leave the hotel. I hope this isn't a problem?"

"No problem at all. It'll give me a chance to open up the house and air it out a little."

She had no idea what that might entail. The management company had always prepared the place for hurricane season and had probably left it that way when the business folded. Two-plus years of summer heat and humidity were bound to have done a job on the house.

"Excellent," Gérard said. "I'll see you soon."

Ten minutes later, Alex pulled onto the drive that led to the

Shimmy Shack, and heard the familiar crunch of crushed shells beneath her tires. Like everywhere else in the Keys, there was no real landscaping at the house, more of a controlled, natural growth, featuring a jungle of palms and multicolored bougainvillea trees.

The house itself was a yellow box that stood on cement stilts several feet from the shore. And as Alex had suspected, large sheets of now graying and dilapidated plywood covered the windows and front door, to protect the place from seasonal hurricanes.

The house had been built by her grandfather in the late sixties, and no one had ever bothered to install proper storm shutters. Grandpa Eddie had always said a solid sheet of plywood was good enough for him, and apparently the management company had agreed.

Alex pulled into the carport and cut her engine. She'd have to pry the wood from the door to get inside, but she hadn't thought to bring any tools—a boneheaded move if there ever was one. Hopefully, the kit her father had always kept on the premises was still here.

She climbed out of the rental and made her way to the storage shed built into the right wall of the carport, then found the key on her key ring and unlatched the padlock.

The enclosure was nearly as deep as the house was wide, and was full of over forty-five years' worth of junk. Moldering cardboard boxes were stacked haphazardly, flaps hanging open, still bearing the signs of Alex's and Danny's childhood rummaging.

Even the old turntable was there.

No sign of "Shimmy, Shimmy, Ko-Ko-Bop," however.

Alex stepped over to a workbench on the left, cleared away a couple boxes, and was relieved to find her father's battered gray toolbox sitting atop it. She carried it around to the front of the house, took the steps up to the front door, and went to work.

Five minutes and several rusty nails later, she set the slab of plywood aside, unlocked the door and...

Something stopped her as she was about to push it open.

A gut feeling. A sense that something was out of place.

Having learned long ago to pay attention to her senses, Alex took a step back and looked at the windows to the left and right. The graying plywood covering them was peeling in spots and otherwise looked the same as the board that had covered the door. But the one to her right didn't seem as tight to the frame as the other one, so she walked over for a closer inspection. Several nails were missing, and those that remained appeared a bit loose in their sockets. This could have been from normal wear and tear, but her gut told her it wasn't.

She grabbed the edge of the board, intending to give it a good yank to test its strength, but she'd barely started when the whole board fell off the wall and revealed a shattered windowpane.

Shit.

Someone had been inside.

Might still be, for all she knew.

She reached into the toolbox, wrapped her fingers around the handle of the hammer, and returned to the door. She twisted the knob, pushed it open a crack, and listened, knowing her caution was probably pointless after all the racket she'd been making. If someone had been inside when she arrived, they'd be long gone by now.

Then again, if that someone was hostile, he might be waiting for her.

Hearing nothing suspicious, Alex widened the gap and slid sideways into the living room, keeping the hammer raised as she swiveled her head, alert for any sign of movement. The tarp that covered the sofa had an obvious dent in it where someone's ass had taken residence, and an empty bottle of Swamp Head ale sat on the wooden-plank coffee table her grandfather had made.

She supposed it could have been left by the laborer who had put up the plywood, but she didn't think so. Not with that broken window.

Peering into the kitchen, she saw a spent candle on the countertop—to compensate for the lack of electricity—and another empty bottle of ale, along with a crumpled pack of cigarettes.

Tightening her grip on the hammer, she started down the narrow hallway that led to the two bedrooms and the deck that overlooked the ocean. Both bedroom doors were hanging open, the mattresses stripped of sheets. She almost continued on, but something on the floor of the room she and Danny used to share caught her eye. She stepped inside and her jaw tensed.

A sleeping bag.

Surely whoever had slept here had plans to come back. Or maybe he was outside, hiding in the thick tangle of bougainvillea trees, hoping she would soon leave.

Angry now, Alex snatched up the sleeping bag with her free hand and dragged it down the hallway toward the small den that was used to access the back patio. Not surprisingly, the door to the deck was no longer boarded. After throwing it open, she stepped outside, looked out at the bay and the trees, and flung the bag over the rail to the ground below.

"Okay, asshole, time to find yourself a new place to crash." She raised the hammer, shaking it at the trees. "And if you come back again, you'd better have health insurance, because you're definitely gonna need it."

She hadn't expected an answer and didn't get one. All she heard was the rustle of leaves in the wind, and the distant raspy cry of a mangrove cuckoo. But again she had that gut feeling. That sixth sense she had picked up during her tour in Iraq.

Someone was out there and had heard every word she'd said.

She hoped he'd taken her seriously.

She was in the storage shed, trying to decide whether to go through the boxes or simply dump them all, when she heard tires on the driveway and the thrum of an engine.

Wiping her dusty hands on her jeans, she stepped outside and waved hello as a Ford came to a stop next to her car, and the man she assumed was Thomas Gérard emerged.

He was much better looking than she had pictured him. Definitely European, with a bit of a Clive Owen vibe.

He said, "Nice to finally meet you, Ms. Poe."

His smile was disarming, and she had no doubt it had served him well. She stepped forward and shook his hand. "Yes. It's good to see a face to go with the voice."

"And the e-mails. Don't forget the e-mails."

"You've been persistent, I'll give you that." She turned now and looked at the house, seeing little more than an old shack in need of some tender loving care. "Although I'm not sure what you see in the place."

He smiled again. "Location, location, location…"

They laughed and she said, "Apparently you aren't the only one who feels that way."

His brows went up. "You've had another offer?"

"No, but I've had an uninvited guest. Someone broke in and has been sleeping here. I'm not sure for how long."

"Have you called the police?"

She shook her head. "I doubt there's much they can do."

"But what if he comes back?"

"He'll find out soon enough that I'm no damsel in distress," she said, then gestured toward the house. "Shall we take the ten-cent tour?"

"By all means."

He followed her up the steps, and they spent the next several minutes moving from room to room, Gérard snapping photos with his phone. He had seen only the exterior of the house, and yes, he had assured her, it was practically a done deal, but he wanted to make sure his client knew exactly what he was getting into.

Alex was almost embarrassed by the condition of the place, which could only be described as Early Garage Sale. No wonder the rentals had dried up. Funny how she hadn't noticed this when she was nine years old. Or even the last time she was here.

Gérard had a quiet confidence about him that went well with the smile and good looks. She didn't often find herself admiring men—her life was too complicated for such pursuits—but there was something about this guy she found...beguiling.

When he was done snapping photos, he said, "I don't see anything here that would change my client's mind, but I'll have to send these to him and make sure he's still interested."

"So, is this what you usually do? Hunt for houses for anonymous clients?"

"That all depends, but yes, I specialize in properties that are often difficult to acquire. And houses in the Keys are hard to come by."

Alex was about to respond when they heard a loud clunk and hum as the ancient refrigerator in the kitchen came to life.

"Thank God," she said. "I was hoping the electricity would kick in before dark. They told me it might take a while."

"So you're staying overnight?"

"For a couple days, at least. If I'm gonna unload this place there's a lot to do. We've collected quite a bit of junk over the last few decades."

"Something I'm not familiar with," he said. "I move around too much."

Alex nodded. "What kind of accent is that you're hiding? On the phone I thought French, but now I'm not so sure."

He gave here another smile. She wished he'd stop doing that.

"I was born in Belgium, but I've lived and traveled all over the world. I seem to collect bad habits in lieu of possessions."

She wasn't sure what he meant by that, but before her imagination could run wild, she started moving toward the front door, making it clear their meeting had come to an end. She had work to do and wanted to get started.

He got the hint and followed her, offering a hand to shake.

She shook it and said, "How soon will you hear from your client?"

"Tomorrow, perhaps. Maybe even as early as tonight."

"I'll look forward to your call, then."

He glanced toward the back of the house. "What about your intruder? You're sure you'll be safe here alone?"

"Don't worry, I can handle myself."

He studied her. "You haven't told me what you do for a living."

"I'm kinda like you," she said. "But I hunt for people instead of houses."

By his look, she could see he didn't quite believe her, but he didn't push it. Instead, he simply flashed that smile one last time and headed through the doorway. But as he reached the top of the steps, he stopped and turned. "I have a thought."

"Yes?"

"Since you're staying over, how would you feel about having dinner? Or drinks, if you'd prefer. I'll be in the bar at the Largo Inn tonight and I hate to drink alone."

I doubt you do it very often, she almost told him, and while the offer was more than tempting, she shrugged and gestured to their surroundings. "I appreciate the invite, but I've got too much to do. Another time?"

"Of course," he said, looking a little disappointed, then turned and headed down the steps to his car.

FIVE

ALEX WAS BACK in the storage shed when she found it. A rectangular metal case she didn't remember ever seeing before, despite the fact that at one time or another, she and Danny had been through every inch of this place, dodging lizards and hunting for treasure.

Ironically, that's what the case looked like—somebody's treasure box, complete with a locked clasp, and no bigger than a hardback book. She'd found it inside an unopened cardboard box at the back of the shed, buried beneath a stack of her grandparents' faded and dog-eared *LOOK* magazines, as if it had been deliberately placed there in an attempt to hide it from the casual explorer.

Had her grandfather put it there? One of her parents?

She could only assume it had been hidden years ago, and that she and Danny had missed it because of their complete lack of interest in the fifties and sixties, the two decades covered by most of the magazines. Faded photos of Sinatra and Kennedy and Audrey Hepburn weren't exactly top draws for curious kids.

Alex turned the treasure box in her hand and the contents rattled.

Coins? Jewelry?

She carried it to the workbench, set it down, and took a screwdriver from her father's tool kit, jamming it into the space behind the clasp. After a single tug, the lock snapped.

She didn't lift the lid right away. Instead, she stared at the box, excitement welling up inside her. In that moment she was nine years old again, with Danny beside her, and her mother and father upstairs making lunch or lounging on the patio or playing a spirited game of Shanghai, and all was good in the world.

All was good.

She held on to the feeling as long as she could, not opening the box until the sensation passed. When she lifted the lid she found four items inside: a tattered newspaper clipping, a key, a worn 5x8 manila envelope. . .and a ring.

Her mother's ring.

Alex's throat constricted and tears filled her eyes. She remembered this ring vividly. Her mother had always worn it on her right forefinger, an ornate silver band with a polished turquoise stone from Nishapur. A gift from Alex's great-grandmother.

But why was it here? Her mother, an anthropologist, had been killed by a terrorist's bomb in Lebanon during a research trip. Wrong place, wrong time. She would've had this ring with her. Would never have left it behind.

Had it been recovered from the rubble? From the body itself?

Apparently so. But why hadn't Alex known about it?

She stared at the ring, unable to choke back the tears, remembering the many times she'd sat on her mother's lap, running her fingers over the smooth stone, wishing it could be hers. Remembering Mom's promise that one day it would be.

"It is family tradition, Alexandra. My grandmother had only sons, so she passed it on to me right before she died. And one day it will be your turn to wear it."

"I don't want you to die, Mommy."

Her mother had smiled. "Don't you worry, child. I'm not going anywhere for a long, long time."

But only a few years later, she was gone.

Alex took the ring from the box, held it up for a moment, then slipped it on her right forefinger. The fit was a little snug, but she had no intention of ever taking it off again. The promise had been fulfilled, a thought that brought a whole new wave of tears.

Wiping them away, she reached into the box again and took out the clipping. It was from a Lebanese newspaper, written in Arabic, the photo showing what was left of the cafe where her mother and two others had been slaughtered.

Alex studied it a moment, wondering if any of the victims had felt anything, remembering the friends she and Cooper had lost to IEDs in Iraq. She briefly closed her eyes, then set the clipping on the workbench and returned her attention to the treasure box.

The next item was the key. She took it out, studied it, and saw a series of numbers etched into the head, along with the letters S&G.

The key to a locker of some kind?

A safe deposit box?

Maybe whatever was inside the manila envelope would give her the answer. She took it from the box and opened it, dumping its contents onto the workbench.

A stack of photographs. Small, square snapshots, some black and white, some color, all faded by time. Photos of a baby, a young girl, a teenager. All with the face of Alex's mother, many with an Iranian backdrop—a mosque, an open fruit market, a street in Tehran.

Her mother had rarely talked about her childhood, but here was a glimpse of it. One Alex had never seen before.

Looking into the eyes of that beautiful young girl got Alex's heart thumping. What was her mother thinking all those years ago? Did she know she'd one day wind up living in the United States, married to an American soldier? Did she dream of having children?

All at once, Alex felt cheated, thinking it should be her mother sharing these photographs with her. She wanted to reach into the past and warn her not to go to Lebanon. To stay away from that fucking cafe.

Yet despite the pain, no tears came this time. She was the stoic Alexandra now. The soldier. A trait she'd inherited from her father. And she knew that wallowing in what-ifs was a waste of time. She couldn't change what had happened to her family.

Nobody could.

But as she came to the last photo in the stack, that stoicism wavered. What she saw was her mother at twenty years of age, or maybe a bit younger, standing on the steps of a large house that looked very Persian. The word "palace" came to mind. And she was wearing an elaborate white wedding dress and veil.

What the hell?

This wouldn't normally be anything earth shattering, except for the fact that Alex had seen photos of her parents' wedding, and this was *not* one of them. They were married at Baltimore City Hall, and her mother had worn a simple yellow sundress that hung in her closet years after she was killed.

Alex flipped the photograph over, hoping to find a date on the back, but there wasn't one.

What she found instead was an odd series of letters and numbers that looked like a website link, truncated by Google's URL shortener:

goo.gl/ALUAfk

Alex didn't move. The presence of her mother's ring had indicated that the box could have been hidden away for a over a decade. But what about this web link? Google's URL shortener had only been available for a few years, which meant the box had been left here more recently.

Maybe within the last few months.

Or even days.

Did the person who had broken into the house leave it here for Alex to find? Was the interloper someone she knew?

Could the owner of that sleeping bag be…

No.

That was ridiculous. He wouldn't risk coming here. He wouldn't step foot on US soil, not while he was still running from the DHS, the CIA, and every other acronym in the intelligence community, both public and private.

So who had put this here?

And more importantly—why?

Alex took her computer tablet from her backpack in the rental car and carried it upstairs to the living room, her hands trembling as she brought the tablet to life. She set the wedding-dress photo face down on the coffee table, pulled up the Web browser, and carefully keyed in the truncated URL written on the back of the photo.

She paused, sucked in a breath, then touched the GO icon and waited as the browser took her to a site called *DataLock*, one of the many file-sharing repositories on the web. The page held a download link for a video file, several megabytes in size, called *SHADI.mp4*.

Shadi?

A Persian name, but Alex didn't recognize it. Her mother's name was Mitra.

Still, it had to mean something.

She tapped the download link and a pop-up screen told her to enter a password.

Shit. Now what?

She thought for a moment, but she was no computer hacker and had no clue what the password might be. In a fit of inspiration, she tried typing in *Mitra* and a message in red came up on the screen:

ERROR: Incorrect password. 2 attempts remaining.

Dammit.

She was convinced now that whoever had left this link had wanted her to find it and download the file, so the clue to the password had to be in that treasure box. She thought about the items she'd found—the photographs, the key, her mother's turquoise ring—but nothing sparked any ideas.

Was there something in the photo itself?

She picked it up and studied it again. Her mother standing on the steps of some kind of Persian palace. A smile on her face, but a bit forced, as if she wished the camera wasn't pointed at her. Her hands clasped a bouquet, and she was wearing the ring.

Could that be it?

Alex started to type *Mitra's Ring* into the password field, but reconsidered halfway through and erased it. The choice seemed unlikely and she didn't want to waste an attempt.

So, what else could it be?

The photographs, the key, the ring...

The key, the photographs, the ring...

The ring, the photographs—

And then it hit her.

The key. It had to be the key. It was meant to open a lock, but maybe not a *physical* one.

Tucking the tablet under her arm, Alex flew through the doorway and down the steps, back to the room where she'd spent most of the afternoon. She moved to the workbench, picked up the key, and squinted at the initials and numbers etched into its head—S&G 4576. She rested the tablet on the workbench and called up the password screen again.

She took a deep breath and typed in *S&G 4576.*

ERROR: Incorrect password. 1 attempt remaining.

Shit, shit, shit.

Okay, she told herself, *think this through, then take another deep breath and try again.*

Feeling a knot form in her stomach, she started typing again, this time omitting the space between the letters and numbers: *S&G4576.*

A little hourglass appeared—*Hallelujah*—then turned over several times until finally, thankfully, another pop-up filled the screen, asking her to approve the download.

Alex nearly shouted in triumph as she clicked the SAVE button. As soon as the *SHADI.mp4* file finished downloading, she didn't waste time wondering what to expect. She simply tapped the link and watched the video player blossom.

After switching it to full-screen mode, she waited as the tablet went black for a moment, then came to life with what looked like poorly transferred footage from an old VHS camcorder. There were streaks in the video and the sound was wobbly.

But that didn't matter. What she saw captivated her.

Stunned her.

It was her mother, in the very same wedding dress and veil, sitting on a chair in a large, palatial room, in front of a Persian rug covered with ornate trays full of baked goods and fruits and spices and coins and a mirror flanked by two burning candelabra.

A traditional Persian wedding.

Her mother was surrounded by Iranian family and friends who watched in delight as the ceremony was performed, the groom seated on the chair next to her.

And as Alex stood there watching it all unfold, her heart started thumping again, leaving her confused, troubled, and even a little angry.

Because the man in that chair was not her father.

SIX

IT SEEMED SILLY to be so upset by the video.

Alex had spent two years on active duty, and had seen things that would make most people want to curl up in a corner. And after years of that kind of conditioning, it should have taken more than a thirty-year-old wedding ceremony to get her going.

But as she drove toward town, she felt angry tears threatening to cloud her eyes, and had to will them away with everything she had.

It wasn't her mother's previous marriage that bothered her so much. It was that she had been *lied* to. All of her life. Told a story about a young college student who had left Iran right before the Islamic Revolution. But there had never been any mention of a dress and a veil and the handsome Iranian groom in that video.

Not one word.

Why would her mother hide such an important part of her past? Was she ashamed of it? Had she come here under a cloud of scandal?

And what about Alex's father? Had he known and been part of the deception? Or had he been as clueless as Alex?

Her mind a swirl of questions, she turned the wheel of her rental car, and pulled into the parking lot of the Largo Inn. She had no idea why she had come here. She was running on autopilot right now and had only wanted to get away from that house and all of its memories.

As she parked the car, it occurred to her she wouldn't have come to Key Largo if it hadn't been for those e-mails from Thomas Gérard, looking to buy the Shimmy Shack for an unnamed client.

Could *he* be the one behind this? Or maybe the client?

She must have unconsciously been thinking it, because here she was at the very place Gérard had said he would be, her anger quickly building into all-out rage.

Easy, Alex. You need to relax.

If Gérard was in that bar, going in there with her finger on the trigger would not get her any answers.

Taking several slow, deep breaths, she shut off the engine and tried to center herself. Her friend Cooper had long been a proponent of meditation, a discipline he had adopted after their tour in Iraq. And in the months since they'd begun working together again, he had urged her to join him, telling her it was the perfect way to purge both mental and physical toxins.

Alex had bristled at the thought, assuming it was Cooper's passive-aggressive way of telling her she was too tightly wound.

But maybe that was true.

Especially now.

Though she had no idea why Gérard would be part of some conspiracy to reveal the truth about her mother, she was far more likely to get information from him by taking the innocent approach than by rushing in and slamming his head against the wall.

With this thought in mind, she twisted the rearview mirror to make sure her eyes were clear, then popped open her door and climbed out.

Gérard had staked out a table near the windows overlooking a small man-made beach and the bay. The sky was full of the remnants of what had undoubtedly been a dazzling sunset that Alex had been far too preoccupied to pay any attention to.

Gérard was draped in his chair, a large tropical drink in hand, his feet up on the arm of the chair across from him. He seemed lost in thought as he stared out at the water, reminding Alex of those Shimmy Shack nights on the patio with her father.

Not that Gérard was anything like Dad. Far from it.

Seeing him looking so relaxed made her doubt he had anything to do with planting that treasure box. But it didn't mean he wasn't an unwitting accomplice.

He must have seen her reflection in the windows because he abruptly turned his head and gave her a wave.

"Ms. Poe," he said, keeping it formal.

Taking his feet off the chair, he sat up, gesturing for her to join him. He looked a little drunk. Maybe more than a little.

"Alex," she said as she approached. "Call me Alex."

"All right, Alex it is. Have a seat, order a drink."

She sat down and a waiter appeared out of nowhere, as if Gérard had him on private retainer. "What can I get for you, ma'am? Key Lime Colada? Mermaid Tail?"

"Jameson. Neat," she said. "And tell the bartender to make sure he wipes the dust off the bottle before he pours."

The waiter gave her a stiff half smile and went away.

"I think you upset him," Gérard said, chuckling. He raised his drink. "They seem to enjoy pushing these fruity monstrosities—which, by the way, cost a small fortune."

"I'm sure you've figured out by now that the Keys don't exactly embrace frugality. If you're looking for a cheap vacation, you'd better apply elsewhere."

He smiled that smile of his. "Is this an attempt to persuade my client to raise his offer?"

"It probably should be, but I'm not greedy. And the sooner we get this done, the better. Have you spoken to him yet?"

"I sent the photos, but he hasn't responded." He took a sip of his drink and leaned forward, his eyes glassy. "But if you don't mind, I'd rather save our business for the light of day. I'm not a fan of discussing such things once the sun goes down."

Or when you're half in the bag, Alex thought.

She looked out the windows and saw that the sun had indeed disappeared, the sky now a mix of deep purples and blues, with a sliver of moonlight reflected by the water. The beach below looked empty and inviting, even if the sand *had* been shipped in from farther north.

The waiter came back and set Alex's drink on the table in front of her.

As she took a sip, Gérard said, "Not that I'm complaining, but why the change of heart?"

"Change of heart?"

"About having a drink with me."

"I don't suppose you'd believe I just got in the car and started driving and this was where I wound up?"

He smiled again and lifted his glass in a toast. "So you're a free spirit. A woman without purpose."

"Only on my bad days," she said.

He laughed but then studied her. "Unless my instincts are fuzzy, there's something troubling you. Did the intruder come back?"

She shook her head. "The only thing troubling me is that I don't know who your client is. That's the real reason I'm here."

"But I've already told you. He prefers to remain anonymous."

"And I prefer to know who I'm doing business with."

He paused. "So then this really is an attempt to raise the price."

"No," she said, "it's an attempt to find out who wants my house and why he had you contact me. Why now instead of a year ago? Six months?"

Gérard shrugged. "As far as I know, he wasn't in the market then. And I'm not sure why this is so upsetting to you."

He was right. She *was* upset and it showed. She was handling this like a ham-handed amateur, but interrogation had never been her specialty. She was the grab-and-go girl who left such things to the experts.

She took a deep breath. "Look, I'm sorry. It's just that being back at that house has been very painful for me, and call me old-fashioned, but I feel uncomfortable selling to someone I've never met."

"So you've changed your mind?"

"No, I just want to know who he is."

"Believe me, Alex, if I could tell you, I would. But I signed a confidentiality agreement and I'm a man of my word. I can relay your concerns to him when he calls, but I doubt he'll budge, even if it means losing the property. He's very private."

Alex sighed. Why was she pushing this poor guy? He seemed to be telling the truth and she wasn't about to get anything out of him like this. Maybe his emails and phone calls were just some weird coincidence, and maybe the person she *should* be interrogating was whoever had broken into the house.

It certainly wasn't Gérard.

She drained her glass and got to her feet.

He looked up at her. "You're leaving?"

"I'm sorry," she said again. "Here you were enjoying the view and I come along and start bullying you like some psycho cop. I'll let you drink in peace."

"But I told you, I prefer not to drink alone."

"Trust me, you don't want me for company right now."

"On the contrary," he said. "That's exactly what I want." Now *he* got to his feet. "But if you aren't interested in drinking with me, what do you say to a walk on the beach?"

Though he wobbled slightly as he held out a hand, he was so damn charming in tone and demeanor that she couldn't help but forgive his excesses. That Clive Owen vibe was working overtime right now, and despite the anger and confusion this trip had already wrought, she found herself giving into him.

"I guess I could use some air," she said.

There was something soothing about beaches at night.

Back in Baltimore, before their involvement with Stonewell International, Alex and Deuce would sometimes grab a six-pack and drive out to Rocky Point after a hard day's work. They'd spend half the night camped out on the sand with several of their cop and bail enforcement friends, drinking beer and swapping war stories in front of a fire. The park was technically closed after sunset, but the beach patrol was more than willing to extend a bit of professional courtesy to their public-safety brethren.

At some point in the night, Alex would usually find herself alone and walking barefoot along the water's edge, letting the cool breeze off Chesapeake Bay remind her that the world was not always about bail jumpers and chases down blind alleyways and bondsmen with tight purses. Sometimes you had to let go of all the bullshit and revel in those small moments of escape.

She figured it was no different tonight. As she and Gérard worked their way down a set of wooden steps to the beach outside the Largo Inn, she decided to allow herself to let go for a moment. To be that free woman Gérard had spoken of.

He said, "So, what do you really do for a living?"

Alex stifled a smile. She'd known he hadn't believed her. "I told you. Same as you, only I hunt people instead of properties."

"You're with the police?"

She shook her head. "I'm a fugitive retrieval specialist. Or what the people in the cheap seats call a bounty hunter."

He looked surprised. "That seems an usual profession for…" He paused, as if he were afraid to finish the sentence.

"For what?" she said. "A woman?"

They were walking on the sand now, the beach curving along the coastline, dotted by clusters of dark palms, an ocean breeze rendering the late summer humidity almost bearable. Gérard had sobered some, but still could have benefitted from a cup of coffee or two, although his drunkenness was more endearing than obnoxious.

"Not at all," he said, stopping. "What I meant to say was…for someone so beautiful."

From anyone else this would have seemed like a well-practiced line, and it probably was. But Gérard came across as sincere instead of smarmy, and Alex had to admit she liked the sound of it. Maybe it was the Irish whiskey talking, but if he kept it up, she might let go completely.

Gérard was silhouetted against the backdrop of the bay as they looked at each other for a moment that was probably a lot shorter than it seemed. In a movie, he would try to kiss her now and she would resist but finally give in, despite her conflicting emotions. And the boyfriends and husbands in the crowd would undoubtedly be squirming in their seats, wondering what the hell kind of flick they'd agreed to see.

But Alex was no ingénue, and the man who emerged from the shadows of the palm trees six seconds later, pointing a gun in their direction, proved this was no chick flick.

"Down on your knees. Both of you." The guy was wearing gloves, a ski mask, and a very ugly attitude.

Alex glanced at Gérard, and then at the hotel, which was farther away than she'd realized.

The mugger took a step closer. "Nobody can see us down here, bitch. Now get on your fucking knees." He turned to Gérard. "You, too, asshole."

Alex had learned long ago that you don't mess around with a guy with a gun, especially at almost point-blank range. If things escalated, she'd do whatever needed to be done, but a few bucks and some credit cards were not worth getting shot over.

She sank to her knees and gestured for Gérard to do the same. But instead of complying, Gérard's gaze took on a look she didn't like.

Oh, shit.

He had been about to make a move on a woman he barely knew, and now had to prove himself worthy, the proverbial knight in shining armor.

Before she could stop him, he crouched slightly, as if he were about to kneel, then sprang forward like a soccer goalie diving for the ball. Judging by the mugger's reaction, he hadn't expected the move any more than he'd expected to use the gun. He let out a yelp as Gérard wrapped his arms around him and knocked him to the sand.

The gun went off, and the shot came perilously close to giving Alex an unsolicited tracheotomy. She fell back with a grunt, then scrambled to her feet just in time to see her inebriated hero trying to wrestle the gun from the mugger's hand.

The mugger lost his grip and the weapon went flying into the darkness as he and Gérard tumbled into the water, the mugger's hands disappearing from view.

Gérard suddenly groaned in pain and rolled away as the mugger jumped to his feet, holding a blade.

"Stay back," he told Alex, adjusting the mask that had come askew. "Stay the fuck back!"

Alex glanced at Gérard, who was still moving but clutching his side.

"Thomas? Are you okay?"

He groaned again. "...I'm cut."

Alex looked up sharply, the anger she'd stifled earlier coming back full force. The mugger must have recognized the threat, because the eyes behind his ski mask went wide.

"Stay back!" he said, his voice wavering. "Or I'll cut him again!"

If Gérard was hurt, she didn't have room to argue, but she didn't have to let the mugger know that.

She took a step forward, keeping her voice level. "You'd better run, you son of a bitch, or I'll tear your head off."

The mugger stood there for a moment, the hand with the blade trembling. Then, without warning, he heeded her advice and took off running, disappearing into the darkness down shore. Alex briefly considered chasing after him, but knew she couldn't. Instead, she moved to Gérard and pulled him away from the water.

"...Is okay," he grunted, the stress of the moment bringing out more of an accent. "I will be okay."

She pushed him against the sand, checked his shirt, and spotted a tear in the fabric near the upper right rib cage. She ripped open the shirt and checked the wound. It was a fairly long slice but didn't look deep, thank God. A couple minutes with a medic and he'd be fine.

"I think you'll live," she said. "But we need to notify the police and get you some medical attention."

"No…no police."

"But— "

"He was an amateur. He was scared. I don't think he'll be trying this again."

"I can see you haven't been around too many perps."

Gérard shook his head. "The police will never catch him and will only make our lives miserable for the next few hours."

He was right about that, even more so where Alex was concerned. As soon as they found out what she did for a living, the questions would likely change in both character and tone. Alex had a decent relationship with the cops in Baltimore, but there was no telling how local law enforcement felt about bounty hunters.

Looking at the wound, Gérard said, "It doesn't seem too bad. Leave me and I'll be fine. I have a first-aid kit in my room."

He sat up, groaning again as blood seeped from the wound.

"At least let me patch you up," she said. "I've had a little experience in the field."

He shook his head. "I almost got you shot and I've already taken up too much of your night with my drunken foolishness."

"I insist."

He looked down at the blood on his hand and relented. "All right. You might have to help me up."

"Hold on for a second."

She pulled her cell phone from her pocket, switched it to flashlight mode, and made a quick sweep of the beach until she found the discarded gun. There were children staying at the hotel, and she didn't want them to find it.

"All right," she said. "Give me your hand."
Twenty minutes later, she was in his bed.

SEVEN

It was nearly three in the morning when Alex abruptly came awake.

She had been dreaming of her mother, twenty years old, wearing that veil and wedding dress. Alex sat on her lap, admiring the turquoise stone on her finger, saying, "I don't want you to die, Mommy." But when she looked up again, she was sitting alone.

Or so she thought.

To her surprise, she saw a Persian wedding rug spread out before her, covered with the traditional bowls of bread and nuts and coins and incense and two burning candelabra with a mirror between them.

But the face reflected in the mirror was not hers.

It was the groom from her mother's wedding video.

Alex sucked in a sharp breath and opened her eyes and found herself lying in the dark of Gérard's hotel suite. Gérard was on his back beside her, chest rising and falling but making no sound as he slept. And as the dream receded, regret kicked in, and she could only ask herself *why*?

Why had she decided to sleep with this man? He was a virtual stranger.

Alex had always been impulsive. For as long as she could remember. But she had never been reckless about her choice of bed partners, which, for better or worse, were few and far between.

So what was it about this one that had made her cave?

Hell, cave wasn't even the word. If anything, *she* had been the aggressor.

After they had found the mugger's gun, she had helped

Gérard—wet and bleeding and smelling of the ocean—through the hotel lobby and up to his one-bedroom suite.

She'd sat him on his bed and told him to strip off his shirt. "Where's your first-aid kit?"

He winced and gestured toward the closet. "In the suitcase."

She retrieved it and checked inside, happy to see it contained some cotton swabs and several butterfly bandages. She then crossed to the bathroom and found a towel and two washcloths. After soaping one of the cloths, she filled a glass with water, and carried everything back to the bed.

She said, "Lift yourself up a little."

He did as he was told and she scooted the towel underneath him and flattened it out. When he lay back down, she inspected the wound under the nightstand light and found a lot of sand, but was relieved to see it was even shallower than she had first thought.

"A couple butterflies should do the trick," she said. She poured water on the cut to wash away the sand, then swabbed it with soap and rinsed again.

He winced. "You've done this before."

She nodded. "Combat training."

"Combat training?"

"Army. Two-year stint."

He laughed and shook his head. "I have to tell you, Alex, the more I know of you, the more fascinating you become. Whatever possessed you to join the military?"

"It's a long, boring story."

"Nothing about you is boring. Tell me."

She shrugged. "I could say it was a family tradition, but the truth is I wasn't ready for college, and figured a two-year stint would do me good. I could always use the GI Bill to help get me an education later."

She left out the part where she had heard rumors that her father had fled to the Middle East, and how she had naively believed she might somehow be able to contact him once she got over there. She had been so young and stupid then.

"So did you?"

She dried the wound and applied some ointment. "Did I what?"

"Get an education."

She nodded again. "I had thoughts about joining the FBI,"—another naive notion that it might help her gather information about her father—"so I majored in Legal Studies, with a minor in Anthropology. I figured since I had a military background and I'm fluent in Farsi, getting in would be a slam dunk."

"You speak Farsi, too?"

"My mother was Iranian. She made sure to teach me."

He studied her carefully. "Yes, I see it now. She must have been very beautiful."

Alex wasn't sure why his gaze made her uncomfortable, but it did, though not in a bad way.

"And did the FBI accept you?"

"Not even close. They rejected me outright."

He frowned. "Why?"

She took out one of the butterfly bandages and ripped open the wrapper. "That's another long and boring part," she said, the edge creeping back into her voice, "and I'd rather not get into it, if you don't mind."

"We can stop talking altogether, if you prefer." He gestured to the wound. "You have my life in your hands."

She laughed and started applying the first bandage. "Trust me, this little thing isn't even close to life threatening. You probably won't even feel it in a day or two. I doubt it'll leave a scar."

He let her work for a moment, then said, "If you don't mind my asking, how do you go from Legal Studies and Anthropology to working as a…fugitive retrieval specialist?"

"Simple. I met a guy at a party, we got to talking and hit it off."

"A boyfriend?"

She laughed again. "No. Turned out he'd been doing trace work for a bondsman, but wanted to strike out on his own and needed a partner. With my background and training, he thought I might be a good fit."

"I suppose in a profession like that, being a woman has its advantages."

"Being a woman always has its advantages." She finished up and patted his bare chest. "And it looks like my work here is done."

Gathering the wrappers, washcloths, and first-aid kit, she got to her feet, but before she could take a step, Gérard grabbed hold of her wrist. It was a gentle enough move, but most men would have regretted making it.

"There's no hurry," he told her. "I'm too wired to sleep. Stay for a while. Talk."

She looked around the bedroom. "In here?"

He gestured to the doorway. "We can go out to the sitting room if you like. I wouldn't want you to get the wrong impression."

He was smiling again. She thought for a moment, then set the washcloths and first-aid kit on the nightstand.

"No," she said. "This is fine."

Then, in a move that surprised *her* even more than it did Gérard, she climbed onto the bed and kissed him.

He didn't seem to have any trouble kissing her back.

Now here she was, lying in the dark, still unsure what had possessed her to climb into his bed in the first place.

Maybe it was simple. Maybe at that moment she had needed to be close to someone. Maybe his charm and drunken attempt at gallantry and her own attempts at playing nursemaid had gotten all the right synapses firing and the rest was inevitable.

Whatever the case, it was done, and she needed to get the hell out of there. And when Gérard came back for more, assuming he would, she'd explain that everything from here on out was strictly business. She just wanted to make this deal and go home.

When it came down to it, he probably wanted the same

thing.

After pushing the sheet aside, she carefully extricated herself from the bed and searched the floor for her clothes. She found her jeans and underwear lying on one side of the room, her T-shirt on the other, and didn't remember removing any of them.

Jesus, Alex. What are you, an animal?

She heard Gérard stir and suddenly felt vulnerable standing there in the buff. She got dressed as quickly as possible, scooped up the mugger's gun from the dresser, and tucked it in her waistband. Tiptoeing over to the nightstand, she kept her gaze on Gérard, then quietly slid open the drawer, and removed a pad and pen, both stamped with the Largo Inn logo.

She stood hunched over the pad, pen ready, trying to figure out what to write. She got as far as *Dear Thomas* and stopped, ripped off the sheet and crumpled it in disgust before returning the pad and pen to the drawer.

After checking to make sure she wasn't leaving anything behind, she went to the door and let herself out.

When Alex was gone, the man who was calling himself Thomas Gérard opened his eyes and reached for his mobile phone on the nightstand. Punching in a speed-dial number, he climbed out of bed and went to the window overlooking the hotel's front parking lot.

He waited through three rings before the line came to life and a voice said, "Yeah?"

"She's leaving the hotel."

"Why so early?" A hesitant pause. "You think we're blown?"

Outside, Alex Poe emerged from the hotel entrance and crossed toward her car, her hair a clear victim of the night's acrobatics.

"Judging by the way she climbed all over me, I highly doubt it."

"Just be careful," the voice said. "She's a fierce little

bitch."

"In more ways than you'll ever know, but she's a lot more vulnerable than she lets on. And *she* isn't the one who cut me."

"Hey, you wanted it realistic, remember? A little blood goes a long way."

Gérard touched the bandages on his rib cage and pushed out a dry, humorless laugh. "That's easy to say when it isn't your blood."

EIGHT

ALEX HAD TURNED off her cell phone in Gérard's hotel room, and now discovered she had five new messages waiting for her—two texts and three voice mails.

All from Jason McElroy.

Given that it was the middle of the night, she was tempted to call him right then and hang up once she knew she'd awakened him, but the prudent course was to continue ignoring him. Whatever the asshole was hot to talk about could wait until she was back in civilization.

She wasn't being obstinate. Well, maybe she was, but when it came down to it, she got no joy from working for the guy. It was a relationship of convenience and little else, and after the mix-up in Istanbul, she wasn't anxious to hear what he had to say.

Stonewell International was a large, highly respected, multinational security firm that, among other things, specialized in black ops fugitive retrieval. If you wanted someone found and wanted it done off the grid, Stonewell was first on your list. As long as you could afford the fee, of course.

Last year, McElroy had gone to great lengths to bring Alex into the fold. He had only succeeded because he'd had information she wanted: the identity and location of someone who'd had recent personal contact with her father. Someone who might know his whereabouts.

Nearly a dozen years ago, her dear old dad, Colonel Francis Edward Poe, had been branded a traitor by the US government for reasons that had never been clear. Most of his file was classified, and Alex's attempts over the years to dig up the truth had resulted in a big fat zero. But she knew one thing for sure: her father was not a traitor. She didn't argue that he had changed after her mother's death, but he had always been a good soldier, and betraying his country was simply not in his DNA.

Alex had all but given up trying to find him when McElroy approached her. His scheme was simple. He wanted Alex to bag a known terrorist who was temporarily being held under an assumed name at a woman's prison in Crimea. All Alex had to do was pose as an inmate, gain the woman's confidence, and break her out of the place—a task that had proven difficult but not impossible.

Unfortunately, the end result had not been a rendezvous with her father, as Alex had hoped, and the only thing that kept her working for Stonewell was McElroy's promise that she had full use of the firm's data network to aid her in correcting that result.

But Alex was no longer the naive eighteen-year-old who had joined the army in hopes of finding the old man. She knew Frank Poe was a considerable prize that someone like McElroy could use to help feather his cap, so she had no illusions about her and her boss's relationship. He was exploiting it as much as she was, and would use whatever information she managed to uncover to find Frank Poe for himself.

All she had to do was beat him to it.

Shortly after three a.m., Alex pulled her rental car into the carport under the Shimmy Shack, still feeling the sting of her impulsiveness. She couldn't deny the sex had been good, but her ability to fall into bed with a guy she'd known for less than three hours left her worried about her sense of self-preservation.

For all she knew Thomas Gérard was a serial killer.

As she climbed out of the car and started up the steps, she again thought about the treasure box and the website link and the wedding video and wondered if he'd had something to do with them. It didn't seem likely, but what if she had been betrayed by his charm and good looks and her own damnably fragile psyche since she'd found that photograph?

She was halfway up the steps when all thoughts of Gérard abruptly vanished.

The Shack's front door was ajar.

Though she'd been upset when she left, she knew she'd locked it, so this could only mean one thing: the intruder was back.

Son of a bitch.

Quietly reversing course, she returned to the car and retrieved the mugger's gun from the glove box. There was sand on the weapon, but she brushed it off and tucked it into her waistband, then went around to the rear of the house to see if the sleeping bag was still on the ground.

It was.

Okay, so what did that mean? Had he not had a chance to retrieve it before he saw her pull in? Or, if he was still upstairs, had he even seen or heard the car at all? That was certainly a possibili—

A muffled crash from above.

There was no *if* about it. Someone was definitely up there, and she'd be damned if she'd let him get away.

She moved through the darkness to a set of wooden steps that led up to the patio—the same steps she and Danny had taken to the beach every day. Switching to stealth mode, she ascended them quickly and quietly, hoping the weather-punished wood wouldn't creak under her weight. It did, but only faintly, and she doubted it could be heard inside the house.

When she reached the top of the stairs, she peered through the sliding glass and saw nothing but the silhouettes of the den sofa and chairs. She took out her keys and unlocked the door, slid it open just wide enough to fit through, then pulled the gun from her waistband and slipped inside.

Movement. She definitely heard movement. Coming from the front of the house.

She stepped into the hallway, pressed her back against the

wall, and worked her way toward the living room. She was halfway there when she heard the sound of running water coming from the kitchen.

She paused long enough to pull her cell phone from her pocket and call up the flashlight app, but didn't activate it. She edged her way down the rest of the hall and made the turn into the kitchen.

Raising the gun and phone simultaneously, she switched on the flashlight and said, "Move and you're a dead man."

There was a loud yelp and a guy in a suit stumbled back against the counter, a wet cloth in one hand, the right leg of his pants rolled up to reveal an almost hairless shin with a nasty red cut in the pasty white flesh.

"Jesus, Alex, it's me! It's me!"

Jason McElroy.

She let out a breath and lowered the gun. "What the hell are you doing here?"

"Just so you know, half the damn lightbulbs in this dump are missing and the rest are broken. I was searching for a working lamp when I ran into that piece of crap you call a coffee table."

"I repeat," Alex said, "*what* are you doing here?"

"Right now I'm trying to keep from bleeding to death."

She stepped forward, and raised the gun again. For all she knew, *he* was the one who had planted the treasure box. "You'd better explain, Jason, or you'll be bleeding a lot more."

"Put that thing down, will you?" He shut off the faucet, hobbled to a chair at the table, then sat and inspected the damage to his shin. "You know, if you answered your phone once in a while, we could have avoided this unpleasantness. I'm here because I need you. It's that simple."

As he dabbed at the wound with the wet cloth, Alex had zero urge to repeat her nursemaiding efforts on McElroy. The threat of nuclear holocaust couldn't make her go down that road.

She crossed to the stove, turned on the hood light above it, then put away her cell phone and said, "You always need me. Why do you think I didn't call you back?"

She, Deuce, and Cooper had handled three successful acquisitions since the op at Slavne prison last year. The grab in Turkey was supposed to have been the fourth.

He said, "You're still angry about what happened in Istanbul."

"Shouldn't I be?"

"Okay, fine, I understand. I was angry, too. But until the government starts asking me for diplomatic advice, there's not a whole hell of a lot I can do about it."

"Diplomatic advice? You think consorting with a known terrorist is diplomacy?"

McElroy sighed. "We consorted with bin Laden until he became inconvenient. Same with Saddam Hussein. The world isn't good guys versus bad guys, Alex. It's all about who has what we need when we need it."

"I'm not sure I want to live in that world."

"Oops, too late." He tossed the cloth into the sink and rolled down his pant leg. "I'm not here to debate politics, all right? If you're looking to catch bad guys, I've got a major acquisition lined up and I can guarantee this one won't turn out like the last. Fair enough?"

With reluctance, she laid her gun on the counter.

"Maybe I'd rather sit this one out," she said. "Sit them *all* out."

"And do what instead? Go back to rounding up fugitive junkies for a few hundred bucks a head?"

"Keep in mind I know who I'm talking to when I say this, but it's not all about the money."

McElroy forced a laugh. "Okay. Fine. We can pretend that's true. What about information, then? That's part of the reason we're in business together, remember? Quid pro quo."

She gestured toward the front door. "Don't bump into it on the way out."

She turned down the hall, heading toward the den and the patio beyond. When she heard McElroy shuffling behind her, she picked up speed.

"Alex, wait."

"I'm done talking, Jason."

"Maybe so, but if you think I can get a cab out here at this time of morning, you're out of your mind. I had a hard enough time getting one from the airport."

She stopped and turned in the doorway. "So what am I supposed to do, offer you a cup of coffee and a donut? You've got Stonewell International at your beck and call. Get somebody to pick you up."

She went out to the patio and stood at the rail. It was too late to sleep and too early to be alive. She tried to enjoy the view but could feel McElroy standing somewhere behind her, undoubtedly trying to figure out how to get her to change her mind.

She was about to turn and tell him to get lost when her phone rang. She pulled it out of her pocket, checked the screen, and saw Deuce's face staring up at her.

Now what?

She answered it. "Do you know what time it is?"

"I figured you'd be awake. And you sound pretty alert."

"A lot more than I want to be."

"I'm calling to give you the heads-up. Our supreme commander chartered a helicopter and he's at your beach house, looking for you. He just called me. There's something major brewing and he's pissed because you haven't—"

"The heads-up is supposed to come *before* I get ambushed, genius."

"Oh, shit, you're there? Did he tell you what the gig is?"

"No," Alex said. "And I don't want to know."

A pause. "You're still pissed about Istanbul, aren't you?"

"Why does everyone keep asking me that? It just happened a couple days ago. Give me time to get over it."

"Look, Alex, nobody wishes it could've turned out different more than I do, but I think you should listen to what the man has to say. He's already promised to double our salaries for this gig, and between you and me, I could use the cash."

"What happened to all that money you saved?"

"I don't want to talk about it."

"Deuce..."

He sighed. "Okay, I ran into an old buddy yesterday and he talked me into sitting in on a game of Stud. And you know what a lousy poker player I am."

Alex couldn't believe it. "Are you telling me you lost it all?"

"I can probably make my rent this month if I don't go crazy, but that's about it. Which is why I'm begging you, kiddo. Hear the man out and seriously think about taking the gig. He won't include me if you're not there."

"Then he's a fool," she said.

"Yeah, well, that goes without saying. But it is what it is. So do me a solid and listen to his pitch."

Alex wanted to reach through the phone and strangle Deuce. He was a great partner and one of her very best friends, but for a smart guy, he could be such a brain-dead moron sometimes.

"All right," she said. "I'll listen. But only because it's you."

"Thanks, Alex."

"That doesn't mean I'm agreeing to anything. If I don't like the sound of it, you'll have to scrape up next month's rent some other way. Sell your body or something."

"Isn't that what we already do?"

He hung up without saying goodbye. She stuffed her phone back in her pocket and wheeled around, knowing McElroy was waiting in the doorway.

"So is that how it works? First, you use Cooper to help recruit me, now you use Deuce to convince me to stay? What did you do, hire some card shark to cheat him out of his savings?"

"You give me too much credit," he said. He had his nose in his phone and was typing something.

She scowled. "I should've shot you in the kitchen. Answer one question before we get into this."

He looked up. "All right, what?"

"Why haven't you asked me where I was tonight?"

McElroy shrugged. "Is it any of my business?"

"Is anything ever your business?" She thought about asking him outright if he'd planted the treasure box, but if he wasn't involved, she'd just as soon keep it to herself.

"Look, Alex, one of these days you're going to have to learn to trust me a little. I really couldn't care less where you were tonight. All I care is that you're here now. So why don't you do us both a favor and put the hostility in check for a minute? I've got two words I think you'll want to hear."

"Which are?"

"Reinhard Beck."

"The anarchist? I remember reading about him when I was kid."

"Anarchist, assassin, child killer, friend to genocidal tyrants—take your pick. He's done it all and he's still doing it." He gestured. "I just sent his dossier to your phone. The usual encryption."

Alex dug out her phone again, saw the alert, and tapped in the password to retrieve the file. "I assume I'm supposed to be excited about this?"

"You should be. This guy's wanted in about fifteen different countries. And thanks to you, we've got the exclusive on him."

"Thanks to *me?*"

"I probably shouldn't tell you this, but my guy from DHS asked for you personally as a condition of the deal. You're building quite a reputation for yourself. Even the snatch in Istanbul is considered a win since you already had the target in hand."

"Don't get me started."

Her cell phone screen filled with a fuzzy black and white photo that looked as if it had been grabbed from an ancient surveillance video. Reinhard Beck stood in a bank with a sawed-off shotgun pointed at one of the tellers, his head turned toward the camera, giving her a full view of his face, as if to say *fuck you*. He was a tall, athletic looking man with light hair pulled back in a ponytail, and eyes as cold and dull as a Burmese python's.

"Is this the most recent photo you've got?"

"It's the *only* photo, except for a couple of school shots from when he was a child."

She nodded, then moved past McElroy and went inside, sinking into a chair as she flipped through the surprisingly thin file for such a major player. It was little more than a rundown of Beck's most heinous crimes, and a series of unconfirmed sightings over the last twenty years. He was a founding member of the German terrorist group known as the Black Hat Battalion. The organization appeared to have no particular political affiliation other than mayhem, and seemed to focus its talents on weapons and explosives trafficking, from which it made a great deal of money. Beck himself was known to his associates as Valac, a nickname with roots in demonology.

Lovely, she thought and looked up at McElroy. "Okay, I can see why you'd want to grab this guy. So where do we find him?"

"Does that mean you're in?"

Alex hated being so predictable, but she had a weakness for chasing after badasses, and this one was about as bad as you could get. If things went right, catching the bastard might even make up for the last debacle. And there was Deuce to consider.

Of course, that didn't mean she had to cop to it.

"Where is he?" she repeated.

"Not far from here. You've heard of St. Cajetan?"

"It's in the Bahamas, right? Club Med for the super rich."

"That's the one." He gestured to the chair across from her. "Mind if I sit?"

She did, but granted him permission anyway, and watched him hobble across the room, still clearly in pain after his battle with her grandfather's coffee table.

Good.

"Here's the thing," he said as he sank into the chair. "This

isn't the usual track-and-grab job. It's slightly more complicated."

Alex didn't like the sound of that. "Explain."

McElroy told her a story about the recent bombing in New
York, and how one of the people involved had led investiga-
tors to a Serbian nationalist. This, in turn, put them on to a
maze of phone calls that clued them in to an upcoming
meeting between Reinhard Beck and a man named Frederic
Favreau. Favreau was looking for a buyer for a set of codes
he'd managed to acquire, and Beck, aka Valac, was first in
line.

"What sort of codes?" she asked.

"That, I don't know. Top secret, eyes only, don't pass Go,
all the usual nonsense. I'm not sure why they don't just arrest
Favreau and be done with it, but I have a feeling our friends
at State have gotten greedy. They're looking for a twofer."

"And for the sake of political expediency, they want us to
execute it," Alex said. "We grab Valac and the codes, and
take the blame if it all goes south."

"Right. Only not in that order."

"What do you mean?"

"They don't want Valac to have the codes in hand even for
a minute. That's how paranoid they are. Our job is to snatch
the codes *before* we snatch Valac, make sure they're secure,
then go after the prize."

"So we take Favreau down first."

McElroy shook his head. "That may spook Valac and
nobody wants to take that chance. This is the closest we're
ever likely to get to him."

"Then how do you propose we handle it?"

McElroy took something from his jacket pocket and
tossed it to her. "These are hot off the press."

Using her phone for light, Alex opened an artfully forged
and distressed passport and saw her photograph above the
name ALEXANDRA BARNES. Tucked into the back pages
was a laminated ID card with the same photo and name,
showing her as a "Correspondent" for Travel Planet

Lifestyles, an online travel site.

"Travel Planet Lifestyles?"

"It's a Stonewell front," he told her. "We've used it as cover for a number of ops when discretion is needed. It's fully operational, so if anyone checks, it's legitimate. It took some quick and dirty finagling, but we managed to snag you a couple days on the island. You'll be doing a video profile of St. Cajetan for the site, complete with camera crew."

"You've gotta be kidding me."

"Not in the least," he said. "We want you to cozy up to Frederic Favreau at the hotel, locate and switch the codes, then let him lead you straight to Valac."

Alex arched a brow. "Cozy up?"

"I'm told you're just his type."

"Oh, brother," she said, tossing the passport and ID card into his lap. "I think you've got the wrong candidate for this job."

"What's the difference between this and throwing on a prison smock or pretending to be a radiology technician?"

"For one thing, I didn't have to 'cozy up' to anyone."

"I'm not asking you to do anything you're uncomfortable with. Just flirt with the guy. Lead him on until we can determine how he's transporting the codes and make the switch."

"And who's the 'we' in this scenario? Are you leading the operation?"

McElroy shook his head. "I'm leaving that to Cooper. He'll be coordinating and using Deuce and Warlock for support. They'll be posing as your production crew."

"Warlock? Who the hell is Warlock?"

"Oh, that's right. You haven't had the pleasure yet. Warlock's a prodigy. We recruited him straight out of HMP Nottingham, where he did time for back-dooring a supposedly hack-proof MI6 database when he was seventeen. His only mistake was bragging about it online. He'll be handling surveillance and comm tech and anything else computer related."

Alex didn't like the idea of working with strangers any

more than she liked having to play dress-up again, but the more she thought about it, the more she realized she needed this distraction. It didn't hurt that she might be doing something worthwhile.

"If Valac is hot for these codes, why the face to face?" she said. "Why doesn't Favreau just transfer them electronically? Wouldn't everyone be safer that way?"

"The answer's dead simple. Valac's old school. He doesn't trust the Internet. Or Favreau."

"Okay, so what's the method of delivery, then? Data chip? Thumb drive?"

"We don't know."

"*What?*"

"That's something you'll have determine before they finalize the deal. Once Favreau arrives on the island, Valac will likely want to keep him at arm's length until he's sure Favreau isn't up to anything that might compromise him. So hopefully you'll have a couple days to figure it out."

She looked at him. "You're not asking for much, are you?"

"If I didn't think you were up to the job, I wouldn't be asking at all."

She huffed. "I thought my participation was a condition of the deal?"

"I'm trying to give you a compliment, Alex. Can't you be gracious enough to accept it?"

"That would require me to pretend I like you," she said. "And I don't."

"I'm painfully aware of that fact."

NINE

IT HAD BEEN only a few days since Istanbul, but it felt good seeing Deuce again. There was always a certain comfort in that big, goofy grin of his.

He was waiting for Alex on the tarmac outside the Key West airport terminal, standing under a sign that read GOLD KEY CHARTERS. He wore a yellow and blue Hawaiian shirt and a pair of khaki cargo shorts, his pockets loaded down with photography gear and peripheral equipment. A bulky Canon 5D camera hung at his neck and two large packing cases sat at his feet. Alex assumed they contained video and lighting gear.

During a telephone briefing with McElroy and Cooper, they had all agreed to travel in character in case anyone was watching, and Deuce was playing his part to the hilt.

After giving him a hug, Alex asked, "Do you even know how to use any of this stuff?"

He shrugged. "What's to know? It's like a gun. Point and shoot."

"Come on, Deuce, this has to be convincing or it'll never work."

"Don't sweat it. I've been studying the manuals. Besides, nowadays, anyone sees me hefting anything bigger than a cell-phone camera, they'll figure I *must* be a pro. Otherwise, why bother?"

True enough, she thought, wishing she had some kind of prop that would sell her role in this as easily.

A full day had passed since her early morning meeting with McElroy. She had spent a lot of that time going through the rest of the junk in the Shimmy Shack's storage shed, trying to decide what to keep and what to toss, half wondering if she'd stumble across another mysterious gift.

She didn't, but then one such gift was already more than enough.

She had watched the video at least ten times since the first viewing, and still couldn't fathom why her parents had never told her about the marriage, or why whoever had planted the box wanted her to know. It was obvious her mother had a whole other life prior to coming to America that she had kept a secret, but what did that have to do with Alex all these years later?

Repeated viewing had not yet produced an answer.

Alex had been in the middle of one of those viewings when Thomas Gérard called her, wanting to know why she had sneaked out of his hotel room. He thought they had "found a connection" and wanted to see her again.

Exactly what she'd been afraid of.

"Will you meet me tonight?" he asked. "We could actually have dinner this time."

Alex struggled to find a way to let him down easy. She carried way too much baggage for the average relationship. Instead, she said, "As much as I'd like to, I can't. I'm leaving the country tomorrow."

"Oh?" He sounded surprised and disappointed. "Where will you be going?"

"Stockholm," she lied. "I've got some business to take care of."

"Bounty hunting business?"

"Fugitive retrieval, remember?"

"Yes, that's right, you're a specialist." She could almost hear the smile in his voice. "You seem to specialize in a number of things."

It was a pointed remark and felt a little out of character for Gérard, but she didn't make an issue of it. He was, after all, a man. And no matter how refined, men always want to talk about it afterward, most often in the form of ham-handed innuendo.

It wasn't a game Alex had any interest in playing. "Have

you heard from your client yet?"

The abrupt change in subject distanced him. "Yes. I have. He hasn't had a chance to look at the photographs, so he promised to call me back tomorrow."

"I'll be gone by then."

"So you said." Another pause. "Alex, did I do something wrong?"

It's not you, it's me, she almost told him, a worn cliché that so often proved true in her case.

"No, of course not," she said. "I'm just a little distracted right now, trying to get ready to go. I'm switching phones for the trip, so I won't be available at this number. Why don't you e-mail me when you've heard from your client?"

An even longer pause. "Of course."

"Thanks, Thomas. It was great meeting you. We'll talk soon."

"I hope we do," he said quietly, then hung up.

Now, standing outside GOLD KEY CHARTERS with Deuce, she felt like a jerk. Why couldn't every relationship she had be as easygoing as the one she had with Deuce? He was an unpretentious guy who rarely expected anything of her except that she pull her weight, which she was more than happy to do. Sure, there was no romance, but maybe she was better off avoiding those kinds of entanglements entirely.

"You ready?" he asked.

She was traveling light, told by McElroy that all necessary wardrobe needs would be waiting for her in St. Cajetan. Cooper and the new guy, Warlock, had flown to the island the night before to secure a room as close to Frederic Favreau's as possible and begin preliminary surveillance. Favreau had reportedly landed first thing that morning and had gone straight to the hotel.

"I'm not sure," she said, in answer to Deuce's question. "I'm still trying to get a handle on who Alexandra Barnes is supposed to be. How do I play this?"

"Think of yourself as the travel industry's answer to Lois Lane."

"So what does make you? Jimmy Olsen?"

Deuce winced and said, "Let's just get on the plane."

They flew to the island on a De Havilland Otter DHC-3 floatplane. Alex and Deuce were two of eight passengers strapped into narrow seats, all with clear views of the cockpit.

Looking around, Alex guessed there was enough jewelry in the cabin to fund a small war, which wasn't surprising given that St. Cajetan was known for its luxurious accommodations. GOLD KEY CHARTERS, on the other hand, favored function over luxury. While the plane appeared perfectly maintained, it had a vintage, pre-sixties vibe to it that clashed with the haute couture of its passengers.

Deuce spent most of the hour-long flight dozing as Alex pulled out her computer tablet and once again fired up the wedding video. Each time she watched it, one thing became clearer and clearer: Her mother was not your typical blushing bride. The look in her eyes suggested she didn't even want to be there.

Alex ran it through again, and this time, something new caught her eye. She had been concentrating so much on her mother and the man beside her that she hadn't noticed it before. As the camera panned past the bride and groom for a brief shot of the attendees, she was surprised to discover that one of the men in the crowd looked familiar.

More than familiar.

She froze the video and stared at the fuzzy image of a man with curly blond hair who seemed out of place in the sea of Iranian faces. A foreigner. An American.

An American she knew.

She found she had to reach into the memory banks to place him, but it didn't take long. He had been to their house when she was a child. And not just one time, but many.

Uncle Eric.

Not a real uncle, but one of her father's oldest and closest friends. He called her Allie Cat, and had dubbed her brother

Dan the Man, a name that had always provoked laughter from Danny. And there had been magic tricks, too, a new one every time he came to visit.

Alex hadn't thought much about him since her mother died, and she couldn't remember the last time she'd seen him.

Could this really be him?

And if so, what the hell was he doing at her mother's Iranian wedding?

"Who's the guy with the bad seventies haircut?" Deuce asked. He was awake now, sitting across the aisle from her, his eyes on the computer tablet. "I don't remember him from the briefing."

"He's not," she said. She put the tablet to sleep before he could get a good look, and tucked it into her backpack.

"So, who is he?"

"Somebody I knew when I was a little kid. Friend of my parents. I'm trying to remember his last name."

"Why?"

"I'm thinking of sending him a postcard. 'Wish you were here.'"

"Then you'll need more than a last name," Deuce said. "An address might help, too. Who is he really?"

Alex usually told Deuce everything, but wanted to keep the events of the last couple days private for a while. Until she could figure it all out.

"He's got nothing to do with us," she told him. "I promise."

"In other words, mind your own business, Deuce."

She smiled. "You catch on fast, don't you?"

From the air, the island of St. Cajetan looked like a deformed pear.

The floatplane approached from the Southeast, giving them a view of the uninhabited side of the island and its jungle of coconut palms and casuarina trees growing out of a thick, vibrant green undergrowth that would take a finely sharpened machete to hack through.

The plane banked left and began to circle toward the far side of the island, and as they approached civilization, Alex was struck by the notion that it looked very much like the photographs she'd seen of 1950s, pre-Castro Havana.

But as the plane continued to descend, she could see that this initial impression wasn't quite true. The Hotel St. Cajetan and the buildings and city surrounding it seemed to be part of a faux, manufactured replica of a bygone era, like an Art Deco Disneyland, or a massive outdoor movie set at Warner Brothers studios—every speck of dirt, every luxurious pool, every sweaty cantina likely the product of a Hollywood production designer.

Now she understood why this plane hadn't been modernized. It wasn't out of place. It was just another part of the image and illusion of St. Cajetan.

Alex knew from the Stonewell briefing that at eighty miles long and thirty miles wide, St. Cajetan was one of the larger of the seven hundred islands that made up the Commonwealth of the Bahamas, and had been sold to a private developer in the early eighties for a rumored five hundred million American dollars. It was now a sovereign state with its own government and paramilitary police force and economy. Over the last three decades, the developer, an egocentric billionaire named Leonard "Leo" Latham, had built the place into the exclusive tourist mecca it was today, and had reportedly tripled his investment and then some.

Over the intercom, the pilot welcomed them all to "paradise." The floatplane made its descent and landed smoothly on the glassy surface of the water in Latham's Cove—yes, the developer had named it after himself—and cruised toward a large wooden dock. Several hundred yards beyond a wide stretch of sand, the Hotel St. Cajetan greeted them in all its Habana-wannabe glory, while dockside, a cadre of smartly uniformed bellboys waited with their suitcase carts as the plane came to a stop and cut its engine.

"Welcome to paradise" was repeated several times as Alex, Deuce, and their jewelry-jangling fellow passengers unstrapped their seat belts and stepped onto the dock.

Alex knew she was supposed to have her game face on, but she was distracted by lingering thoughts of Uncle Eric and his presence in the wedding video. It bothered her that she couldn't remember his last name. She knew it was sitting somewhere at the periphery of her mind, but until it came forward, she wouldn't be able to run a check on the guy. She had considered using Stonewell's facial recognition software, but knew the video was too old and fuzzy for reliable results.

Setting it aside for the time being, she reminded herself she was now Alexandra Barnes, travel correspondent extraordinaire, and waited as Deuce supervised the loading of his equipment onto one of the bellboy's carts. She then followed them up the dock toward the hotel lobby.

Let the games begin.

TEN

Cooper greeted them with a big smile. "Alexandra...
Sticks... Glad to see you finally made it."

The hotel lobby was about half the size of an airport
hangar, impeccably decorated with French leather club sofas
and chairs, flanked by what looked like authentic Edgar
Brandt side tables and lamps. The textured tile floor was
polished to such a high shine that Alex almost felt guilty
walking across it.

As Cooper told the bellboy there were more bags in the
hotel's storage room, Alex said quietly to Deuce, "Sticks?"

"McElroy's contribution to my cover," he told her. "Apparently a lot of camera guys get saddled with the name because
of the tripod."

She rolled her eyes. "He watches too much TV."

"What he lacks in imagination he makes up for with a
nice, fat discretionary spending budget. If I didn't like the
money he's paying me, I'd have to kick his ass."

"If you let yourself get lured into another poker game, I'll
have to kick *yours*."

Deuce grimaced. "Don't worry, I'll never make that mistake again."

While the bellboy was away fetching their things, Cooper
said, "The good news is, Warlock hacked the hotel's reservation system and switched us to a four-bedroom suite on
Favreau's floor. The bad news is, it's across the hall instead
of next door, so setting up surveillance could get complicated."

"Why couldn't he get the suite next door?" Deuce asked.

"It's been occupied for the last month by some British rock

star I've never heard of. Except for the parade of groupies going in and out of the room, he's holed up in there like a hermit."

Deuce sighed. "I knew I should've kept up those guitar lessons."

They took the elevator to the tenth floor, and made their way down a wide hallway with more leather club chairs and a hand-tufted, black and cream Art Deco carpet. It was clear to Alex why staying here cost a small fortune. This stuff didn't come cheap.

As they approached their room, Cooper nodded toward the corner door at the end of the hall to their right, indicating Favreau's suite. Without better surveillance access, they'd have to get creative. Hopefully the new guy, Warlock, had the goods.

"I think Favreau may be a hermit, too," Cooper whispered as he unlocked their door. "He's had the Do Not Disturb sign on since he got here and hasn't left the room."

"That could be a problem," Deuce said.

Cooper nodded. "We'll just have to give him a reason to go out."

They stepped inside their suite and found themselves in a small foyer with yet another Edgar Brandt table along the wall, this one tall and narrow with a mirror above it. After stepping around a corner into the living room, Alex couldn't help but pause. The room was an immaculately furnished Art Deco wonderland. The walls, the curtains, the flooring, the furniture all screamed "luxury accommodations."

Unfortunately, the pleasing visual line was interrupted by the presence of a large rolling metal cart in the middle of the room, and the slender, leather-jacketed street bum slouched on a stool in front of it.

Sitting atop the cart was an open laptop and three monitors mounted side by side on a stand. The street bum—Warlock, Alex assumed—was so wrapped up in whatever he was typing on the laptop that she wasn't sure he even realized they were there.

"Hey, Warlock," Cooper said as they approached. "I want you to meet Alexandra Poe and—"

Without moving his gaze from the screen, Warlock raised an index finger to silence him.

Cooper, Deuce, and Alex exchanged looks as Warlock continued to type for a moment, then finally looked up and said in a thick British accent, "Sorry 'bout that. I lost the connection to the CCTV feed and wanted to…"

He paused, eyeing Alex as if he had only now noticed her, then broke into a grin. There was a sparse patch of beard on the point of his chin, while his hair looked as if he'd recently been caught in a windstorm. He reminded Alex of Scooby Doo's friend Shaggy, and if she had run into him on the street, her first thought would've been *heroin addict*.

The only thing that shattered that notion was the sleek, futuristic pair of glasses he wore.

"Hold on now," he said. "What's this?" He gave her the once-over. "I heard you were a looker, but you're a right fit bird, aren't you?" He got off the stool and offered a hand to shake. "Alex, right? I'm Warlock."

She shook the hand as he lowered his gaze slightly.

"And if you don't mind my saying, that's a cracking pair of baps Mother Nature blessed you with."

Alex frowned, not quite sure she'd heard him right. "*What*?"

He wagged a finger at her chest. "Baps. Bristols. What I believe you Americans call hooters, although yours are more like delicate—"

Alex had her hand around his throat before he could finish the sentence. She flung him backward onto the sofa and pinned him there by the neck, his glasses askew, his face turning red as he tried to breathe.

"Listen to me, you little shit…"

"Alex…" Cooper said.

"…You talk to me like that again…"

"Alex…"

"…and I swear to God you'll find yourself sipping your dinner through a…"

"Alex, *enough*. We need this guy."

She held on a second longer before letting Warlock loose. He scrambled to his feet and backed away, coughing and staring at her with wounded, disbelieving eyes. "Bloody 'ell! What was that for?" His voice was a strangled rasp.

She glared at him. "You seriously don't know?"

He pulled off the glasses and inspected them as if they were a precious heirloom, then turned to Cooper. "This slag is mental. You expect me to work with her?"

"If you want to get paid, I do."

Deuce smirked and sank into a nearby chair, crossing his ankles as he leaned back. "Have we got any popcorn in this joint? I think I'm gonna enjoy this show."

"He keeps talking to me like that," Alex said, "I guarantee you will."

"Talking to you like what?" Warlock slipped the glasses back on and pressed a button on the frame. "I don't know if you realize it, but I was trying to give you a compliment."

"If that's what passes for a compliment in your world, then…" She paused as she noticed his eyes widening slightly, his gaze now fixed on the upper right corner of the glasses, as if he saw something moving there.

Cooper noticed it, too. "What's wrong?"

Warlock gestured to the cart. "Seems our boy Freddy is on the move."

They all looked at the computer screens, each showing close-circuit shots of the hallway they had just traveled through, the center camera facing the right corner door. A slightly overweight man in chinos and a navy blue polo shirt stepped into the hall, checked the DO NOT DISTURB sign on the knob, and started the trek toward the elevator.

Frederic Favreau.

Cooper and Warlock moved to the rolling cart, Cooper snatching up a black plastic packet and tossing it to Deuce.

Deuce nearly fumbled it as he got to his feet. "What's

this?"

"Comm set. We're running the surveillance."

"Where's mine?" Alex asked.

He scooped up another packet and tossed it to her. "You're on comm, but you're staying here. You can help Warlock."

"You're leaving me with *him?*"

"You want this ruse to work, don't you? We can't risk Favreau seeing you yet."

She understood his reasoning, but that didn't mean she had to like it. She nodded, reluctantly, and threw a look at Shaggy's evil British twin, who was busy pulling a metal case from the bin at the bottom of the cart.

Cooper checked the monitors, then handed Deuce a holstered SIG Sauer and gestured. "He's nearing the elevator. We'd better get moving."

Deuce tucked the rig into his waistband at the small of his back and popped in a miniature earbud. The earbud was so tiny it could only be retrieved by the short piece of nylon thread attached, and was invisible to the naked eye.

He grinned at Alex and Warlock. "Keep it civil until I get back, kids. I don't want to miss anything."

Alex showed him a middle finger and he laughed as he followed Cooper out of the room.

She turned to Warlock, who was laying the case on the sofa she had pinned him to.

"Okay, genius, so what's *our* plan?"

"I take it we're calling a truce?"

"If you can keep your so-called compliments to yourself, we'll be just fine. What's the plan?"

As if all were forgiven, he grinned at her and threw the metal case open to reveal a stockpile of miniature cameras and microphones and other surveillance goodies Alex wasn't familiar with.

"I don't know about you, but I've got a very serious desire to invade Freddy boy's privacy."

ELEVEN

WHEN COOPER AND Deuce emerged from the stairwell on the main floor, they found that the elevator had come and gone and Favreau was nowhere to be found.

"He moved faster than I expected," Cooper said and scanned the crowded lobby, seeing no sign of the guy. He touched the transmitter in his pocket and spoke into his mic. "Hey, Warlock, you still in the room?"

"Not for long."

"Check the security cams for Target One. I don't have a visual on him."

"Give me a mo," Warlock said. Then, a few seconds later: "Front entrance, left side of the tarmac. He's queued up for a cab."

"Thanks."

Cooper and Deuce hustled to the hotel entrance, where a large stone fountain bubbled in the middle of a circular drive, and saw a roped-off area to their left, where several guests were lined up next to a sign that read TAXI.

Favreau was at the end of the line.

Cooper said to Deuce, "Get in behind him. I've got a car in the hotel garage, but if I'm not back before he's gone, try to grab a cab and follow him."

"Why don't I just put a tracker on him? Shouldn't be a problem."

Cooper shook his head. "I don't want to risk him finding it later. We'll do this old school."

Deuce grinned. "My stock in trade."

Less than three minutes later, Cooper was behind the wheel

of his rental, a perfectly maintained blue 1950 Buick Super that was as common here in St. Cajetan as a Lincoln Town Car in DC. Pulling around to the hotel's front drive, he spotted Deuce near the fountain, waving him over.

"Take a right," Deuce said as he climbed into the passenger seat. "Yellow cab headed northwest."

Cooper hit the gas and made the turn, only to discover a sea of yellow cabs on the street ahead, all American classics like the car he was driving. This city seemed to be living in a self-induced time warp.

Deuce pointed toward one of the cabs, an old Plymouth that looked very much like the two in front of it and one in the adjacent lane. "There. That's the one."

"You sure?"

Deuce frowned. "Do I *look* like an amateur? Bent license plate and rusty dent on the left side of the bumper."

Fair enough, Cooper thought, taking visual note of the cab's deformities as he nudged the accelerator and sped after it.

"He made a phone call while we were standing in line," Deuce said. "Had the number on speed dial."

"What'd he say?"

"Just confirming a time and that he was on his way."

"So it's a meet," Cooper said. "This could be a problem."

"You think it's Valac?"

"I don't know, but if it is, it's out of character. According to his profile, Valac is extremely careful about who he does business with, and so is Favreau."

"Maybe Favreau's already been vetted."

Cooper shook his head. "Other than the phone calls the NSA intercepted, there's been no indication of any other contact between them, and Favreau's only been here since this morning. McElroy thinks the reason he was summoned here at all is to give Valac a chance to check him out before they close the deal."

"So why the concern?" Deuce asked.

"Because McElroy's been wrong before."

The cab made a left at the next intersection, taking them down a narrow, pockmarked street crowded on either side by tall, moldering tenement buildings. There was a different feel to this part of the city, as if they had crossed some invisible line and entered the real St. Cajetan, the one that wasn't carefully controlled and maintained by the island's corporate overlords. You'd never find this street on any of the brightly printed tourist maps the hotel provided.

"He's stopping," Deuce said.

Cooper eased off the accelerator and pulled to the curb as Favreau's cab came to a halt in the middle of the street. After a moment, the rear passenger door opened and Favreau emerged, looking about as in sync with his environment as a ballet dancer in a hardware store.

"I guess we're on foot," Cooper said. He killed the engine and opened his door.

"Wait," Deuce told him. "What if he's just being careful? He may switch to another cab."

Cooper nodded and tossed him the keys. "You stay with the car. I'll follow him and give you the heads-up if he pulls anything. We should know soon enough."

As Cooper climbed out and closed his door, he saw Favreau rounding a corner at the end of the block. Cooper looked around for any prying eyes, noticed nothing but a couple of locals sitting on a nearby stoop sharing a joke and a joint, and headed after his target.

He slowed as he reached the corner, cognizant that Favreau might suspect he was being followed, and made the turn as nonchalantly as possible.

The adjacent street was empty.

"Shit," he murmured.

"What's wrong?" Deuce asked in his earpiece.

"He's gone again."

"What?"

"You may've been right. He may have had another cab waiting for him. I don't see him any…"

Cooper heard the peal of laughter, and spotted a man and

woman emerging from an alleyway about half a block down. The man, squinting against the sun, looked like a slumming tourist who hadn't seen daylight in quite some time. The woman was dark-skinned and local, clad only in a sheer red camisole and panties, and a pair of high heels that were tall enough to cause a nose bleed. She had her hands all over the tourist, coaxing him to come back into the alley.

Cooper knew there were two possibilities at play here. The alley either led to a whorehouse or a strip joint.

Or a combination of both.

"Hold on," he said to Deuce as he headed toward them. "I think I know where our target is."

TWELVE

WARLOCK MAY HAVE been a rude punk, but once the clock started ticking, his ability to abandon all distractions and stay focused on his task impressed Alex.

After checking the CCTV cams on those strange, futuristic glasses, and telling Cooper where Frederic Favreau had gotten to, he returned his attention to the case on the sofa and continued picking through the gear. He inspected each piece, setting several micro video cameras and a handful of audio transmitters to the side.

"These should do the trick," he said, then looked up at Alex. "Are you ready?"

"Just waiting on you."

"You aren't going to try to strangle me again, are you?"

"Stop making me want to," she said.

A few seconds later they poked their head out the door, checked to make sure the hallway was clear, and headed for Favreau's corner suite.

"Keep an eye on the elevator," Warlock told her. "I've put a loop on the security cams up here, but we wouldn't want anyone to catch us breaking into Freddy's room."

"And how exactly do you plan on doing that?"

He smiled and held up a fat felt pen. "My secret weapon."

"A permanent marker?"

"This isn't just any marker." He removed the cap to reveal what looked like the cylindrical connector for an AC adaptor in place of the usual felt tip. "My sonic screwdriver."

"Your what?"

"I take it you're not a fan of The Doctor?"

Alex had no idea what he was talking about, and was

starting to feel the urge to hurt him again. "Just get it done and explain it to me later, all right?"

He smiled. "You're a feisty one, aren't you?" She gave him a look and he raised his hands. "Sorry, sorry. My ex-girl-friend always said I'm a shameless prat who doesn't know when to keep my mouth shut."

"I have nothing but sympathy for her. Now are we gonna do this, or wait until Favreau gets back and ask *him* to open it?"

"Consider it done," he said, and stepped up to the door. He was about to use his so-called sonic screwdriver when he froze. "Hmmm."

"What's wrong?"

"Looks like Freddy's a belt-and-braces man."

"Belt and braces?"

"Overly cautious. Not that I can blame him." Warlock got closer to the door and studied the frame, top to bottom. "Unless I'm mistaken, and the likelihood of that is zero to none, he has an inexpensive but crudely effective wireless perimeter alarm hooked up to this door."

"How do you know?"

"My glasses rarely lie."

She looked at the door and saw nothing, but was willing to take his word for it. "Okay, so can't you use your fancy pen?"

He eyed her with disdain. "This is for locks, not cheap counter-espionage devices. If we try to breach this entrance, Freddy'll likely get a notification on his cell phone that someone has invaded his space, and we'll never see him again."

"So we fly blind? That's not gonna work at all. We need eyes in that suite."

Warlock nodded. "I really do wish I could have procured the room right next to this one. " He looked across at the rock star's door. "They're bound to share a ventilation system."

"So maybe he'll let us in," Alex said. "I can distract him while you do your thing."

"Who? Bellamy?"

"Is that his name?"

Warlock nodded again. "Liam Bellamy. A Liverpudlian git who thinks playing a single chord and howling like a strangled cat is music."

"I take it you're not a fan?"

"Hardly. Considering where he comes from, you'd hope that some of the influence would have rubbed off, but this twat makes millions proving there's no direct relationship between talent and environment."

"You think you could pretend to be one? A fan?"

"Of Bellamy's?" He looked as if she'd asked him to clean out a septic tank. "I suppose I could, but I'd have to seriously consider suicide afterwards."

"Works for me," Alex said. "Hopefully you'll wait until this op is done."

"Anything for Stonewell. What do you have in mind?"

"Just follow my lead."

Alex moved to the rock star's door and knocked. Loudly. She waited a few seconds, got no answer, and knocked again.

Still no answer.

She turned to Warlock. "Apparently he isn't a hermit after all. Looks like you're off the hook." She gestured to the marker in his hand. "So show me some magic."

"With pleasure."

He stepped up to Bellamy's door. "This hotel, like many around the world, is equipped with a key-card lock with a particular flaw that anyone with a little talent in electronics and a connection to the Internet can exploit. I discovered this trick online."

"And here I thought you were an evil genius."

"Genius? Yes. Evil? Only when necessary. But I'm afraid I can't take credit for this one." He uncapped the pen again and held it under the door's lock mechanism. "There's a small hole under here and all I have to do is poke the tip of my wand into it, and as my dear departed grandmother used to say…Bob's your uncle."

A green light came on and Warlock turned the knob, opening the door.

"Well, I'll be damned," Alex said. "Thank God for insolent punks who know how to use the Internet."

Warlock arched a brow. "If you aren't careful, sooner or later you're going to hurt my feelings. Wasn't throttling me enough?"

"Somehow I don't think so. Shall we?"

She pushed the door wide and they stepped into a foyer and a living room very similar to theirs, except for three significant differences: It was a corner suite, had only one bedroom, and was a complete dump. Furniture was overturned, room service trays held piles of dirty dishes, empty beer and liquor bottles were strewn about, clothing hung off barstools and lamps, a broken acoustic guitar stuck out from under the sofa, the wall-mounted television monitor had cracked glass, bath towels were piled in a corner, and the overall stink rivaled the Quarantine Road landfill back in Baltimore.

Warlock sniffed. "Tell me that isn't dead body I'm smelling."

They heard a very loud snore coming from beyond the bedroom doorway.

"Not dead yet," Alex said, "but definitely circling the drain."

They crossed to the bedroom, peered inside, and saw a very naked rock star sprawled faceup across a king-sized bed, clutching a half-empty bottle of Chivas Regal.

Warlock gestured, keeping his voice low. "Ladies and gentlemen, I present the Liam Bellamy in its natural habitat. Don't get too close or it's liable to impregnate you."

Alex eyed him flatly. "You do know you're not nearly as clever as you think you are, right?"

"Now you're just being cruel."

"Uh-huh. So what's the plan, here?"

Warlock gestured to the wall behind the bed. "Freddy's

suite is beyond that wall." He indicated an air-conditioning duct up near the ceiling. "Looks as if I was right about the ventilation system, which means I'll need to find the crawl space into the ducts, which I assume is somewhere around here." He nodded toward an open doorway. "Maybe the loo."

"Okay," Alex said. "Go do your thing. I'll stay here and babysit in case our boy from Liverpool beats the odds and wakes up."

"And if he does?"

"I guess I'll have to improvise."

THIRTEEN

FREDERIC FAVREAU WAS not a patient man.

He knew this about himself and attributed it to his up-bringing in a home for wayward youths in Newark, New Jersey. He had always tried to adjust accordingly, but there was only so much abuse he could take before his true nature took over.

He was dangerously close to reaching that point with Reinhard Beck, and he hadn't even met the man. What he had hoped would be a simple transaction via the phone and encrypted e-mail had turned into what could only be characterized as an elaborate, time-sucking audition.

And for what?

The honor of selling the great god Valac a piece of information?

Ridiculous.

Wasn't it enough that Favreau had tortured and killed someone to get that information? He was not, and never had been, a fan of such brutal methods of extraction, but he did whatever needed to be done. And if that bastard scientist had been smart enough to take the money Favreau had offered, such drastic measures would never have been necessary.

You'd think Valac would appreciate Favreau's initiative, but no. You don't get an audience with a superstar unless and until you've jumped through all the necessary hoops.

True, a short vacation in St. Cajetan was nice, but Favreau had no desire to play the part of the trained monkey, ready to dance on command. If Valac's initial bid on the merchandise hadn't been much higher than anyone else's, Favreau wouldn't even be here. But his patience was wearing thin and he was willing to take only so much before he'd tell the son of a bitch to fuck off, then take the next plane home.

The place that had been chosen for the preliminary meeting was a dive. Favreau had spent time in his share of strip joints over the years, but this one looked like something from the outer rim of hell. Most of the women were dogs, for one thing, like the one on stage, pimping for Bahamian dollar bills. There was nothing less appealing than a stripper with the face and body of a pit bull.

He sat at a table, drinking scotch, staring morosely at what looked like a hair on the rim of his glass that was clearly not his, when a couple of hard cases walked in through the front entrance, spotted him, and came over to the table.

Favreau had never seen Valac before, had only spoken to him on the phone, but neither of these guys looked like they fit the voice.

The tall one, obviously in charge, scraped a chair back without an invite and sat across from him as the other one hung back a little, keeping his eye on the door.

"Good afternoon, Frederic."

The accent was American. If Favreau had to guess, he'd say the guy was ex-CIA, one of the many who had either gone rogue or hired themselves out to men like Reinhard Beck.

"Where's Valac?" he asked.

The tall man smiled. "Dealing with other matters at the moment. He sent me to continue the negotiation."

"Continue?" Favreau said. "He made his bid and heard my counter. Either he accepts it or I'm gone. I know a man in Chechnya who would kill for what I'm selling."

"I assume you're talking about Dakalu?"

Favreau tried to keep the surprise off his face. How could they possibly know whom he'd been in contact with?

"Dakalu is no longer in contention," the tall man said. "He's had an unfortunate accident."

"Accident?"

"Something to do with his car exploding. I don't know the

exact details."

Favreau felt a chill run down his spine. What the hell was going on here?

The tall man was still smiling. "I believe you'll find that Owusu and Budiono have withdrawn from the bidding as well. So that leaves only Valac."

What started as shock was turning into anger. Favreau said, "So is this your idea of negotiating? You brought me here to try to intimidate me?"

"Of course not. Valac loves the island and wants others to enjoy the experience just as he does. It isn't often that men like us get a chance to relax, but St. Cajetan is something of a safe haven, and he thought you might appreciate it here."

"Bullshit," Favreau said.

"There's no need to be hostile, Frederic."

"Look, I don't care if your boss is the last man on Earth, if he thinks he can lowball me—"

The tall one raised a hand. "It's not like that. Valac is a man of honor. He simply wants a couple days to consider your latest price and asks that you humor him. In the meantime, he hopes you'll indulge in the many pleasures the island has to offer."

Favreau gestured to the woman on stage. "You mean like dog face over there?"

"I'm sure some men find her very appealing. But if she isn't your type, there are bound to be others on the island who are. A tourist, perhaps. There's quite a selection this time of year, and they all have money."

"The only money I'm interested in right now is Valac's. Either he wants what I've got to sell or he doesn't. Tell him I expect an answer by tomorrow."

"I'll be sure to relay the message," the tall man said as he got to his feet. "We'll be in touch again. Very soon."

"You'd better be. Or competition or not, I'll withdraw my offer and leave."

The tall man gave him one last smile. "I'm afraid you might find it difficult to secure a flight, Frederic. You can certainly try, but I wouldn't recommend it at this point."

Favreau felt something stir in his intestines. "Is that some kind of threat?"

"Now why would we feel the need to threaten you? We all want the same thing, don't we?"

He nodded to the other man and the two crossed the bar and exited.

When they were gone, Favreau let out a long, shaky breath, then flicked the hair off the rim of his glass, knocked the rest of his scotch back, and ordered another.

From his table across the room, Cooper watched Favreau down his drink and said into his comm mic, "Deuce, you out front now?"

"That, I am."

"There are two guys coming your way, one tall, mid-to-late fifties, curly gray hair. The other mid-thirties, dark, looks like muscle."

"I got 'em, they just exited. The tall one looks a little familiar but I can't place him. I'll take photos for facial recognition."

"I'm guessing they're Valac's men, so you'd better follow them."

"I figured as much, but how can you be sure?"

"Because Favreau looks like he's about to drop one in his pants. Once he leaves, I'll catch a cab, see if I can keep up. But from the look on his face, I figure he's done for the day."

"You sure he isn't done for good?"

"I don't think so. Nothing exchanged hands. No money, no merchandise. So I think we're okay."

"Roger," Deuce said. "I'll be off comm for a while. Talk to you on the other side."

Keeping his gaze on Favreau, Cooper touched the transmitter inside his pants pocket and sent a signal to Alex.

After a moment, she responded. "You rang?"

"How are things going back there?"

"Hunky-dory," she said. "I'm babysitting a naked rock star,

and the twit with the fancy glasses is banging around inside the ventilation system as we speak."

"You're in the *rock star's* suite?"

"That would be a yes."

"What the hell happened?"

"Favreau booby-trapped his door so we had to improvise."

"Jesus," Cooper murmured. "Warlock, are you on comm?"

"The twit with the fancy glasses is a little busy at the moment," Warlock told him.

"Just give me an assessment."

"All right, but you won't be happy. I have limited choices up here, meaning one. I can snake a single cam into Favreau's living room through the AC vent, but I don't know how good the signal will be. He has some all-purpose jammers in place that've buggered up my equipment. Which means a compromised picture and little or no sound."

"That's the best you can do?"

"I'm afraid it is. The vent is too small for physical access to his room and the rest of the vents are cut off."

Cooper sighed. "We'll just have to get you in there somehow." He saw that Favreau had finished knocking back another drink and was climbing to his feet. "In the meantime, Target One is on the move, so unless he makes a stop, you've got about ten minutes to get that camera in place. I don't want to chance him getting even a *hint* of what we're up to."

"Almost there," Warlock said.

"Good. See you soon."

Alex had hold of Warlock's legs and was helping him climb out of the crawl space above the toilet—and trying to avoid the blinding sight of his butt crack in the process—when the snoring abruptly stopped in the bedroom behind them and the rock star groaned.

"Shit," she said.

She left Warlock hanging and sprinted out of the bathroom, closing the door just as Liam Bellamy came awake.

He blinked groggily at her, his expression a mixture of drunken confusion and outright surprise. "Who the 'ell are *you*?"

"You don't remember? I'm insulted."

He frowned and thought about it. "Did we shag last night?"

Alex swallowed a tiny bit of bile. Between Warlock's butt crack and this guy's almost hairless body, she was beginning to have her doubts about the UK's male population. Surely they could do better than this.

She put on her best post-coital smile. "We did, and it was amazing."

"Brilliant," he said. "You up for another go?"

She almost choked. "Sorry. I have to get to work."

He shrugged and wagged his fingers at the door. "All right, then. You can see yourself out."

Without another word, he rolled over, buried his face in the pillow, and was snoring again within seconds. Relieved, Alex pushed the bathroom door open, and found Warlock still hanging there, his pants threatening a plunge toward his knees.

Maybe agreeing to take this job hadn't been such a good idea after all.

FOURTEEN

DEUCE FOLLOWED THE gray-haired man and his muscle-bound buddy as they drove several blocks then took a turn onto St. Cajetan's only highway. According to his GPS, the road wrapped around the entire island, with only a single gap on the south side that would require a four-wheel drive to traverse. Not something in large supply around here.

Deuce kept a healthy distance from them, enjoying the view of the ocean as he drove, not particularly concerned about being spotted. His car looked like a hundred others he'd seen on the road today, and he doubted the gray-haired man or his buddy would notice him. He was just another tourist exploring the island.

The two men made no stops, keeping a steady pace until they'd traveled about thirty miles into a less densely populated area, where they finally turned onto a narrow road that looked very much like a long driveway.

Whatever it led to was hidden by dense tropical foliage.

Deuce sped past the turn, drove for a few seconds, then pulled to the side of the road and waited for the highway to clear before making a U. He headed back and came to a stop at a roadside fruit stand located only yards away from the driveway.

After cutting the engine, he grabbed his camera, and filed through the shots of the two men he'd taken outside the strip club. The muscle didn't look familiar, but he was positive he'd seen the gray-haired man's face before. He just couldn't remember where.

He got out of the car and approached the fruit stand, which was manned by a local boy of about nine or ten. He raised the camera and kept the driveway in frame as he took several shots of the boy climbing off his perch and approaching with a plate of sliced mango. "You like a taste?"

"Sure." Deuce fingered a slice and popped it into his mouth. Damn, it was good. Gesturing toward the driveway, he asked, "You have any idea where that goes?"

The boy nodded and grinned, showing him big white teeth. "Pappy Leo's house."

"Who?"

"Pappy Leo. King of St. Cajetan."

Deuce realized he was talking about Leonard Latham, the billionaire who owned the island.

The kid pushed the plate toward him. "More?"

Deuce ate another slice and said, "Have you been up there before? To the house?"

The boy nodded enthusiastically. "Pappy Leo asked me to bring him fruit. Paid me twice what I wanted. He's a very nice man."

"So what does the house look like?"

"Big," the boy said. "Very big."

Deuce gestured toward the driveway again. "And is that the only way in?"

The boy shook his head. "They have a service road in back. No trucks allowed this way." He pushed his plate forward again. "The mango is good, yes?"

"Yes," Deuce said after sucking down another slice. Probably the best he'd ever tasted.

"Will you buy some?"

Deuce tucked the camera under his arm and reached for his wallet.

"I do believe I will," he said.

Deuce found the service road on a street full of rundown shacks at the rear of Pappy Leo's estate. He parked the car in front of an abandoned lean-to and traveled on foot, stepping past a sign at the mouth of the road that read PRIVATE. DELIVERIES ONLY.

About a quarter mile in, he heard the echo of voices and the slam of a door. A moment later, an engine started and accelerated in his direction. He backed away from the road and hid in the underbrush as a van rumbled past, the name ST. CAJETAN MAIL SERVICE printed on its side.

When it was gone, he waited for a moment then returned to the road, and continued traveling along it until it widened slightly and began to rise up a small hill. He moved into the bushes again and worked his way to the crest of the hill, then crouched amidst a cluster of coconut trees and peered down toward a large white mansion that looked as if it belonged on a Southern plantation.

Though he saw no fence around the perimeter, there was a checkpoint manned by two uniformed security guards at the end of the service road.

He heard voices again and shifted his gaze. Three men sat at a table on a large veranda at the rear of the mansion, drinking beers as they talked.

Deuce raised his camera to study them more closely through the telephoto lens. The one facing him was the gray-haired man he'd been following. To his left was a man Deuce recognized from photographs—Leonard Latham, or, as the kid had put it, Pappy Leo. The man sitting directly across from them had his back to Deuce, but his gray-streaked hair was pulled into a ponytail.

Valac?

Deuce wished he could hear what they were saying.

He snapped off several shots of them, then trained his lens on the mansion and its lush grounds. He counted four exterior CCTV cams covering the courtyard and walkways and the lap pool at the rear of the house. He didn't see any more guards, but that didn't mean they weren't there. If ponytail really *was* Valac, Deuce didn't imagine he'd go without protection.

As Deuce lowered the camera, the gray-haired man jerked his head up, looking in his direction.

Shit, Deuce thought as he ducked out of sight.

Did he see the reflection of the lens?

Deuce heard a shout that sounded like a command, and the jungle around the mansion came alive as uniformed guards rushed out from behind trees and started toward him.

Son of a bitch.

Slinging the camera around his neck, he headed back the way he'd come. Fast.

Not wanting to chance using the road, he made his way through the underbrush, hacking at it with his hands to clear a path. He heard a radio squawk behind him, closer than he expected, and dove to the ground, rolling under the protection of a large bush as he reached toward the small of his back for the piece Cooper had given him.

It was gone. The holster must have been dislodged when he rolled.

He scanned the ground but saw no sign of it.

Seconds later, two guards appeared on the roadside only yards away, checking the trees and undergrowth for any sign of movement. They clutched what looked like FAMAS Infanterie assault rifles.

These guys weren't fooling around.

Deuce held his breath and remained perfectly still, wondering if they'd stay where they were or go off road.

And if they did, then what?

He couldn't allow himself to be seen or this op was blown. It was bad enough that the gray-haired guy had noticed the glint of sunlight off the camera lens, and Deuce cursed himself for being so careless. Like Alex and Cooper, he had spent time in the military—a stint in Kabul with the US Marines—and he should've known better than to make stupid mistakes.

He heard voices. Radios squawking. More guards approaching. One of the two on the road turned in his direction and stepped into the underbrush.

Wonderful.

The guard was getting closer, but making the rookie mistake of looking into the distance instead of down at the bushes directly around him. He wasn't checking his flank, either, and if circumstances were different, Deuce would've had him on the ground by now.

The guard took another step forward and Deuce's heart stopped.

The SIG and holster he'd lost lay in the dirt only three yards away, a foot or so from the guard's boot. Another step and the guy would trip over them.

Finding that gun would prove that what the gray-haired man had seen was a real concern, not just a trick of light. That someone might still be hiding nearby. And if the guard came to that conclusion and kept looking, Deuce would have no choice but to deal with him.

Preparing himself for the worst, he watched as the guard continued to inch forward, looking as if he were about to take that fateful step. The gun was right in front of the guy, partially covered by leaves, but plainly visible in the sunlight.

Then a voice blared out of the radio, telling everyone to report in.

The guard stopped, and took another quick look around before pulling the radio from his belt and thumbing the call button.

"All clear," he said as he turned and walked back toward the road.

Seconds later, several more all clears were transmitted, then a voice said, "All right, false alarm. Return to your positions."

Deuce quietly exhaled as the guard joined his partner and two others who were now waiting on the road. They had a brief conversation, and one of them laughed, then they headed as a group toward the house.

Deuce waited a full ten minutes before he climbed out of the bushes, grabbed his gun and holster, and hightailed it back to his car.

FIFTEEN

ALEX HAD ALL but given up on trying to remember Uncle Eric's last name when something Warlock said triggered it.

They had returned from the rock star's suite, a frustrated Warlock blathering on about how he didn't appreciate being left hanging in that bathroom, and how he wished he could've gotten a better video feed into Favreau's suite. "The luck we're having, Freddy boy's bound to get skittish and play rabbit before we find out how he plans to deliver those codes."

"We'll figure it out," Alex had said. "One way or another."

But the word "rabbit" remained in her mind, niggling at her for several seconds. And then, without warning, the name she had been seeking surfaced in a flash—

Rabbit. Hop. *Hopcroft.*

Eric Hopcroft.

She wasn't sure what else she may have said to Warlock, because the moment she remembered that name, she snatched her backpack off a chair and carried it into the nearest bedroom.

Behind her, Warlock said, "Why are you going into my—" but his voice disappeared as she closed the door.

As she sat on the edge of the bed, she pulled her computer tablet from the backpack and brought the device to life, tapping the icon that gave her immediate, encrypted access to Stonewell's databases.

Stonewell International had been collecting information in the field for over thirty years, enough to fill a warehouse full of databanks, and unfettered access to this resource was the main reason Alex was willing to put up with McElroy and participate in ops like this one.

After she logged in with the proper decryption key, she called up the search menu and typed in the name HOPCROFT, ERIC.

The search engine took only milliseconds to deliver a profile photo of the man from her mother's wedding video, accompanied by identifying text:

> NAME: Eric Arthur Hopcroft
> DOB: 3/18/56, San Gabriel, Calif.
> DOD: 8/17/01, Republic of Yemen

Date of death?

That would explain why she hadn't heard anything about him after all these years. The odd thing was, he had died only a week before her mother was killed.

A coincidence?

Alex searched for the cause of death and saw two words that momentarily froze her.

Gunshot wounds.

She called up the summary and read a brief report claiming Eric Arthur Hopcroft had been on a field assignment for the CIA when he was gunned down by two unknown assassins in Sana'a, the capital of Yemen. The nature of his assignment was currently classified.

So Uncle Eric was CIA.

Okay.

But why had he been at her mother's wedding?

Was he on assignment then as well?

And what was his relationship to her father? Her dad had always treated Hopcroft as his best friend.

Alex thought of the many times the man had come to their house. Holidays. Dinner parties. Weekend barbecues. He'd even shown up at one of Alex's piano recitals, back when her parents shared the delusion that she had some musical talent.

But why?

Had he come because of Dad, as she had always believed, or because of *Mom*?

It was possible Uncle Eric had been a friend to both her mother *and* father, and might well have been the reason they met, but something about this situation didn't feel right. Especially when she factored in Hopcroft's profession.

So, why had he attended her mother's wedding?

Was it an official visit? A clandestine one? Personal?

And why had he been killed only days before the bombing of the cafe in Lebanon?

What, if anything, was the connection?

Contrary to what Alex had hoped, there were even more questions flooding her brain now, and as she tapped through the pages of Hopcroft's file, she saw nothing that helped her. He was long dead, and any answers he might provide had been buried with him.

Feeling depressed, she sighed, closed the file, and logged off the database.

It was times like this that she wished she was still in Baltimore running skip traces and bagging local fugitives, back when she had adjusted to the idea that she would never again see her father, and the memories of her mother were simply reminders that she and Danny had once been loved.

Now she felt as if she didn't know her parents at all, that they had been strangers who had merely pretended to be part of their happy family.

How had it all gotten so complicated?

By the time she returned to the living room, Cooper was back, and Deuce was just coming in, looking disheveled and dirty. His expression was as serious as Alex had ever seen it, no trace of his usual, easygoing grin.

"What the hell happened to you?" Cooper said.

"You don't want to know. But it looks like Valac's a guest of Pappy Leo and has an army protecting him."

"Pappy Leo?" Alex said.

"Leonard Latham. King of St. Cajetan. That's what the

locals call him."

"He's staying at *Latham's* place?"

"I couldn't get a face shot to confirm, but my gut tells me it's our man."

As Deuce set his camera on the end table, Alex noticed several cracks in the lens.

She grabbed it and tilted it up. "What did you do? Fall on it?"

"As a matter of fact, yes," he said, taking control of the camera again. He flicked open a compartment on the body, ejected an SD card, and handed it to Warlock. "I'd lay odds that if you do a facial scan and ID the gray-haired guy outside the strip club, you'll find Reinhard Beck on his list of known associates."

"I'll get it started," Warlock said, moving to his laptop. "But this isn't like what they show us on the telly. It could take some time."

"That's fine," Cooper told him. "In the meantime we'll operate on the assumption that Deuce is right."

Alex frowned. "From what I read about Latham, he's a bit eccentric, but I don't see him as the type to be hanging out with a known terrorist."

Cooper shrugged. "Maybe he's getting a thrill out of it. Or maybe Valac is using an alias and Latham has no idea who his guest really is."

"A guy who just happened to show up with an army?"

"I'm guessing most of them are Latham's men. A typical show of power. I don't imagine people call him the king of St. Cajetan for nothing."

"You should see his house," Deuce said. "*Big* plantation style."

"How many men are we talking?" Alex asked.

"At least half a dozen. Probably more. But the good news is, they're not that competent. If they were, I wouldn't be standing here right now."

"Where you spotted?" Cooper asked.

"No, but it was close enough to get me sweating." Deuce

looked at Warlock. "You have any luck rigging Favreau's suite?"

"Luck isn't the word I'd use," Warlock said.

"So what word *would* you use?"

Alex told him about the snafu and the workaround, and Deuce plopped heavily into a chair. "Well, isn't that wonderful. If we tell McElroy any of this, he isn't gonna be happy."

"I'll deal with McElroy," Cooper said, then turned to Warlock. "Are you online with that feed you managed to run?"

"Watch and weep." Warlock tapped a key on his laptop and gestured to the center screen, where a high-angle shot of the living room in Favreau's suite appeared. The problem was, there was enough snow and horizontal interference to make it nearly impossible to see. "Our boy Freddy's one paranoid little wanker. I don't know many blokes who travel with a perimeter alarm and a jammer in their kit." He smiled. "Besides us, that is."

Cooper pointed to the monitor. "Is that the best you can do?"

"I've been trying different frequencies, but it looks as if he's running interference on all of them."

Alex studied the screen and was reminded of the scrambled adult cable stations she'd stumbled across as a kid. You could see movement, but it required some imagination to fill in the blanks. She thought she saw Favreau crossing toward an alcove in the wall that mirrored one in their room.

She gestured to the screen. "I think he's headed for the safe."

Deuce leaned forward in his chair and squinted. "Or doing a mean mambo."

"He could be keeping the codes in there."

"Or storing them in the cloud," Warlock said, "with industrial-grade encryption."

Cooper shook his head. "He's got no control over the cloud. And a guy who goes to this much trouble for security is worried about getting ripped off. I don't know about the safe, but I'm guessing they're somewhere in that room."

"So we're back where we started," Alex said. "We still need access."

Cooper nodded. "Which means we have to up our game. It's time to play dress-up."

Her expression blank, Alex said, "I can't tell you how thrilled I am to hear you say that."

Deuce grinned. "At least it ain't undersized hospital scrubs."

SIXTEEN

IT MAY NOT have been undersized hospital scrubs, but the on-camera attire Stonewell had chosen for Alex was unambiguous in its message: Alexandra Barnes, travel correspondent extraordinaire, was not a modest woman, and what she may have lacked in talent was surely made up for by what little she seemed to wear.

Thanks, guys.

The suitcases they'd sent were full of bikinis and tight cutoffs and evening attire that straddled the line between Madonna and whore. All of it may have been appropriate for an island vacation, but Alex was more of a jeans and T-shirt kind of girl. The last time she'd worn a nice dress was at a law enforcement cocktail party three years ago, so slipping into a Terani red strapless mini that hugged every curve had her feeling self-conscious.

When she stepped off the elevator and walked into the hotel lobby, Cooper, Deuce, and Warlock all stopped what they were doing and stared at her for an excruciatingly long moment.

"Easy boys, it's just a dress."

It took Cooper a few seconds to find his voice. "I guess that's where we'll have to disagree."

Warlock had sense enough to keep his mouth shut, but his face said it all as Deuce whistled. "Wow, kid, you clean up good."

"Thanks...I think."

The three of them were in costume as well, which meant they wore basically the same things they'd been in all day. Cooper, the "producer/director," had added an electronic

clapboard to his ensemble, while Deuce and Warlock had chosen job-appropriate accessories to enhance their wardrobes—a hefty video camera balanced on one shoulder for Deuce, and a long pole with a microphone mounted on the end for Warlock.

Cooper seemed to be having a hard time taking his eyes off Alex. She rarely regretted being female, but at moments like this, she hated it. This dress made her feel more like a display piece than a human being.

She said to Warlock, "What's going on with Favreau?"

His gaze shifted to the upper right corner of his glasses. "He's heading for the elevator as we speak."

Warlock had managed to hack a line into the phone in Favreau's suite, and they'd heard him make a dinner reservation at the Cajetan Cafe for nine p.m. He was dining alone, so they had figured this was their best chance for Alex to make her move.

They got into position near the elevators, Deuce pointing his camera in Alex's direction as Warlock held the boom mic above her head. To a professional crew, they probably looked like amateur hour, but the Internet was undemanding, and everyone else was bound to think they knew what they were doing.

"He's on his way down," Warlock said.

Cooper got in front of Alex and held up the electronic clapboard. "Alex in Wonderland, take one."

He clapped the board and stepped away. Alex took a breath, focused on the teleprompter mounted on Deuce's camera, and began to read the copy, doing her best to sound like a semi-talented talking head with some major T&A appeal.

"I'm Alexandra Barnes, and we're here in the lobby of the Hotel St. Cajetan, an Art Deco masterpiece that boasts over three thousand rooms, two casinos, seven restaurants, and an old-world Caribbean vibe that has most visitors believing they've been transported to the island via time machine."

The elevator doors behind Deuce and Warlock slid open,

and a small crowd of passengers that included Frederic Favreau spilled out. They all looked at the camera and boom mic, and began to buzz a little as they filtered past. In Favreau's case, it was his eyes doing the talking, taking in Alex in much the same way Cooper's had.

So far, so good.

"On our visit here," Alex continued, "we'll be showing you every facet of the hotel and its luxurious accommodations, as well as the must-see beaches and landmarks around the island that make St. Cajetan one of the most popular vacation destinations for millionaires and billionaires from around the world."

She offered the camera her best fake smile and held it until Cooper said, "All right, cut it."

She briefly made eye contact with Favreau, trying to show a hint of interest, then turned to Cooper. "I feel like we need one more. What do you think?"

"I think it was fine and I'm beat," he said. "If we need any retakes we can do them in the morning."

Alex was about to reply when she turned and saw that Favreau was already halfway across the lobby, headed for the Cajetan Cafe.

"So much for attracting his attention," she said quietly.

Cooper smiled. "Believe me, you got it. I thought his eyes were gonna pop out of his head. Not that I can blame him. Deuce is right, you *do* clean up good."

"*My* eyes are up here, Shane."

His gaze shifted. "Hey, what can I say? I'm human."

"Let's concentrate on Favreau, okay? I'll give him a few minutes then make my entrance."

Favreau was in the middle of his dinner by the time the maitre d' sat Alex at a small table across from him. It had taken a fifty-dollar tip to get the table she wanted.

As Favreau looked up, the maitre d' draped a napkin over Alex's lap and said, "Will you be dining alone this evening?"

"Yes."

He handed her a menu encased in leather. "Enjoy your meal."

She stopped him before he could leave. With Favreau within earshot, she wanted to sell her cover while she had the chance. "Excuse me, but my producer would love to include your cafe in our profile of the hotel. Who would he contact to arrange a tour of the kitchen?"

The maitre d' seemed unimpressed. Maybe she needed to slip him another fifty. "The general manager. He's available during office hours. Is there anything else?"

She told him no, thanked him, and when he went away she opened the menu and pretended to ignore Favreau as she read through her options. Several times, she felt Favreau's gaze on her but she kept hers on the menu. The man wasn't exactly eye candy, and according to Stonewell's information, had come to expect to pay for the women in his life. So she couldn't make it seem too easy for him. Sure, Alexandra Barnes could be bought—but not too cheaply.

When she finally looked up from the menu, Favreau was concentrating on his meal again. She let him catch her watching him before she looked again at the menu and pretended he wasn't there.

She counted to sixty, then put the menu down and called across to him. "Excuse me."

He had just taken a mouthful and seemed surprised she had spoken to him. He swallowed and said, "Yes?"

"Do you mind if I ask what you ordered? I'm having a hard time deciding."

"The mutton," he said. "But it's a little on the spicy side, so you might want to try something else." He grinned. "Unless you like it spicy."

He was about as subtle as a sledgehammer, and Alex felt like rolling her eyes, but she resisted. "Hmm, I don't know. Maybe you're right. I'd better order something else. Any suggestions?"

"I can think of a few I'd like to make, but no, this is the first time I've eaten here."

"Oh? When did you get in?"

"This morning."

"Are you here on holiday or business?"

"A little of both, I guess. What about you?"

She smiled. "Strictly business, I'm afraid. I couldn't afford this place otherwise."

"I saw you in the lobby. Are you with some kind of news station?"

"I wish. I'm still working my way toward the networks. In the meantime I'm doing destination profiles for a travel website. Maybe you've heard of us. Travel Planet Lifestyles?"

He shook his head. "Can't say that I have, but I'll be sure to check it out now that I've seen what they have to offer. You have a lot of videos on there?"

"Actually, this is my first gig for TPL."

"Well, I'm sure the camera loves you. I'm thinking you may be one of the most beautiful women I've ever—"

"Alex?"

The voice came from across the room and she swiveled her head, surprised to see none other than Thomas Gérard, in all of his Clive Owen glory, brushing past the maitre d' and heading in her direction.

What the hell?

"Alex," he said again as he stepped up to the table, blocking Favreau from view. "I can't believe you're here. I thought you said you were going to Sweden."

This wasn't good. This wasn't good at all. If the words *bounty hunter* or *fugitive* came out of his mouth, her cover would be blown.

"Change of plans," she said quickly. "What are *you* doing here?"

"A client invited me. He has a house he wants me to look at and I was near the island, so…" He paused. "I really can't believe it's you. After that last phone call, I was convinced I'd never see you again. I keep thinking about what a wonderful night we had and I—"

"Thomas, not here, okay?"

"What?"

She tried to send him a message with her eyes. "I don't want to talk about this right now. I'm here on a job."

"You mean—?"

"Yes. I'm working. And right now I just want to eat in peace, if you don't mind."

He put his hands on the table and leaned toward her, lowering his voice. "Listen, I don't know what I said or did to upset you, but—"

"Thomas, I mean it. Not now."

He looked at her as if she had slapped him. "Then when?"

She sighed. "I don't know. But I have work to do and I can't have you interfering. Do you understand?"

He stood up. "I suppose I do. Yes."

"I'm sorry, Thomas, I really am, but this just isn't the right time. How long will you be on the island?"

"A few days."

"Then we'll talk before I leave. Are you staying at the hotel?"

He nodded.

"All right," she said. "I'll call you. I promise."

He stood there and she could see he wanted to say more, but he didn't push. Instead, he bowed slightly, said, "Enjoy your meal," then turned and walked out of the cafe.

Alex felt like the world's biggest bitch, but at the moment that was the least of her worries.

When she looked over at Favreau's table—

—he was gone.

SEVENTEEN

"WHO THE HELL was that?" Cooper asked as Alex emerged from the cafe.

Deuce and Warlock were nowhere to be found.

"You heard all that, huh?"

He tapped his ear. "You're on comm, remember? Who is he?"

"Believe it or not, he's my real estate broker."

"The guy who contacted you about the Key Largo house?"

She nodded.

"Jesus, Alex. Did we just get blown?"

"No. You heard everything. I think we're okay. He didn't say anything compromising."

"I don't care," Cooper told her. "This is sloppy. What's he doing here? Did he *follow* you?"

"Were you listening or not? He thought I was in Sweden. It's a stupid coincidence."

"And you're sure he's just your real estate broker? Because that isn't what it sounded like."

Alex frowned. "What difference does it make?"

"Because if this guy is gonna be following you around like a dog in heat—"

"He didn't follow me."

"So you say. But he didn't sound like someone who's all that anxious to go away, either. And that could be a problem, Alex. A *big* problem."

"For the op?" she said. "Or for you?"

Cooper was silent. Which was where he always went when he got angry. She'd seen it a hundred times in Baghdad.

But she had to say it. His anger seemed more personal than usual.

"Look," she told him, "everything'll be fine, so let's do what we came here to do, okay? Where's Favreau?"

Cooper did not look happy. "Deuce, are you reading this?"

"Oh boy, am I," Deuce said in their ears.

"What's Favreau up to?"

"He's on the beach, taking a smoke break. What do you want me to do?"

"Hang back and let me think about this."

One of the elevator doors opened and Warlock stepped off and approached them. "Bloke went up to his room. He's on the eighth floor."

Alex realized he was talking about Gérard and glared at Cooper. "You had him followed?"

"Of course I did. It's standard protocol." He turned to Warlock. "You got any cigarettes on you?"

Warlock patted his jacket pocket. "Always. Why?"

"Give them to me."

Warlock brought out a battered pack of Doinas and handed them to Cooper, who, in turn, offered them to Alex.

"Go down to the beach and ask him for a light," he said.

"Won't that be a little obvious?"

"We don't have much choice, thanks to your real estate friend. Just put on the charm and believe me, he won't care."

"We're talking about a guy who's so paranoid he rigs his hotel room like it's Fort Knox."

"Trust me. If he thinks he's got even a fifty-fifty chance of landing someone like you in the sack, all that paranoia goes right out the window."

"At the risk of getting choked again," Warlock said, taking a prudent step backward, "I have to agree."

Alex shot him a look but said nothing.

"You'd better get down there before he leaves," Cooper told her.

"Fine," she said. She snatched the pack of cigarettes out of his hand and dropped them into the clutch purse she was carrying.

As she headed toward the rear exit, Warlock called out, "Don't lose those. I'll be wanting them back."

She resisted the urge to show him her middle finger.

She found Frederic Favreau sitting on a retaining wall near a kayak stand that was closed for the night. After stopping several yards away, she took out the pack of Doinas, popped one into her mouth, then rooted around inside her clutch.

On the way down she had decided it would be best to use Gérard as a prop, as if his sudden appearance in her life had rattled her.

Which wasn't that far from the truth.

She had passed his presence off to Cooper as a coincidence, but she wasn't convinced of that herself, and wondered if Gérard really *had* followed her here. The question was why.

As she dug through her purse she could feel Favreau watching her again. After a moment, she cursed under her breath and looked up, pretending to notice him for the first time.

She took the cigarette from her mouth. "Oh. Hello again."

"Hi, there."

"You wouldn't happen to have a light, would you?"

"I'm starting to think you're stalking me," he said with a grin. "It's usually the other way around."

She approached him. "I think *I'm* the one who's being stalked. You saw what happened in the cafe, right?"

He took a lighter from his pocket and flicked it. "Hard not to. Old boyfriend?"

She leaned in and lit the cigarette. She'd never been a smoker, but figured she could tolerate a few puffs before she felt like puking.

"No," she said, deciding to stick as close to the truth as possible. "Just somebody I met in Key Largo." She took another puff and exhaled. "Men sometimes get attached to me. I'm not quite sure why."

"Oh, I think you know." He pocketed the lighter. "Before we were so rudely interrupted, I was about to tell you you're one of the most beautiful women I've ever seen."

She smiled. "I never know how to react to that."

"But you're used to hearing it, aren't you?" He held out a hand. "I'm Frederic, by the way."

She shook it. "Alexandra."

"Nice. I like it. What did you end up ordering, Alexandra? At the cafe?"

"Nothing. I didn't have an appetite after Thomas showed up."

"That's not right. You want me to talk to this guy? Tell him to back off?"

She laughed. "No, I appreciate it, but I'm sure he got the message."

"Maybe, maybe not. Some guys have selective hearing when it comes to certain women. I could tune up his eardrums a little."

"I appreciate the sentiment, but no thanks."

Favreau shrugged. "Just trying to help a damsel in distress. I thought I heard him say something about Sweden. Is that where you're from? Because I would've pegged you as American. Although you look like you've got some Middle Eastern blood in you, too."

"You're very observant."

"You're very observable."

She laughed again. He might not be the most attractive or subtle guy in the universe, but he definitely had game.

"Sweden was supposed to be my first gig," she said. "But the girl assigned to St. Cajetan dropped out at the last minute, so here I am."

"And here *we* are." He took a last drag off his cigarette and flicked the butt into the sand. "And it kills me to say this, Alexandra, but it's been a long day and I'm beat."

He got to his feet.

"You're leaving? I thought we might get a drink."

"Trust me, I'm tempted, but it took me twenty-eight hours

and three stops to get here this morning, and all I really want to do right now is sleep. Will you take a rain check?"

She hesitated. "...Of course."

"Good," he said with a nod. "My offer still stands about the ex. Just let me know." He grinned again. "You have a good night now."

Alex watched him in a state of disbelief as he stepped past her and headed up the beach to the hotel.

When he was gone, she said into her comm mic, "Does somebody want to tell me what the hell just happened?"

EIGHTEEN

IT WAS WELL past ten when they all stepped into their suite, feeling depressed and discouraged.

"You know," Deuce said, "I can't really blame the guy. Alex is a wild card right now. For all he knows, she could be law enforcement, or even working for Valac."

Warlock dropped two equipment cases by the door. "The poor git's probably Googling Alexandra's life story as we speak."

"If he is," Cooper said, "He'll find a nice little social media profile Stonewell cooked up. Facebook, Linkedin, Twitter, and credits that include regional television stations in three different states." He turned to Alex. "There's no reason for him to think you're anything other than what you say you are."

"A lot of good that does us now." She kicked off her heels and headed for the living room. "The longer it takes us to find those codes, the closer he gets to making the sale."

Deuce followed her and plopped into a chair. "We could try the fire alarm gambit. Maybe he'll forget to rig his door."

Warlock laughed. "Good luck with that, mate. Freddy boy strikes me as a creature of habit."

"You have any better ideas?"

"Probably. But none that comes to mind at the moment."

Deuce gave him a look and said to Cooper, "Maybe we should grab the bastard and smack him around a little. Get the codes and force him to run point for us."

Cooper shook his head. "We have specific instructions about that. McElroy doesn't want to risk tipping off Valac."

Alex sank to the sofa and leaned back. "Well, maybe

McElroy should get his butt out here and come up with a better solution, because so far his way isn't working. I'm with Deuce. I've always preferred the hands-on approach."

"Technically speaking," Warlock said, "isn't that what you're going for?"

Alex glared at him. "You really do walk the edge, don't you?"

"Has anyone ever told you you're a bit humor impaired?"

"When you say something funny, maybe I'll laugh."

Cooper raised his hands. "All right, children, save it for the playground. We have work to do."

"By the way," Warlock said to Alex. "I believe you still have my ciggies. I'd like them back."

"Sure," she said. She popped open her purse, took out the pack of Doinas, crumpled it into a ball, and tossed it at his chest. "They're all yours."

Warlock's eyes narrowed. "That was my last bloody pack, you—"

"All right, you two, enough," Cooper said. "I know we're all feeling frustrated right now, but you can save this bullshit for somebody else's parade. Are we clear?"

Alex and Warlock were silent, but Alex knew Cooper was right. She and Shaggy were acting like five-year-olds.

Not that Deuce had any problem with it.

"Damn," he said, "I really gotta get me some popcorn."

There was a knock at the door.

They all turned in surprise, then Warlock touched the frame of his glasses, shifting his gaze to the upper right corner. His eyes went wide and he rushed over to the rolling computer cart in the middle of the room. "It's him. It's Favreau."

Alex sat up. "*What?* You're sure?"

"I'm not blind. He's standing in the hallway with a bottle of bubbly."

There was another knock and Alex and Deuce jumped to their feet as Warlock rolled his rig toward his room. While the others cleared out, Alex went to the door, took a deep breath, and said, "Yes?"

"It's me, Frederic, your new smoking buddy. I hope it's not too late to cash in that rain check."

"Oh...uh...I thought you were going to bed?"

"Turns out I wasn't as tired as I thought I was. I got my second wind."

"Okay..." she said. "Give me a minute, all right?"

"Take your time. I'm in no hurry."

Alex stepped away from the door, wondering how she should play this. It was one thing to share a lighter on the beach and maybe get a drink at the hotel bar, but showing up at her room was a bold move. One that told her Frederic Favreau was used to getting his way.

She left the foyer and crossed to her bedroom. She closed the door behind her, slipped out of the dress, then pulled on one of the hotel robes from the closet. Taking her cell phone from her purse—which doubled as a comm transmitter—she dropped it into a pocket.

When she opened the door again, Cooper stood only a few feet away.

"Perfect," he said, eyeing the robe. "This guy'll never know what hit him." He tossed something to her and she caught it. "These should buy us some time."

A bottle of pills. "What are they?"

"Think roofies, only a lot stronger and a lot faster acting. We're talking seconds, not minutes."

Alex was surprised. "You carry these around, do you?"

"They were a gift from McElroy. Something the Stonewell labs cooked up, just in case."

She slipped them into her empty pocket. "Thanks. You've just made my job infinitely more palatable."

"Thank McElroy," he said, then tapped his ear. "I'll be on comm."

As he disappeared into his room, she crossed back to the front door, took another breath, then opened it to find Favreau staring down at the screen on his cell phone.

He quickly pocketed the phone and looked up, taking in

the robe and the subtle swell of her breasts. "Damn, I think I like this even better than the dress." He held up the bottle of champagne. "I hope you have glasses."

"How did you know what room I'm in?"

He grinned. "I'm a pretty resourceful guy. Place like this, you just have to know who to bribe. And when I found out we were hall mates, I thought we might as well get to know each other."

In the cafe and on the beach he hadn't struck her as a man who lacked confidence, but now he displayed a cockiness Alex hadn't seen before. She figured Warlock was right— Favreau had done some checking and found she was safe. At least where it counted. He likely assumed she was nothing more than a gold digger and decided he'd take advantage of the situation.

All she had to do was run with it.

"I guess I should be flattered," she said.

"I guess you should be, because I'm not usually this proactive. But then a woman of your caliber doesn't come along every day." He gestured. "Are we gonna do this or what?"

She stepped aside and let him pass, taking the bottle of champagne from him as they moved into the living room. "Have a seat. Let me find those glasses."

He looked around. "Whoa, this place looks bigger than mine. You're not here alone?"

"I wish," she said, heading into the kitchen. "I'm sharing it with my crew. But don't worry, they've all gone to bed. Early call tomorrow."

He sank to the sofa and leaned back. "The three guys from the lobby?"

"That's right."

"Did you tell them about me?"

"No," she said. "Should I have?"

"I don't want to be stepping on anyone's toes. Things can get ugly that way, and I don't like complications."

She laughed, set the bottle on the counter, and began searching the cupboards for wine glasses. "I'm new, remember? I barely know these guys."

"You don't know *me* at all."

"Yet I already like you better. Besides, two of them are gay and the other one's married."

"Okay, I'll give you the gay guys, but the married one, trust me, he's checking you out. He'd be crazy not to."

She found the glasses and set them on the counter. "You really like to say what's on your mind, don't you?"

He shrugged. "I'm a man of many faults and few regrets."

"You're also good for a girl's ego."

He grinned again. "I aim to please."

"And I aim to drink." She tore the foil from the bottle, removed the crown, and popped the cork. As she poured into the first glass, she dipped her free hand into her robe pocket and thumbed the cap off the bottle of pills.

"Go easy with mine," he said. "I wouldn't want you taking advantage of me."

She laughed again, then took the hand from her pocket and dropped a pill inside the glass as she poured. From his vantage point on the sofa, Favreau couldn't see a thing, and by the time she crossed to him, the pill had completely dissolved.

She handed him the doctored drink. "What shall we toast to?"

He raised his glass. "To gay guys, married men, and painfully gorgeous women."

They clinked glasses and drank and she sat next to him, close enough that their thighs were touching. He put a hand on her leg and a small shiver of revulsion ran through her. She hoped Cooper had been right about the pills. The faster this happened, the better.

He finished his drink in two long gulps, set his glass on the table, and turned to face her. He took her glass from her hands and set it next to his.

"I'm not finished with that."

"Finish it later," he said, then pushed her against the cushions and leaned in to kiss her. His breath smelled of mints and tobacco and champagne, and Alex braced herself for impact, silently cursing McElroy and Cooper and even Warlock and Deuce. But most of all, she cursed herself for saying yes to this nonsense.

What had she been thinking?

But before his mouth could touch hers, Favreau got an odd look his face and said, "Jesus, that champagne is stroooo…"

Then collapsed against her chest.

NINETEEN

"HE'S OUT," ALEX said, then climbed out from beneath him as the others emerged from their rooms and joined her at the sofa.

Patting him down, she took out his cell phone and handed it to Warlock, who turned it on and scrolled through the menu. "It looks like a burner and he's wiped the memory. Nothing of use here, but I'll put a tap on it so we can monitor his calls."

Alex removed Favreau's wallet, quickly thumbed through it and found two hotel key cards, several hundred euros, a French ID card with his name, address, and date of birth, and a handful of credit cards, each with a different name.

Warlock looked hopefully at the wallet. "Any SD chips? Thumb drive?"

"What you see is what you get."

"No real surprises so far," Cooper said. "He's not stupid enough to keep the codes on him. We need to get past his perimeter alarm and search his suite."

Warlock gestured to Favreau's pockets. "Check to see if he has any keys."

Alex found a ring full of them and handed it over. "What are you looking for?"

He searched a moment then held up what looked like a key fob. "This. It deactivates the alarm."

"Then we're in," Deuce said.

"We're in," Warlock told him.

They breathed a collective sigh of relief, then Cooper gestured to Deuce. "Let's get him into Alex's room and get his clothes off."

"*Dude*," Deuce groaned.

"Stonewell's paying you double, remember?"

"Yeah, but still…"

"Hey," Alex said, "at least you didn't have him on top of you with his tongue wagging in your face. I'll never get those few seconds back."

Deuce grunted and grabbed hold of Favreau's ankles. "May I reiterate, if I'm ever near a poker game again, just shoot me, okay?"

"Believe me, it's already on the list."

Cooper took Favreau by the armpits. "Alex, you start the search while Warlock's rigging the suite. We'll get over there as soon as we can. And play nice, all right?"

Warlock and Alex exchanged a look. He showed her a tight, tobacco-stained smile and wagged a finger at the wallet in her hands. "Be a dear and grab one of those key cards, luv. We may as well make this as painless as possible."

As they approached Favreau's suite, Warlock pressed a button on the fob he'd found and they heard a faint beeping sound from the other side of the door.

"That takes care of the perimeter alarm. He'll never know we were here." He gestured to Alex. "Card."

She handed him the key card, but when he ran it through the slot, the light flashed red, refusing them entry. He tried again and got the same result.

Alex sighed. "I'm really starting to hate technology."

"If it weren't for technology, you'd still be cleaning your teeth with twigs, and squatting in the dirt to spend a penny." He handed her the defective card, and pulled out his souped-up permanent marker. "And don't forget, there's always this."

Uncapping the device, he poked the end into the hole at the bottom of the lock mechanism. The light flashed green and the latch unlocked.

He grinned. "And here you were ready to give it all up and go back to nature." He gestured to the key card in her hand.

"Make sure you return that to his wallet. Not that it'll do him any good."

"Just get inside," she said.

Warlock picked up his case full of surveillance goodies and led her into Favreau's foyer. Except for the size, the suite appeared to be identical to theirs. He pointed to the mirror above the table and said, "I should be able to rig a camera behind there without it being obvious. It won't be the best angle but at least we'll get a view of—"

"Do whatever you have to. Just get me inside the safe first."

"With all due respect, breaching that safe is a waste of energy."

"What makes you so sure he didn't put the codes in there?"

"You've spent a bit of time with the man. Does he strike you as someone who's careless?"

"Not particularly."

"Then why would he leave his most valuable bargaining chip in a hotel room safe? That's much too obvious and not even remotely secure."

"Do me a favor and open it anyway."

"On one condition."

Alex willed herself to be patient. "And what would that be?"

"You buy me a new pack of snouts."

She frowned. "I'm starting to think you should come with subtitles. Say what?"

"Fags. Ciggies. They don't come cheap, you know."

"They'll also kill you," she said. "If I don't do it first."

He shrugged. "My grandmother smoked two packs a day and lived to be ninety-five."

"She obviously didn't spend much time around you. Will you *please* open the safe?"

"I don't have to," he said. "You can do it yourself."

"And how am I supposed to do that?"

He smiled. "Every hotel safe has a default password in case the guest forgets his, and it's rarely changed from the original factory setting."

"You're kidding."

"Go to the keypad, tap in six zeros, and open sesame."

"Seriously?"

"Give it a try."

"How can you be sure they didn't change this one?"

"Because it worked on ours."

She studied him a moment, thinking he must be pulling her chain, then turned and crossed to the alcove in the living room.

After opening the cabinet door, she looked at the small, rectangular safe built into the wall, and wondered how in God's name a hotel could be so lax with its security. If doors and safes were so easy to breach, what was the point in staying here? People might as well pitch tents, fire up a generator, and save some money.

She tapped six zeroes into the keyboard, and as promised, the safe beeped and the latch released. She opened the door, found a single sheet of paper, and pulled it out.

It was a handwritten message:

Tell your boss the price is now double.

She stifled a laugh. The note was obviously meant for Valac's men, in case they decided to get greedy and tried to rip him off before the deal was complete.

But Warlock had been right. No sign of the codes.

So now what?

She returned the note to the safe, and as she closed the door, it occurred to her she needed to lock it again or Favreau would know somebody had been inside. But how would she do that without overriding his password?

"Hey, Warlock," she said.

He called out from the foyer. "Six ones. He'll never have a clue."

Apparently the Brit was a mind reader, too. She tapped six

ones on the keypad, heard the reassuring *thunk* of the lock engaging, then turned and looked around the suite, wondering where Favreau could have hidden the damn codes.

"So help me out here. How do you think he's storing the data? SD card?"

Warlock came out from the foyer carrying his case full of gear. "My guess would be a micro SDHC, which is small enough to hide just about anywhere." He held up his left thumb and forefinger to indicate size. "But his equipment is consumer grade, the kind you get from a high street spy shop, so I'm inclined to think he's the type who goes in for hidden compartments in fizzy drink canisters or toothpaste tubes. You might try the loo or maybe the kitchen cupboards."

She nodded, then spotted a computer on the coffee table. "What about his laptop?"

"It's worth a look, but I'll clone the drive before we leave."

As Warlock went into the bedroom, Alex crossed to the computer, crouched in front of it and opened the lid. It came to life showing a page from the website for Travel Planet Lifestyles, her own face smiling out at her above a pair of breasts and shoulders that definitely weren't hers. The Photoshop wizards at Stonewell had put her in a bright red bikini on a beach somewhere tropical, microphone in hand.

Thanks again, guys.

The bio accompanying the photo claimed that Alexandra Barnes had been a runner-up in several regional beauty contests, had a degree in journalism, and was the newest addition to the TPL roster.

It was all very convincing.

Alex checked the computer's SD slot, but it was empty. She closed the lid, flipped it over and checked the screws on back, but there was no sign of any wear or tampering that might indicate something was hidden inside.

She looked around the suite again, and thought she might as well have been searching for the proverbial needle in a haystack. In a movie or spy novel she would have found the codes by now, but fiction didn't always reflect reality, a point proven by this goat rodeo of an op.

Alex's whole life was a testament to the fact that nothing ever comes easy.

And she had a feeling this would be a very long night.

"How much time before he wakes up?" Deuce asked.

Favreau was heavier than he looked, but carrying him to the bed had been the easy part. Getting the clothes off a guy who was nothing but dead weight had been another thing altogether, an experience Deuce could have done without.

Favreau wore tighty whities, for godsakes.

Nobody should *ever* wear tighty whities.

Cooper draped a sheet and blanket over him and said, "The drug should last until morning. McElroy says the chemists at Stonewell really know their stuff."

"Remind me to make friends with those guys. You think Favreau will suspect anything?"

"He'll wake up groggy and hung over and wondering what the hell happened, so we'll have to convince him he had the best night of his life."

"And how are we supposed to do that?"

"By filling in the blanks. Just follow my lead when the time comes."

Deuce nodded and they crossed to the door, turning out the light as they left Alex's room.

"I gotta be honest with you," he said. "This op is giving me no joy. Alex is like a little sister to me, and I don't feel all that comfortable seeing her dress her up like a Barbie doll and putting her in this kind of situation."

"She's a big girl and can handle herself better than most. Look what she did to Warlock."

"Yeah, I know, but you're feeling it, too, aren't you?"

"What do you mean?"

Deuce chuckled. "Come on, Shane, you think I'm some dummy who isn't paying attention? I saw the way you looked at her when she got off that elevator tonight."

"You were looking, too."

"It's not the same and you know it. You've been looking at her like that since I first met you."

Cooper went into the kitchen and opened the refrigerator. "You don't know what you're talking about. Alex and I may have gone through a lot of shit together in Baghdad, and yeah, we're friends, but that's as far as it goes."

"So why did you almost go ballistic when her real estate agent showed up?"

"I was concerned about our cover being blown. Favreau was sitting right across from them."

"Or maybe you were reacting to what the guy said about them having a wonderful night together. Sounded to me like they did a little more than talk about property values."

Cooper huffed and grabbed a Coke from the refrigerator door. "That's none of my business. Or yours, either."

"But you'll check into him, won't you? You've probably already given McElroy the heads-up."

Cooper shrugged. "That *is* my job. Gérard's a complication. And you know as well as I do that I'd be compromising the mission if I didn't take a look at him, find out if he's who he says he is."

"And if he is?"

Cooper popped the top of the Coke can and took a sip. "Then we chalk it up to one of life's crazy coincidences and hope he stays out of our way."

Cooper was doing a good job of maintaining his cool, but Deuce had been around him enough to understand his body language. And while the mouth was saying one thing, the rest of him was clearly on defense. Deuce had poked at a wound the guy couldn't hide. Not from him, at least.

"Listen," he said, "I only bring this up because I think you're a pretty decent dude and I feel your pain."

"You got it all wrong, man."

"Yeah? Alex never discusses her love life with me, but I just want to say that if she ever decides to hook up with somebody long term, she could do a lot worse."

Cooper sipped his Coke. "Coming from you, that's a ring-ing endorsement. But I'm telling you, there's nothing to this, okay?"

"Whatever you say. But I've got a feeling that seeing her in that dress kinda solidified it for you. Because she *does* clean up good."

Cooper sighed. "Oh, for chrissakes, will you give it a rest already?"

"I'm just sayin'."

"If you want the God's honest truth, Deuce, the real object of my affection is you."

Deuce was momentarily thrown.

"That's right," Cooper went on. "Didn't you hear what Alex told Favreau about us? Man bait is what you are. It's the Hawaiian shirt that *solidified* it for me."

Deuce gave him a look, then grinned. "My old man was hardly ever sober, but when he was, you know what he always said to me?"

"What?"

"Don't knock anything 'til you've tried it at least once."

They both laughed.

Cooper finished his Coke and set the can on the counter. "On that note, why don't we go give my new girlfriend and Warlock a hand?"

"I thought you'd never ask."

They searched Favreau's suite from top to bottom looking for a data chip of one kind or another—every cupboard, every drawer, every closet, every nook and cranny. Under sinks, behind air conditioning grates, between mattresses, sofa cushions, under throw rugs, tables, table legs, and lamps. They searched every inch of Favreau's suitcase and clothing, including the lining, before carefully returning each item to its proper place.

And they found nothing.

No canisters or tubes of toothpaste with hidden compart-ments. No secret pouch sewn in the hem of a jacket. No false bottom in a bag—

—Not. A. Thing.

They gathered in Favreau's living room at three a.m., exhausted after a long night, and Cooper finally called it. "That's it, we're done. Looks like Warlock was right. Either Favreau's storing the information somewhere off campus or on the cloud. This almost makes me miss Istanbul."

Warlock said, "No worries, mate. If it's on the cloud, he'll have to access the data through his computer and I've already cloned it. If there's a connection point, I'll find it."

"But what if you don't?" Deuce said. "We'll be up a creek without a motorboat."

Alex shook her head. "Sooner or later he'll sew up the deal with Valac and make his move. We'll just have to be there when he does."

Cooper nodded and said to Warlock, "How are we on cameras?"

"Two in every room."

"And his jammers?"

"I found one in here and one on the nightstand. I reprogrammed them to let our feed through."

"Won't he notice?" Deuce asked.

Warlock looked at him as if he'd asked the stupidest question ever. "This is not my first time in the field, *Mr.* Jones. No, he won't notice."

"But if he does?" Deuce persisted.

Before Warlock could answer, Alex said, "If he does, he'll likely think it's Valac's men. He's already suspicious of them."

Deuce grunted. "He's suspicious of everyone, including you. You'd better watch your back around that toad."

"It's the front I'm most worried about."

"That, too. Did I mention he wears tighty whities?"

Alex groaned. "Just kill me now."

TWENTY

Favreau's head hurt.

It was nothing too painful, just one of those underground headaches he sometimes woke up with when he hadn't slept all that well. Yet, oddly enough, he felt as if he'd gone down hard last night and stayed there.

The last thing he remembered was making a move on Alexandra Barnes on her living room sofa. But the champagne, along with the scotch he drank at dinner, had done a number on him, and he could barely even visualize the moment, like it was some crazy dream that was already slipping away from him.

What he did remember was the robe she was wearing, and the way her breasts had moved around beneath it as she walked, and that face of hers with those exotic brown eyes. She was the complete package, that one, coming from a whole different planetary system than the strippers in that club yesterday, and he couldn't quite believe a woman of her breeding would pay any attention to him without having a wad of cash dangled in her face.

When he returned to his suite after their encounter on the beach, he had checked into her and she seemed legitimate, but he couldn't shake the feeling she wanted something from him. That maybe she had decided to hunt for a sugar daddy in her spare time while she was here in St. Cajetan, and he had seemed like an easy mark.

Or maybe she worked for Valac. Some whore hired to spy on him. Try to steal the merchandise while Valac pretended to mull over Favreau's latest counter offer.

Favreau trusted that son of a bitch about as far as he could throw him.

The thing was, Alexandra Barnes didn't strike him as a whore. At least not the kind someone like Valac would be associated with. She was a class act, top to bottom—no pun intended. He couldn't imagine Reinhard Beck going to all the trouble of hiring some call girl just to save a few million bucks.

Whatever the case, Favreau wished to hell he knew where the night had gone. He remembered pushing her against the sofa cushions and going in for the kill…

But after that? Nothing.

And now here he was, naked in his own bed and—

Wait a minute.

Was this his bed?

He looked down at the tangled sheets then scanned the room. While it looked a lot like his, the artwork on the walls was different. The one above the dresser was a reprint of Vuillard's *Le Corsage Rayé,* and if he remembered correctly —and who could tell at this point?—the one in his room was a Marval.

So this definitely *wasn't* his bed.

He looked toward the closet and saw a handful of dresses and beachwear on hangers, including the dress Alexandra had worn to dinner last night. Then his eyes caught the infamous robe in a pile on the floor, and close by a lacy thong, carelessly discarded.

Holy shit. They'd done the deed, all right. His move had been successful and then some.

But why the hell couldn't he remember it?

He turned and looked at the spot beside him and saw that the sheets had been thrown back. He squinted at the clock and saw it was just after seven a.m.

Yawning, he ran his fingers through his hair, then swung his legs around and sat up on the side of the bed.

Jeez, he felt a little nauseated, and his head was really starting to pound now. Hung over, for sure.

Had he had more to drink than he thought?

Taking it slowly, he got to his feet and resisted the urge to upchuck all over the carpet, convincing himself that the nausea was more psychological than physical. He shuffled into the bathroom and stared at his booze-battered face in the mirror as he took a long, much-needed pee. Then he went back into the bedroom, searched the floor for his own clothes, and found them strewn along the foot of the bed. They looked as if they'd been flung there in a hurry. Being that close to jumping Alexandra's bones, he'd undoubtedly wanted to make sure he got the deed done before she changed her mind.

He just wished he could remember it.

He found his briefs, pulled them on, then felt a sudden stab of panic as he stared at his slacks lying on the floor.

His wallet. Had she lifted his wallet?

Snatching up the pants, he dipped a hand inside the pocket, relieved to find the wallet still there. He pulled it out, checked that everything was where it should be, including the money, then returned it to his pocket, stepped into the slacks, and buckled his belt. Next he grabbed his polo shirt and pulled it on.

He heard a laugh from the other side of the door and thought he smelled coffee. Forgetting about his shoes for now, he went into the living room to find a couple of Alexandra's crew members in the kitchen. A big guy in a green Hawaiian shirt, and a soldier type in T-shirt and jeans, both sipping from hotel coffee mugs.

Favreau wondered if they were both gay or only one of them was. Probably the one in the T-shirt. The other, not so sure.

"Well, well," T-shirt said to his buddy, "check it out. The man of the hour is awake."

Favreau rubbed his face. "Yeah, and I feel like a dog's ass. You think I could get a cup of that coffee?"

"How do you like it?"

"The blacker the better."

T-shirt nodded, went to a coffee maker, and poured some

into a mug as Hawaiian shirt silently checked out Favreau.

"Where's Alexandra?" Favreau asked.

"She's in the spare bathroom," T-shirt said. "Getting ready for the shoot."

"Shoot?"

"We're filming a bunch of segments today."

Favreau bobbed his head but immediately regretted it. "She feels anything like I do, good luck with that."

"Believe me, I already read her the riot act." T-shirt pointed at the coffee table. "You guys had quite a party last night."

For the first time, Favreau noticed the overturned champagne bottle and an empty bottle of Jack Daniels sitting next to the two glasses.

Did they actually drink all that?

No wonder he'd had a blackout.

"Jesus," Favreau murmured.

T-shirt handed him his coffee. "I don't think Jesus had much to do with it, but I guess somebody up there likes you. Otherwise you wouldn't be crawling out of my correspondent's bed at seven in the morning."

Favreau sipped. Maybe he wasn't the gay one after all. "Is that a problem for you?"

"As a matter of fact, it is. I like her to be alert and ready to work. Instead she's been dragging her ass around here ever since I woke her up. I won't even get into all the racket you two made."

"Oh God, oh God, oh God," Hawaiian shirt said with a grin. "Sound familiar?"

As he and T-shirt laughed, Favreau wished it did sound familiar. What was the point of bedding a stunner like Alexandra if you couldn't remember a thing about it?

Not that he'd admit it to these guys.

"What can I say?" he told them. "I guess I have a gift."

"That was the sound coming out of *you*," Hawaiian shirt said, and he and his friend laughed again, this time louder and harder.

Favreau didn't normally blush, but he felt heat in his

cheeks and suddenly wanted to punch both of these bastards. Not that he had the energy. Instead, he laughed along with them, and was about to tell the big one how hilarious he was when Alexandra emerged from a hallway and said, "What's so funny?"

That sobered them up fast.

T-shirt said, "Your friend just told us a..." He paused. Frowned. "What the hell are you wearing?"

She looked down at her clothes, a pastel green V-neck and a pair of white shorts. She had a tan, toned body Favreau couldn't get enough of.

"You don't like it?" she asked.

"I told you to wear the yellow bikini top. It looks good on camera."

"I know, but—"

"Come on, Alex, we didn't hire you for your opinion. Bikini tops get page views, okay? That's what it's all about. Now go change before we head out."

Favreau understood what T-shirt was saying—any moron would—but he didn't like the way the guy was talking to Alexandra, and could clearly see she didn't, either.

"Hey, pal, jump back a little, all right?"

T-shirt shot him a look. "Excuse me? I didn't realize you were the producer on this shoot."

"I'm just saying there's no need to—"

"To what? Are you her manager now? Her agent? You bang her one time and think you can come in here and tell me how to do my job?"

Favreau glanced at Alexandra, who had averted her eyes in embarrassment. "No, but—"

"Then get the hell out of here. You've already done enough."

Favreau felt his blood pressure rise. He put his coffee mug on the counter. "You'd better watch your mouth, pal."

"I better watch *my* mouth?" T-shirt glared at him for a second. "You've got a helluva nerve. You show up here, get my talent stinking drunk, you keep her up all hours of the night making enough noise to wake up the rest of us, and now she looks like crap. If the way I'm talking upsets you, I'm sorry, *pal*, but I've got a living to make, and at the moment it unfortunately depends on her."

Favreau struggled to keep from launching himself at the prick, but knew that was probably suicidal, considering his current condition and the size of the guy standing next to T-shirt.

"Just so you understand," he said. "I know people who would happily cut you up into tiny little pieces on my say so."

"Ooooh, you're scaring the hell out of me." T-shirt turned to his partner. "Is he scaring you, too, Sticks?"

Hawaiian shirt grunted. "Oh God, oh God, oh God..."

That did it. Unable to help himself, Favreau shot forward —

—but it was Alexandra who intervened. She jumped between them and put a hand on Favreau's chest, holding him back with more power than he'd expected.

"He's right, Frederic. Stop."

"He's *right*?" Favreau wanted to tear these guys apart.

"People are paying me good money to represent TPL, and I blew it last night by partying too hard. Believe it or not, the camera sees a lot more than we think it does." She paused. "Look, I'm sorry you got in the middle of this. But we have work to do, so why don't you go get your shoes, and I'll walk you to the door."

Favreau glared at the two men, struggling to regain his calm, then returned his gaze to Alexandra. "You're sure?"

"You look like you could use some more sleep."

He couldn't argue with that. "All right, then."

He sucked in a deep breath and let it flow back out as he gave them all one last look before heading into the bedroom for his shoes.

A couple minutes later, Alexandra met him in the foyer. She was wearing the yellow bikini top now, and damn if soon-to-be-fish-bait hadn't gotten it right. She looked amazing in the thing.

He wished more than ever he could remember what was underneath it.

"I'm sorry about this," she said. "But I want you to know I don't regret anything. In fact, I'm hoping we can have dinner tonight."

"Tell me when and where."

"We should be done shooting around six. Meet me in the restaurant at seven?"

"I'm expecting a call, and may have some business to take care of at some point, but I'll be there."

She opened the door, took hold of his hand, and squeezed it. "I'd kiss you, but I just finished my makeup and I don't want Atilla the Hun to get upset with me again."

Favreau chuckled. "At least you got a sense of humor about it. If I were you, I'd brain the guy the minute he's not looking." He squeezed back, wanting more than anything to crawl all over her. "See you tonight, baby."

He pecked her on the cheek and went back to his suite, intending to spend the rest of the morning in bed.

Maybe sleep would help him remember.

When Alex came back into the living room, Cooper said, "If I didn't know what a scumbag Favreau is, I'd almost feel sorry for him. He's on the hook bad."

Deuce nodded. "Just goes to show that if you try hard enough, you can convince anyone of anything."

But Alex wasn't so sure Favreau was convinced. She had a hard time reading the man. For all she knew, he was conning *them*, and this spy vs. spy nonsense was starting to grate on her nerves. They weren't even a full day into this op and she just wanted to smash and grab and be done with it already.

"He told me he's expecting a phone call."

Deuce grunted. "Then we'd better stay on him like a fly on rice. We can't let him get to Valac before you've had a chance to switch out the codes."

"Assuming I ever get access to them."

"We also have to consider our next move," Cooper said. "If Favreau goes to Latham's place to close the deal, Valac won't be easy to get to."

Deuce raised his hand like a kid in high school. "I think I might have a way in."

"How?"

"There's an access road that leads to the back of the house. That's where the guards almost caught me."

"The operative word being 'guards,'" Alex said. "I don't think they're going anywhere."

"Just hear me out. Before I got close, I was almost run down by a delivery van. I figure a place that size, and him being the king of St. Cajetan and all, there must be a lot of vans coming and going. All we have to do is be in one of them. If we time this right, we'll be on Valac before he even realizes it."

"Might work," Cooper said. "We can check Latham's charge accounts to see who he regularly takes deliveries from. If we can go in as a known entity, there's less chance they'll be paying close attention."

Alex said, "It would be easier to grab him when he's out in the open."

"Sure it would," Cooper said. "But who knows if we'll ever get that opportunity? Besides, it would present us with a whole other set of variables to deal with. Unfortunately, we have no choice but to keep this a stealth attack. We can use the photographs Deuce took to get the lay of the land, check out some satellite shots—and blueprints, if we're lucky."

"That's not a lot to work with," Deuce said.

"No, it's not. For the most part we'll be flying blind."

"It's like the streets of Baghdad all over again," Alex said.

"Doesn't hurt to look at it that way," Cooper told her.

"Yeah, but how many times did we go into the Red Zone wondering if we'd ever come out? And some of us didn't."

"So what are you saying? You want to back out?"

She shook her head. "I'm just making an observation. I've already compromised too much of my integrity to back out now."

"What about you, Deuce?"

He shrugged. "Seems like we're trying to put this op together with duct tape and spit, but considering the complete lack of lead time, what real choice do we have? Besides, as you both know, I need the money. And if it all goes south, I guess they can always give it to my goldfish."

"Since when do you have a goldfish?" Alex asked.

"I picked one up after we got back from Istanbul. I was feeling a little pissed about the way things went down, and some brainiac on the Web said that fish are soothing for the soul. I named my guy The Dude."

"And who's feeding The Dude while you're in St. Cajetan?"

Deuce's face fell. "Shit. I didn't think about that."

A door flew open and Warlock stepped out of his room. "Cooper, you might want to take a peek at this."

"What is it?" Cooper asked.

He pointed to his glasses. "I finally got a hit on one of the photos Deuce took and I think you'll find it illuminating."

"All right, show us."

Alex and Deuce followed Cooper into the bedroom, where Warlock's computer cart was shoved up against the closet doors. The screens showed the interior of Favreau's suite, the center one featuring Favreau himself, sitting on the edge of his bed. He looked as if he might fall asleep before he had a chance to lie down. Whatever was in that pill had done a number on him.

"So what've you got?" Cooper asked.

"Turns out the gray-haired man—the one you saw meeting with Favreau—is no longer with us."

"You mean he left the island?"

"No," Warlock said. "He's dead. Been dead for over ten years, as a matter of fact."

Deuce snorted. "Have you been smoking something?"

Warlock dismissed him with a wave. "What I'm trying to tell you is that he's former CIA, reportedly assassinated in

Yemen shortly before 9/11."

Alex's heart went still.

Had she heard him right?

"According to his file," Warlock continued, "he was in Sana'a on an assignment when two gunmen shot him down in the street. They were never found and no one ever took credit for the kill, because apparently it was all staged."

"You're sure about this?" Cooper asked.

"The match is a hundred percent. It's him, and he's very much alive."

Alex couldn't breathe. Felt the room tilting sideways.

Warlock touched the side of his glasses, and two head shots filled the computer cart's center screen: one current, the other showing a much younger version of the same curly-haired man.

"The photo on the right is from the official records," he said. "His body, or rather *someone's* body, was brought back to the States and buried at Arlington with full honors. It took a bit of hacking to pull up his known-associates file, but this is where it gets really wonky."

"In what way?" Cooper asked.

Warlock looked at Alex. "It seems the first name on that list is a Colonel Francis Edward Poe. And the second one is the colonel's wife, Mitra Najafi Poe."

Alex could feel them all looking at her now, but she couldn't take her gaze off those photographs on the center screen. Because staring back at her was none other than Eric Hopcroft.

Uncle Eric.

The man who had once taken pleasure in showing magic tricks to her and Danny.

The man from her mother's wedding video.

TWENTY-ONE

ALEX COULDN'T GET out of their suite fast enough.

Running toward the elevator, she heard Cooper calling to her, but ignored him and kept moving, her heart pounding so hard against her chest it felt as if it might break her ribs.

She pressed the down button and now Deuce was calling her, too, both of the men coming her way. She tapped the button again and again until the elevator doors finally slid open and she boarded the empty car.

She didn't remember the doors closing behind her or the ride down. Images of her mother and father and Uncle Eric and that fucking wedding video tumbled though her mind, over and over, and the next thing she knew she was exiting the rear of the hotel, heading toward a beach crowded with gold-plated tourists.

Even outside, she still couldn't breathe and she needed air.

Was desperate for air.

She knew she was having some kind of panic attack, all the thoughts and feelings that had been swirling inside her these past few days now threatening to strangle her.

Eric Hopcroft was alive and he was here, on this island, working for the kind of man she detested, the kind of man who brought nothing but misery to the world, the kind of man she wanted to crush from existence.

Eric Hopcroft had once been her father's best friend, had attended a wedding Alex had known nothing about—

—So, what did this mean?

What did any of it mean?

Was her *father* working for Reinhard Beck as well?

And what about her mother? How did she fit into all of

this?

Her head throbbing, Alex crossed to the dock where she and Deuce had arrived the day before, and looked out at the still water of Latham Cove as she tried to calm herself and catch her breath. She closed her eyes and told herself to take it slow, try not to breathe too quickly or deeply.

And then she heard Cooper and Deuce calling her again and she wanted to run, wanted to keep them from seeing her like this. Like her father, she had never been the kind to share her vulnerabilities, her anxieties, even though she knew this sometimes cut her off from the people she cared about.

But she didn't run. Instead, she opened her eyes and moved up to the wooden rail that bordered this part of the dock and once again looked out at the still water, drawing strength from it, willing herself to be calm as Cooper and Deuce approached her, out of breath and undoubtedly full of questions.

"Alex, are you all right?" Cooper asked. "What's going on?"

She put out a hand. "Give me your phone."

"Why?"

"Just give it to me."

"Is Warlock right?" Deuce asked. "Is this guy Hopcroft a friend of your father's?"

"Not just my father. Danny and I used to call him Uncle Eric."

"I *knew* I'd seen him somewhere before," Deuce said. "He was in that video you were watching on the plane. The guy with the funky hair."

"What video?" Cooper asked.

"Will somebody give me a goddamn phone?"

Cooper pulled his cell phone from his pocket and handed it to her. She turned away from them and faced the water again, searching through the menu until she found the number she wanted.

"Who are you calling?" he asked.

"Who else?" she said. "McElroy. That son of a bitch is up to something and I want to know what it is."

"You'd better give me a straight answer, you little twerp, or I'll fly to DC right now and beat it out of you."

It had taken McElroy a full ten minutes to come to the phone, his secretary claiming he was in a meeting. But Alex didn't buy it. He had probably been expecting this call for a while.

"Calm down, Alex, take it easy."

She had stepped away from Cooper and Deuce, and was now standing at the end of the dock. She exhaled her fury. "I don't want to take it easy. I *knew* you were up to something. Why do I let you do this to me?"

"Do *what* to you? I have no idea what you're talking about."

She tensed her jaw. "Eric. Hopcroft."

"Who?"

"Don't. Just don't."

"I swear to God, Alex, I don't know who that is."

"Just like you aren't interested in my father anymore? That's what this is about, isn't it? Grabbing Valac and those codes is a sideshow. A bonus. What you're really after is information about Raven, and you think Hopcroft can give it to you. He's the real reason I'm here."

She heard the sound of a computer keyboard. "Look," McElroy said, "I don't know what kind of fantasy you've built up in your head about me, but give me a sec here and I'll try to—"

"Don't pretend you're only looking him up now. You've seen my father's file how many times? Hopcroft's name is bound to be right there in his list of known associates."

"Yeah, you're right, I see it here. But the reason I don't remember him is because I never gave any thought to it. He's of no interest to me. It says here he's deceased."

"You know very well he's alive and here in St. Cajetan."

"*What*? Do you have proof of this?"

"Yes. He met with Favreau at a strip club yesterday afternoon and it looks like he might be Valac's right-hand man. I'm sure Cooper told you about it. And if *he's* in on this, I'm gonna beat his ass, too."

"Will you calm down and listen to me? Nobody's in on anything. This is all news to me."

"I don't believe you."

McElroy sighed. "I swear to you, Alex, I'm completely in the dark about this. And believe me, I don't like it any more than you do. I don't need this guy throwing a monkey wrench into my op."

"This op is a joke," she said. "We're running around like a bunch of fools trying to find a set of codes that probably don't even exist and—"

"They exist. I promise you. If they don't, then *I* was the one who was lied to, and the joke's on me."

"Except you aren't the one standing here half-dressed, trying to cozy up to some Neanderthal in a Polo shirt. You remember what you said about me being a condition of this deal?"

"Of course I do. My contact requested you personally."

"Then if you're telling me the truth, you'd better find out why. Because if I don't hear back from you by the end of the day, I'm gone, and you can kiss Valac and Favreau and those codes and Eric Hopcroft or whoever the hell you're really after goodbye."

McElroy started to say something but she clicked off. In a well-worn pattern, fury had now replaced her anxiety. And at some point, when the fury passed, she'd be back to her old self—more or less—but she wasn't even close yet.

"Alex? Are you okay?"

It was Cooper, coming toward her down the dock.

"You'd better not be part of this, Shane."

"Part of what? Tell me what's going on."

She handed him his phone. "If you don't already know, I'm sure you'll hear about it from McElroy soon enough." She held out her hand. "I need the keys to the rental car."

"Alex, for the last time, *what's* going on?"

"Give me the keys and wait for McElroy's call."

"At least tell me where you're going."

"No," she said. "If I do, you'll try to stop me."

"Alex…"

"The keys. Please."

He reluctantly pulled them from his pocket and handed them to her. "Whatever you do, I'm begging you, don't blow this op."

She stepped past him and started back toward the hotel. "I'm sorry, Shane, but right now that's the least of my worries."

TWENTY-TWO

FINDING THE LOCATION of the Latham house took no time at all. Alex had simply stopped the rental car, stuck her head out the window, and asked the first local girl she saw, "Where does Pappy Leo live?"

Twenty minutes later she drove past the fruit stand the girl had described and the main driveway to the house, then made a left turn on a road that took her through a jungle of coconut and bougainvillea trees behind Leonard Latham's massive plot of land. This seemed to be the only road up here, and after driving past ramshackle houses and their lean-to carports for a while, she began thinking she was lost.

It was then that she noticed a car behind her, another old Buick like hers.

Was it someone who lived up here?

Or was she being followed?

It was possible that Deuce's close call yesterday had spooked Valac and put him on alert. Latham's security men could be patrolling the surrounding neighborhood, checking out anyone who might look as if they didn't belong.

She pulled to the side of the road to see if the other car would do the same, but the Buick sailed past her without slowing and disappeared around a curve. She tried to get a look at the driver, but sunlight glinting on the passenger window prevented her from seeing inside.

She waited a moment in case the car turned around, but when it failed to reappear, she pulled onto the road again. Several minutes later, she finally found what she was looking for: a narrow road on the left with a sign that said PRIVATE. DELIVERIES ONLY.

The service road Deuce had mentioned.

Alex rolled to a stop, staring at the sign and the blacktop beyond. She could see only the first hundred feet before the road curved to the right and disappeared amidst the foliage.

Valac was in there somewhere. And more importantly, Eric Hopcroft.

She sat behind the wheel, engine idling, knowing her fury had gotten the better of her. She had no game plan. None. All she had was the desire to confront Hopcroft and try to make sense of what was going on. To find out the truth.

Studying the lay of the land, she thought about her options. If she went in on foot, it might be best to avoid the service road altogether. The jungle foliage that surrounded it was thick but not impossible to travel through, and it would give her all the cover she needed to approach the estate unseen. And if any guards got in her way, she'd neutralize them.

But as soon as she considered this, she dismissed the idea. If she wanted a confrontation with dear old Uncle Eric, why skulk around in the jungle? Why not take the direct approach and drive straight to the house instead? She would no doubt be stopped by the guards, but if she made enough of a fuss and demanded they take her to Hopcroft, she saw no reason why they wouldn't. At the very least, they would alert him, and the moment he saw her on the CCTV cam, he was bound to recognize her.

Or would he? She had been a teenager the last time she saw him, and she'd been through a lot of changes. The awkward girl he'd known had disappeared long ago.

Well, he would figure out who she was soon enough, wouldn't he?

Spinning the wheel, she nudged the accelerator and turned onto the service road, ignoring Cooper's voice in the back of her head, pleading with her not to blow the op.

She had no idea how far she'd have to travel before she reached the house. A quarter of a mile, maybe? Half? More?

As she wound her way through the trees, she heard the

flutter and squawk of birds through her open window, and wondered if their reaction to her presence would alert the guards. This Buick would never be mistaken for a delivery van, and Latham's men might cut her off before she even reached the house.

She was a good quarter mile in when the road widened slightly and the ground began to rise.

What the hell am I doing?

This all suddenly seemed ridiculous as the temporary insanity that had overtaken her started to fall away.

There was no guarantee she'd even get an audience with Hopcroft. That had merely been wishful thinking. And despite her feelings, there was a part of her that *did* care about Stonewell's op. She couldn't help herself. Embedded in her psyche was the need to do what was right. She wanted that scumbag Valac caught and tried and convicted for his crimes. If she were to barge in on Latham's private property, that would only alert the bastard that something was up and likely cause him to flee.

"You're an idiot," she told herself.

She pulled her foot off the accelerator, intending to make a U-turn and get the hell out of there. But as she eased the car to the side to give her more room for the turn, she heard the roar of an engine, and the Buick she'd seen earlier raced up alongside her, pulled in front, and screeched to a halt. The doors flew open and three men emerged carrying automatic weapons.

She reached for the transmission lever, intending to throw the car into reverse, but froze as the biggest man hurried forward and pointed the muzzle of his gun at her window. "Show me your hands."

There was something familiar about his voice, but she couldn't place it. She had no weapon on her, and she was trapped inside the car, so she did as she was told.

"All right," he said. "Open your door slowly and get out."

"What do you want from me?"

"Don't speak, just do what I say."

Nodding, she pushed the door open and raised her hands as she climbed out.

Did these guys work for Valac?

And where had she heard that voice before?

As the big one gestured her forward, one of the other men slipped in behind the wheel of her car and shut the door.

Alex looked toward the other vehicle and saw a fourth man seated in back, but couldn't make out his face.

Valac?

Or maybe Hopcroft?

The big man waved his weapon and gestured her forward again, directing her toward the other car as his colleague moved to it and opened the rear passenger door.

"Get in."

"Tell me who you are. What do you want? I took a wrong turn, is all. I didn't realize I was doing anything—"

"Get *in*."

She started for the passenger door and was halfway to it when she remembered where she'd heard that voice. It had come from behind a ski mask on a moonlit beach in Key Largo. From a man wielding a knife.

What the hell?

As she climbed inside the car, she suddenly knew she had been set up from the very beginning. The e-mails. The phone calls. The walk on the beach. The chance encounter at the Cajetan Cafe.

Because the man sitting on the backseat was Thomas Gérard.

She clenched her jaw. "You'd better have one hell of an explanation for what's going on here, because I'm in no mood to be kind."

He showed her that killer smile. "It's quite simple, Alex. Your father sent me."

TWENTY-THREE

A PARK BENCH at the National Mall was not their normal meeting place, but when McElroy made the request to get together, Mr. Gray had chosen the spot, saying it would do them both good to get a little sun.

When McElroy arrived, Gray was seated on the bench, peering into the sack lunch in his lap as he dipped a hand inside and rooted around. After a moment, he produced a flip-top can of pineapple chunks and a plastic fork, removed the lid, and dropped it back into the sack.

He held up the fork and can as McElroy sat down. "Would you like a taste?"

"I'll pass, thank you."

"I prefer this over fresh pineapple," Gray said. "I've no explanation for it. I suppose it could be the syrup that I'm addicted to, but I don't think so. There's something sublime about the texture and taste of canned pineapple that always keeps me coming back for more."

"I'm happy for you. But I'm not here to discuss your culinary quirks."

Gray stabbed a chunk and popped it into his mouth, chewing as he spoke. "You know, you worry me, Jason. Your obsession with work will be the end of you." He swallowed. "When was the last time you sat down to dinner with your lovely wife?"

"I don't have a wife. Lovely or otherwise."

"Of course you don't. Divorced, I take it?"

"Like everyone else in DC."

"Don't be so cynical. I've been married for over thirty years."

"The exception that proves the rule," McElroy said. "But I didn't come here to discuss your family life, either."

"Very well, then I suppose we should get down to it. Your call sounded urgent, so what's plaguing you on this fine day? A problem with the acquisition?"

"Considering what's at stake, you seem pretty calm."

"I've learned never to fret over things that are only partially in my control. I've put my trust in you and your people, and I have no doubt you'll get the job done, one way or another."

"Thanks for the vote of confidence." McElroy took the manila file folder from under his arm and held it out to Gray. "But while you're blowing smoke, you want to explain this to me?"

Gray took another bite, chewed, sipped a bit of the syrup, then reluctantly returned his snack and fork to the paper sack and set it to the side. He took the folder from McElroy and opened it.

Inside were the side by the side head shots of Eric Hopcroft that Cooper had sent McElroy, along with a print-out of Stonewell's file on the man.

"I'm surprised it took you this long," Gray said. "Does Ms. Poe know about this?"

"That's why I'm here. She thinks this has something to do with me wanting to catch her father. Cooper says she went off half-cocked, so there's no telling what she might do."

"I'm sure it's not a concern."

"Why would you say that?"

"For someone who works with the woman, you seem to know so very little about her. As I told you before, we've been watching her on and off for quite some time, and based on our observations, she may get the occasional hair up her ass, so to speak, but she usually does the right thing in the end. So I'm sure she'll come to her senses about this little wrinkle before she allows herself to do anything rash."

"You knew about her connection to Hopcroft, didn't you?"

Gray nodded. "Of course we did."

"Is that why you got her involved?"

"If you're a student of human nature, you know that when

an asset has a personal connection to an operation, they tend to hone their focus and up their game. Like an athlete playing in honor of a recently fallen teammate. It's true that Ms. Poe happened to be in the right place at the right time, but we knew of her family history, and hoped that Hopcroft's involvement in the matter would only strengthen her commitment to the task at hand."

McElroy leveled his gaze at Gray. "Sounds like more smoke to me."

"Take it however you like, Jason. As much as I value our relationship, what you think means little to me in the larger scheme."

"Thanks for being honest for once. And while you're at it, why don't you tell me the truth about Hopcroft?"

Gray offered him a benign smile. "I'm afraid that's classified."

"You have clearance," McElroy said, "and you've trusted me before. Have you ever gotten any blowback because of anything you've told me?"

"Next, I suppose you'll be asking me about the codes."

McElroy shook his head. "I don't give a damn about what those codes are for. You made sure of that by dangling Valac as a reward. But contrary to your speech about human nature, this thing with Hopcroft is threatening the acquisition of a very big prize, and I think I have a right to know what's going on."

"And if I don't feel like sharing?"

"I'll tell my team to withdraw and let *you* deal with this mess."

Gray's eyes hardened. "That would be a very big mistake."

"No, the mistake was you people getting greedy. You could have stopped Favreau even before he went to St. Cajetan, but instead of a safe single, you went for the double. Get the codes back *and* take down a man who's been sticking his thumb in your eye for decades." He smiled. "Don't think I'm not grateful for the chance to make all that happen and leave you blameless if anything goes wrong. But Stonewell doesn't live or die on the strength of a single acquisition, or work with a single client, and while walking away may be painful, it won't be fatal."

Gray said nothing for a long moment, no doubt weighing the pros and cons of showing his hand. Then he said, "Hopcroft is deep cover."

McElroy's brows went up. "He's working for you?"

"His assassination in Yemen was meant to facilitate his entry into a terrorist network and give him the freedom to move without restriction."

McElroy was incredulous. "So he's been undercover for *twelve years*?"

"He's very committed. He started out as a kind of free-lance fixer slash security man, and built up quite a reputation as someone who delivers." Gray smiled. "With our help, of course."

"How long has he been working for Valac?"

"Four years now. He began as a free agent, but was able to gain Valac's trust and was brought in full time. And in those four years he's managed to work his way into a senior position. He's next in line of succession after Valac."

"Line of succession?"

"Contrary to all reports," Gray said, "Valac doesn't run the show. He has people he answers to. A shadow group that we believe has strong ties to Iran and other unfriendlies. It's all very John le Carré, but Hopcroft is now in the thick of it, and if Valac goes, he's the one who takes over."

"I don't get it. If he's that close to Valac, why not have him switch the codes and take Valac out himself?"

"And risk destroying over a decade's worth of hard work? I don't think so. Besides, taking Valac alive has its advantages."

"Okay. So is Hopcroft the one who gave you the heads-up on the deal with Favreau?"

"No," Gray said. "That happened exactly as I told you. We haven't heard from Hopcroft for several weeks now, and he's ignored all the usual methods of communication. We can only assume that his rise in the ranks and Valac's cautious nature have subjected him to more scrutiny than usual, and he doesn't want to risk exposure. He knows nothing of this operation or even that we're aware of the deal."

McElroy thought about this and the truth suddenly fell into place. "That's the real reason you wanted Alex on the team. She's your message to Hopcroft."

"Very good, Jason. There's hope for you yet."

"Which means you aren't the only ones who've been keeping tabs on her. He has, too. He cares about her."

"Very much so, as it turns out."

"But why?"

"I'm not sure, but he was around the Poe family quite a bit during her formative years, and I assume he formed an attachment. Our agents aren't always immune to sentiment, I'm afraid."

"But in this case, it works to your advantage," McElroy said. "He must know that Stonewell recruited Alex, and you're hoping that the moment he sees her, he'll realize what the play is."

"We're counting on it."

"And with him in position to take over for Valac, this isn't just a double. It's a home run."

Gray smiled again. "Assuming everything goes as planned. Which, of course, depends on your team. How close are they to finding those codes?"

"They're working Favreau the best they can, but they haven't had any luck yet. And with Alex in the wind—"

"Trust me, she'll do the right thing."

"You don't know her as well as you think you do. It's one thing to observe and another thing altogether to work with her. I'll be the first to admit I don't feel entirely safe around her."

Gray shrugged. "That's because she despises you. But that's another discussion altogether. The clock is ticking. It's only a matter of time before Valac and Favreau meet, and those codes need to be in our possession before that happens.

Even with Hopcroft in place, there's no telling what Valac will do once he has them, and we'd rather not risk that happening."

"Like I said, if the codes are that important to you, don't be so greedy. You've got a man in place. Take Favreau now, wait for Hopcroft to communicate with you, and save Valac for another time."

"And deprive you of your payday? We wouldn't dream of it."

"Uh-huh," McElroy said. "Tell me one more thing."

"Which is?"

"You keep saying 'we,' but how many people really know about this? Does it go all the way to the top?"

Gray laughed. "Come on, Jason. You know better than to ask that."

Then he picked up his paper sack and rooted around inside until he found his plastic fork and can of pineapple chunks.

TWENTY-FOUR

IT'S QUITE SIMPLE, Alex. Your father sent me.

The phrase echoed through her head as they drove, Gérard steadfastly refusing to expand on the comment until they reached their destination.

It's quite simple, Alex.

But there wasn't anything simple about it at all, was there? The four words that followed had frozen her where she sat and she knew she didn't dare push him, didn't dare threaten him, didn't dare do anything that might make him decide to drop it right there and not explain.

Your father sent me.

The last time she had heard from her father had been shortly after the op in Crimea. She had hoped to meet with him at a London pub, but he had left her a note instead, along with a pair of tickets to a Baltimore Orioles game. She and her brother Danny had gone to the stadium, but she'd found it hard to concentrate on the game, her eyes constantly drifting toward the stands, wondering if her father was out there somewhere.

It didn't help when Danny suddenly looked up and said, "Dad?"

"What about him?"

"Dad here?"

His gaze was fixed on the stands across the field, but even if their father *was* out there, there was no way Danny could see him from that distance. Still, her heart began to pound as she raised her binoculars and studied the crowd.

But she saw nothing. No sign of the colonel. Or Raven. Or whatever you wanted to call him. No sign of the man who had tucked them in bed at night in that long ago fairyland that had once been their lives.

"Dad like baseball," Danny said.

She lowered the binoculars. "Yes, he does. He likes it very much."

"Dad not here."

"No, but he wants *us* to be. He wants us to know he still loves us."

Danny got quiet after that, withdrawing into himself as he often did. Alex rubbed his back and watched the game and wished, not for the first time in her life, that she could wipe away his pain.

The note accompanying the baseball tickets had been her father's last communication.

> *One for you, and one for the little lieutenant. Wish I could go with you.*
> *Enjoy the game.*

But it wasn't enough. Both she and Danny needed more. Much more.

And maybe Thomas Gérard was about to fulfill that need.

It's quite simple, Alex.

Your father sent me.

They rode to the leeward side of the island, far away from the fabricated fantasy of the Hotel St. Cajetan and the city surrounding it, and found a table at an unassuming outdoor cafe with a view of the ocean. Gérard ordered them coffee and when the waiter was gone, he said, "You must have a million different questions for me right now."

"I'm trying to be patient."

"Then I'll warn you that I don't have the answers to them all. Very few, in fact." He smiled apologetically. "I'm sure you've deduced by now that I'm not a real estate broker."

"And I'll bet your name isn't Thomas Gérard, either."

"That isn't important. All that matters is that I'm a friend of your father and—"

"He has friends?"

"More than you might think. Quite a network of them after all these years. People who have never believed a man like him would betray his own government."

Alex studied him. "And how do you know him?"

"I was once VSSE, Belgian State Security. Now I work as a facilitator for ex-patriots who've run afoul of their governments. I arrange false identities and secure the proper travel credentials. All off the books, of course."

"And you've been helping him."

"For many years now. He usually contacts me when he needs something done that he can't do himself. Which is why I'm here."

"Why do *you* get to have all the fun? Why hasn't *he* contacted me?"

"For your own protection. And Danny's."

"You'll have to explain that."

The waiter came with the coffee and set their cups in front of them. When he was gone, Gérard said, "Your father has made a number of enemies as well. People who might decide that you or Danny could provide them with leverage against him. But if those enemies believe you aren't important to him, they're likely to leave you alone."

"So his answer to the problem is to abandon us?"

"Not abandon. Distance. He's always had someone keeping watch over you. And he left you the beach house so you'd be more secure financially."

Alex huffed. "Because money's so important to us. What about how we *feel*?"

"The colonel felt your safety was worth the trade-off."

"Pardon me if I disagree."

"He knows he hurt you, Alex. He isn't proud of that fact. But he felt he had no choice. The people who set him up are as ruthless as they are thorough. And they wouldn't just threaten to kill you in exchange for his cooperation. They would happily strap you or your brother to a table and torture you for weeks on end. And Danny's…innocence would mean nothing to them."

"What the hell has he gotten himself into?" she asked.

"I think you can probably answer that question yourself."

She had certainly wondered about it enough times. She remembered the change in him after her mother was killed, but she'd been too busy dealing with her own grief to fully appreciate his. He had seemed so stoic at the time, but she knew now he must have been hurting deeply, and that hurt had been part of why he had withdrawn in those later days. And why he had so suddenly disappeared.

He was looking for her mother's killers. What else could it be?

But what had he done that caused him to be branded a traitor? That was a question she had asked herself at least a thousand times in the last decade. Was it something as simple as stealing and sharing classified intelligence about the incident?

Or had our own government been involved?

After the way the op in Istanbul went down, she had to wonder.

Had the people who set off the bomb in that Lebanon cafe been working for us?

And, if so, why?

She looked at Gérard. "How much do you know about my mother's murder?"

"Only what your father has told me. Which is very little. He's very much a lone wolf, and he shares only what he feels he needs to."

"Are you the one who planted those photos in my storage shed?"

Gérard's eyelids flickered. "Photos? What photos?"

She was surprised he didn't know. "I told you, someone broke into the house. I think whoever it was left behind some photos of my mother, hoping I'd find them. That's why I was so upset when I came to the bar that night. Right before you and your friend played your prank on the beach."

Gérard looked embarrassed. "That was foolish of me. A misguided attempt to gain your trust."

"It got you a lot more than that, didn't it?"

"I'm so sorry, Alex. I didn't mean for it to go that far. But you must admit there's a chemistry between us. We both feel it."

He reached to take her hand, but she pulled it away. "You think far too much of yourself, Thomas. A moment of lust doesn't qualify as anything more than that. And I frankly wish it hadn't happened. Especially now."

"I'm sorry to hear you say that."

"And I'm sorry you're disappointed, but what do you expect? You're a professional liar. You lied to insinuate yourself into my life and you help others lie about who they are. My father may be a good man, but he's the exception, isn't he? Most of the people you help deserve to be locked up."

He started to say something but she cut him off.

"Don't. I don't want to hear any excuses or rationalizations. You are what you are. But explain to me—why the real estate ruse? Why not come to me directly and tell me my father sent you?"

"The ruse was his idea," Gérard said.

"Why?"

He hesitated. "Because of your involvement with Stonewell."

"What's that got to do with any of this?"

"Surely you know that Stonewell has been after the colonel for years. They almost caught him in France shortly before they recruited you. And it's the recruitment that concerns him."

"Why does that matter?"

"Because Stonewell isn't to be trusted. While he was buoyed by your contact with El-Hashim and your close encounter in London, he held back when he realized you had been followed. And he can't be certain of how much animosity you might harbor toward him."

Alex was taken aback. "He doesn't trust me?"

"The colonel doesn't trust anyone completely. Not even

me."

Alex felt as if she'd been stabbed in the heart. She had risked her life to find her father and he still didn't trust her? But her rational mind understood his reasoning. She had every right to hate him, and he had no way of knowing her real motive for joining Stonewell. For all he knew, she was plotting to help capture him.

"He wanted me to approach you carefully," Gérard said, "and he thought the offer to buy the house would be a way in."

"So he's your mysterious client."

Gérard nodded.

"Do you know where he is now?"

"No. He's constantly on the move. We communicate through encrypted text messages only, and I haven't heard from him in several days."

"And you're sure you didn't plant those photographs?"

"I have no idea what you're talking about."

"What about my mother's wedding video? Do you know anything about that?"

He spread his hands. "I'm afraid I'm at a loss."

Strange, she thought. Then who had left them? And why?

"What does all this have to do with Eric Hopcroft?" she asked. "It can't be a coincidence you contacted me only a few days before McElroy showed up."

"A man once said that chance is the nickname of providence."

"Skip the bullshit and just tell me."

Gérard smiled. "One of your father's government contacts alerted him about the call between Favreau and Reinhard Beck. And when Stonewell was mentioned in connection to a possible recovery effort, he correctly deduced that because of your connection to Eric Hopcroft, they would involve you somehow."

"How could he know that?"

"He wasn't sure, of course, but he once worked with the man who initiated this mission and knows how he operates."

"And who is this guy?"

Gérard shook his head. "I don't know his real name, but people call him Mr. Gray. But that isn't important. All that matters is that your father was correct and you're here at the right place and time."

"For what?"

"To do what he's been trying to do for the last several years."

"And that is?"

Gérard pinned her with his gaze. "Kill Eric Hopcroft."

Alex wasn't sure what made her do it.

Maybe it was instinct, or the fury returning, or the simple audacity of the words themselves. But before she could stop herself, she lunged across the table and knocked Gérard backward in his chair, sending coffee cups flying as she planted him on the ground.

The next thing she knew, hands were grabbing at her— Gérard's thugs jerking her away from him.

"Who the hell *are* you?" she spat as Gérard climbed to his feet. "My father would never send me a message like that."

Gérard calmly straightened his clothes and hair. "You know him so well, do you?"

Another stab to the heart. "I know that much. He's not that kind of man."

Gérard turned, and saw other patrons and the waitstaff staring at him and Alex in dismay. He seemed genuinely embarrassed and quickly produced several bills from his wallet, offering them to their waiter and pouring on the charm. "I'm so sorry about this. Please forgive us." He gestured to his men. "Let her go."

As they released her, Alex felt foolish for the outburst, but only because of the attention it had drawn.

Gérard waved his men toward the street. "You and Hugo return her car."

"Are you sure?" the one from the beach said.

"Yes, I'm certain. Go." Once they'd left, Gérard looked at

Alex. "Why don't we discuss this on the drive back to the hotel?"

"I'll catch a cab," she said. "There's nothing to discuss."

"I know you don't think much of me right now, but I'm not lying to you. Not this time."

"And I'm supposed to believe that?"

"I can prove it," he said.

"How?"

"Ride with me to the hotel and I'll tell you."

She hesitated. The truth was, she didn't want proof. Why would she? It would mean she really *didn't* know her father. Didn't know him at all. That in the years he'd been missing, he had become some hardened mercenary she wouldn't recognize. And even though she could understand such a transformation—she had gone through it herself to some degree—she didn't want to believe her mother's death had turned him into someone like that.

But she didn't say no. She nodded, then followed Gérard to the car, and they got in front this time, Thomas climbing behind the wheel.

After they were back on the highway and had driven in silence for a while, he said, "You remember the last night you saw your father?"

She turned. "Of course I do."

"He was in his study, and he'd had a lot to drink." He glanced over at her and then back at the road. "You found him on the floor, leaning up against his desk, photographs of you and Danny and your mother in his lap."

Alex was astonished. "How could you know that?"

"Because he told me. He said when you helped him up, he told you he loved you, then began to recite some lines from a poem. One your mother was fond of."

Alex's throat constricted and she felt tears welling. "Stop."

"'But ere he vanished from her view/He waved to her a last adieu/Then onward hastily he steered/And in the forest disa—'"

"Stop," she said. "I believe you, all right?"

"It was his way of saying goodbye."

"And this is your way of torturing me." She couldn't deny it now. Nobody could have known about that night but her father and her. "Just tell me why. Why would he ask me to kill Uncle Eric? Why would he ask his own daughter to kill a man he once called his best friend?"

Gérard looked at her again. "Because Hopcroft isn't the friend your father thought he was."

"Then what is he?"

"The man who killed your mother."

TWENTY-FIVE

WHEN ALEX RETURNED to the suite, she couldn't get the door open. Her key card no longer worked.

Typical.

Cooper answered her knock and she swept past him without a word and found Deuce and Warlock waiting for her in the living room. She dismissed them with a gesture, told them everything was okay, then locked herself in her room.

She grabbed her phone from her backpack, crawled onto the bed, and curled up on her side as she punched three digits.

A moment later the line connected and a voice said, "Ryan's House, Mrs. Thornton speaking."

"Hi, Mrs. Thornton, it's Alex Poe."

"Oh, hi, Alex. How are things in Key Largo?"

"Great," she said, trying to keep her voice steady. "I've almost got the house packed. Is Danny available?"

"Oh, you know him, he's planted in front of the TV right now watching SpongeBob."

SpongeBob SquarePants was her brother's favorite cartoon. He never seemed to get enough of it.

"Let me talk to him, okay?"

"Of course, dear."

Alex waited as Mrs. Thornton tried to draw Danny's attention away from the television and get him on the phone. In the background she could hear Sandy Cheeks saying something about "ugly on an ape," then Danny's voice was in her ear, a man's husky baritone that sounded so childlike.

"Aleck?"

"Hey, buddy, how are you?"

"Good," he said, drawing out the word and sounding like he was about to laugh.

"You having a good day?"

"Good day! You come home? Aleck come home?"

"Not yet, hon, but as soon as I can. I promise."

"French fry?"

"Of course. We always get french fries."

"French fry, french fry, french fry. Three ketchup."

Alex laughed. She would never be able to speak to him as an adult but she cherished these moments.

"I just wanted to give you a quick call, make sure you're okay. I love you."

She heard cartoon voices again and knew his attention had wandered back to the TV.

"Danny?"

"Aleck. Danny love Aleck."

Alex closed her eyes. "Me, too, hon. More than you'll ever know."

They talked a while longer, but phone calls had always been difficult and keeping his attention was a struggle, especially when she was up against SpongeBob and Patrick. Still, she kept him on the line longer than usual, wanting to maintain the comfort of family and home and the warmest of the memories that had been dogging her these last few days.

She finally said goodbye and clicked off, then fell back against the pillows, thinking about her conversation with Thomas Gérard.

Quoting that Anne Brontë poem had done the trick. She had never told anyone about her father's last goodbye, and nobody could have known about that moment except him. She hadn't even thought about it herself in several years.

But ere he vanished from her view
He waved to her a last adieu,
Then onward hastily he steered
And in the forest disappeared.

It was a favorite of her mother's, one she would recite at will, as if it gave her strength. There had always been an air of melancholy about her as she spoke the words, her eyes looking inward toward some private heartache.

Could she have been thinking about her life before coming to the US?

A life that apparently included her marriage to another man?

That Alex's father had used the poem as his own goodbye spoke volumes about where his mind was at the time. He was grieving deeply, just as Alex was. And Danny.

"Why does my father think Hopcroft was involved in her death?" she had asked Gérard. "The Lebanese government blamed it on Hezbollah."

"Everything in Lebanon is blamed on Hezbollah, and I'm sure they're happy to accept the blame. But when the colonel went there and started to investigate, he realized it was only a convenient cover story. He managed to trace the bomb's triggering device to a group of terrorists who were in league with a man he thought was dead. A man he had considered his friend."

"But why?" she asked. "Why would Hopcroft kill my mother? She was an anthropologist. She meant no harm to anyone."

"I don't know the answer," Gérard said. "All I know is that he wants you to put a bullet in the man's head."

"But why me?"

"He's been keeping tabs on you. He knows about your time in the military, the commendations you received. And he knows you're fully capable of doing what needs to be done. He's very proud of you."

"Proud enough to ask me to kill for him?"

"Not just for him. For you and Danny, too."

"This is crazy," she said. "What am I supposed to do, just walk up to Hopcroft and shoot him? His guards would cut me down before I got within ten feet of him."

Gérard shook his head. "That's why I stopped you from barging in on them. He wants you to continue on as planned. Work with your team and cozy up to Favreau. Leonard Latham is throwing a party at his mansion tomorrow night, and we believe that's when the exchange will take place."

"Why didn't we know about this party?"

"Latham is St. Cajetan's answer to Howard Hughes. He's very cautious about his privacy. You'd only know about the party if he wanted you to."

"Yet *you* know. Which doesn't say much for Stonewell's intelligence division."

"My opinion of Stonewell has never been very high."

"There's just one problem," she said. "If I'm not supposed to know about this party, how do I get myself invited?"

"We believe Favreau *will* be. All you have to do is convince him to take you with him."

"And how am I supposed to do that?"

"Come now, Alex, why are you always so quick to dismiss the effect you have on men? Why try so hard to be one of us when you can use your natural gifts to be so much more?"

"Even if I convince him," she said, "that doesn't mean I'll do what you want me to."

"Not me. I'm merely the messenger."

"Then I want to hear it directly from him. From my father."

Gérard balked. "I'm not sure that can be arranged before tomorrow."

"Try," she said. "Otherwise I'm concentrating on Valac and Valac only."

The message came much sooner than she expected.

She was still lying in bed, Gérard's words swirling through her mind, when her cell phone vibrated, indicating she had received a text.

She called it up with trembling hands, entered the encryption key Gérard had given her, and looked at the screen:

If it's too much to ask, I'll understand.

And that was it. Nothing more followed. She had no real proof this was even from her father, but that poem had been a powerful convincer.

She waited a full ten minutes before she responded.

She thought of her mother being torn apart by that bomb in Lebanon. Of their lives being torn apart by her death.

And she thought of good old Uncle Eric, the man who had once shown magic tricks to Allie Cat and Dan the Man. Good old Uncle Eric, who was supposed to be dead but was very much alive and working for one of the most ruthless terrorists the modern world had ever known.

Then she called up her cell phone's keyboard and wrote:

Consider it done.

TWENTY-SIX

"HELLO?"

"MR. GRAY?"

"I was hoping to hear from you. I assume this line is secure?"

"As always."

"Can I also assume this means you have good news?"

"Yes," Gérard said. "She was much easier to convince than I thought she would be. And with any luck, Mr. Hopcroft will soon cease to be a problem for you."

"Bastard should have stayed dead."

"He will be soon."

A pause. "Perhaps I'm not paying you enough."

"I'm happy to discuss a bonus when the job is done."

"And I'll be happy to arrange for one. You're a valuable asset, Thomas."

"I appreciate that, sir. Just one question."

"Yes?"

"How did you know about the poem? I know you and Colonel Poe were close at one time, but if you haven't seen him since he disappeared…"

"The joys of surveillance, my friend. In the days before Frank fled, we were monitoring his home quite extensively. That moment with Alexandra was a particularly private and touching one. Which is why I chose it."

"Well, it worked like a charm," Gérard said. "I almost felt sorry for her."

"Don't allow yourself to go down that road, son. That was Frank Poe's downfall. He too often let his heart rule his mind."

"And Hopcroft?"

"Always a pragmatist. Which is why he's such a danger to us."

"*Us*, sir?"

"You're part of it now, Thomas. Don't forget that."

"I won't," Gérard said. "How did it go with McElroy?"

"The man's a rube. He supplied his own theory about our request for Alexandra's involvement and I saw no reason to discount it. That's the problem with the private sector. They'll believe anything if there's a dollar attached." He paused. "There's one last thing before we hang up."

"Yes?" Gérard said.

"When the deed is done, there's something I want you to do at your first opportunity."

"And that is?"

"I want you to send a message to my old friend Frank. I want him incapacitated by grief. It took him a very long time to recover from the death of his wife, and I doubt he'll be able to survive another loss, even if time and distance has separated them."

A pause. "Are you saying what I think you're saying?"

"Yes," Gray told him. "I want you to kill his loving daughter."

TWENTY-SEVEN

WHEN ALEX FINALLY emerged from her room, doing her best to offer the others no sign of her continued distress, Cooper took her aside and filled her in on the latest phone call from McElroy.

"He says the Hopcroft thing is pure coincidence."

"He does, does he?"

"That's what his guy told him. They had no idea Hopcroft was even alive, let alone working for Valac." He paused. "But I've known McElroy long enough to sense he's holding something back."

He'd also known *her* long enough, she thought, but he was smart enough not to ask her about it. He hadn't even asked where she'd gone.

"Screw McElroy," she told him. "Let's do this."

"You sure you're up to it?"

"I'm sure."

But she wasn't really, was she? At least not for the part Cooper knew nothing about. She had killed men in Iraq, and done her share of shooting since she'd started working for Stonewell. And she would never hesitate to use a bullet or even her bare hands if she, or those she cared for, were attacked, something she'd proven in Crimea and in Istanbul.

But killing a man in cold blood was a different story. Even if that man deserved to die. And despite the message she had sent to her father, she wasn't fully committed to the task.

Not yet, at least.

Yes, her mother's death had hardened her, but not to the extent it seemed to have overtaken Frank Poe. And when the time came, she wasn't sure she'd be able to do the deed.

Maybe that would change when she and Hopcroft were standing face to face, but she couldn't be sure of anything right now.

So why had she sent that message?

"There's just one problem," Cooper said. "How are we supposed to proceed if this guy Hopcroft knows you?"

"What did McElroy say?"

"He doesn't think it's a concern as long as you don't bump into him on the street."

She nodded. "Even then, I'm not sure he'd recognize me. The last time he saw me, I was a scrawny teenager."

"It still seems a little dodgy. But McElroy wants us to go forward as planned. He thinks if Hopcroft does happen to recognize you, there's a chance it'll work in our favor. Get you closer to the lion's den."

"I agree with him."

Cooper's brows went up and he swiveled his head, looking around the room.

"What's wrong?" she asked.

"I guess I was expecting the planet to explode, but it looks like we're okay."

When Favreau finally came awake, Alex and the rest of the team watched him on the monitors as he sat on the edge of his bed again. After a couple of minutes of barely moving, he jumped to his feet and scrambled into the bathroom.

Warlock jabbed at the keyboard, cutting off the sound a split second too late as Favreau dove for the toilet bowl and started to retch.

They all turned away in disgust.

Deuce said, "Maybe those chemists at Stonewell aren't as good as they think they are."

Warlock shrugged. "Or maybe this is his afternoon ritual. Binge and purge."

When it was safe to look back again, they watched as Favreau spent about five minutes at the sink rinsing and spitting, then went to the phone by his bed, ordered room service, telling them to add the tip to the check and leave his food outside the door.

"Maybe you were right," Deuce said.

Favreau ate a burger and fries, drank a large Coke, smoked cigarettes, and spent the bulk of the afternoon sprawled on his living room sofa, watching the big-screen TV with occasional glances at his cell phone, which was always close by.

He didn't get any calls.

As the day wore on, he started to pace, and they could see by his body language that he was getting angry. He hadn't heard from Valac and it was obvious his patience was nearing its limit. He began checking his phone more frequently now, pacing then checking, pacing then checking...

And he still didn't get any calls.

Valac was really doing a number on the guy. Showing him, through continued silence, exactly who was in the position of power. Letting Favreau know that he needed Valac more than Valac needed him.

"With any luck at all," Warlock said, "he's one of those obsessive-compulsive blokes who has to reassure himself that he still has the merchandise."

Deuce nodded. "By now he must be wondering if Valac has somehow managed to rip him off. So maybe we'll get lucky and he'll show us what we missed."

But apparently Favreau *wasn't* one of those blokes and they didn't get lucky. He began to pace with increasing urgency, but made no move to check anything except his cell phone. He didn't even go near his computer.

As six thirty approached, he glanced at his watch, went into the bathroom, and started stripping off his clothes.

Alex took this as her cue to get ready herself.

Dinner would soon be served.

As Alex headed for her room, Cooper stopped her in her doorway. "Are you sure you're up to this?"

She nodded, and without realizing what she was doing,

she leaned forward and kissed his cheek. "Thank you, Shane."

He was as surprised as she was. "For what?"

"For caring. The way I've been treating you lately, I don't deserve it. But it helps to know I can always count on you and Deuce."

"I'm here whenever you need me. Hell, I'm here even when you don't."

"You may not want to be after all is said and done."

He frowned. "What does that mean?"

She shook her head. "I'm just being melodramatic."

She left him standing there and went to take a shower.

She couldn't get used to playing dress-up.

Each dress she tried on managed to reveal a little bit more than the one before it (did Stonewell not understand the subtle approach?), and despite Thomas Gérard's suggestion that she learn to embrace and utilize her femininity, Alex couldn't get over feeling awkward and uncomfortable and overexposed.

How did so many women *do* this every day?

When she was done fussing with her makeup and only slightly convinced she didn't look like a cheap, Bourbon Street whore, she went back into the living room to search for her purse.

Once again, the three men greeted her transformation as if they'd witnessed a miracle, causing her to wonder how bad she looked when she wasn't on display.

"You guys really need to stop."

"You have no idea, do you?" Cooper said.

"I'm not an idiot, Shane, but this is hard enough without you three gaping at me every time I put on a dress."

"Who says we can help ourselves?" He checked his watch. "We'd better get downstairs. It's almost seven and Favreau's already on his way."

"Wait," she said. "I don't think slipping him a super-charged roofie is going to work twice in a row."

Cooper hesitated. "…I have plan for that. A kind of secret weapon."

"Secret weapon?"

Looking about as uncomfortable as she had ever seen him, he said, "I'll fill you in on the way down."

TWENTY-EIGHT

IT WAS AMAZING how the sight of a beautiful woman could change your mood instantly.

When Alexandra Barnes walked into the cafe and was led by the maitre d' to his table, Frederic Favreau thought he might have to pinch himself to make sure he wasn't hallucinating. All the anger he'd been harboring toward that son of a bitch Valac seemed to fade further and further into the background with each step she took. Had he really been in this woman's bed last night?

Damn.

It didn't matter if all she saw in him was a guy with money who might be able to help her escape those two dipshits she worked for. Hell, she could use him in any way she wanted —tie him up, smack him around, steal every cent he had. He wouldn't put up much of a fuss. At this point, Ms. Alexandra Barnes was the only thing that made the trip to St. Cajetan worth it.

The slinky little dress she wore had an immediate effect on him, and forced him to adjust the napkin in his lap to keep it from being obvious.

He waited as the maitre d' seated her across from him and handed her a menu, then shooed him away and said, "I wish I could order a dozen of you and have one waiting in every city I visit."

Her brow furrowed. "I assume that's a compliment?"

"It was supposed to be, yeah. Did I say something wrong?"

"I guess it's the sentiment that counts."

Was she busting his balls right now? She sure didn't act

like any woman he'd ever encountered before. He was clearly out of his depth with her, but he was trying. Boy, was he trying.

"Sorry," he said. "Maybe I'm not as smooth as the guys you're used to dealing with."

"You mean like Coop and Sticks?"

He laughed. "If I'd been feeling better this morning, I would've brained those two bastards. But I see you survived. How did your day go?"

"About as well as I expected. We drove around the island, got some pickup shots, and tried to snag an interview with Pappy Leo."

"Who?"

"Leonard Latham. The man who owns the island. That's what the locals call him."

"Never heard of him. Did you have any luck?"

She shook her head. "He's pretty reclusive. Spends most of his day cooped up on his estate in the middle of the island."

"I know the feeling. Only I spent my day upstairs."

"Why?" she said, looking surprised. "The island is so beautiful. Why not get outside and enjoy yourself."

Favreau shrugged. "I've never been much for sunburn."

"Well, if I'd known you'd spend your day locked up in your room, I would've insisted you come along with us."

"Yeah, that would've gone over big. Besides, I was wiped and spent a lot of it sleeping. I don't usually get blackout drunk."

"Blackout?" she said. "Are you telling me you don't remember last night?"

Favreau wasn't sure why, but he suddenly felt embarrassed. "I almost hate to admit this, but yeah, I can't remember a thing. And looking at you right now, I sure as hell wish I did."

"Maybe I should be insulted."

"No, I just had too much to drink. I've never been great at holding my liquor."

She looked around as if to make sure no one was eaves-dropping, then leaned forward slightly. "If it's any consolation, it didn't affect your performance. *I* remember every detail."

The thought forced Favreau to readjust his napkin. "I hope I didn't disappoint."

"I wouldn't be sitting here if you did."

Damn, he thought, what he wouldn't give for a video replay.

"Do me a favor," he said. "If I try to take even a single drink tonight, stop me."

"So we aren't ordering champagne?"

"If you want a glass, go right ahead. But I plan on staying as sober as a monk."

"Don't they take vows of chastity, too?"

He grinned. "That's a bit drastic. But I don't want to take any chances. Don't get me wrong. It's not like I black out all the time. I'm usually pretty good at remembering things."

"Oh, you are, are you?"

"Really good, actually. Especially when it comes to numbers. I *never* forget numbers." He grinned. "Comes in handy at the—

His cell phone vibrated in his pocket. He fumbled for it, pulled it out, the ID on the screen reading UNKNOWN CALLER.

"Excuse me," he said, getting to his feet. "I've gotta take this."

"The call you've been expecting?"

"Looks like it."

And about damn time, he thought.

His heart was beating faster as he jabbed the answer button and headed into the lobby. "This is Favreau."

"Frederic, I have news for you."

It was the guy he'd met at the strip club.

"Yeah?"

"Mr. Beck has accepted your counter proposal."

He stopped in his tracks. "You're sure?"

"Would you like him to think about it a while longer?"

"No, no," he said. "It's just that I've been waiting so long to hear from you, I thought he may've changed his mind." He paused. "So, when do we do this?"

"Tomorrow night."

Favreau's voice went up half an octave. "Tomorrow night? If it's all the same to you, I'd like to get this thing done as soon as—"

"Do you want the deal or not?"

"Well, yeah, of course I do."

"Then you'll continue to cooperate and do whatever Valac asks of you. There's an envelope waiting for you at the front desk. That should tell you everything you need to know."

"Okay," he said. "But why all the cloak and dagger? Why can't we…"

He stopped when he realized the line was dead.

"Did you blokes get all that?"

Alex tried not to wince as Warlock's voice exploded in her ear. "We got it," she said. "But lower your volume a bit."

"Sorry. Is this better?"

"I think I'd prefer complete silence, but I don't suppose there's any chance of that."

Cooper said, "Don't start, you two, this is neither the time nor place. Warlock, are you looking at the CCTV feed for the front desk?"

"I am indeed."

"He's approaching it now. Can you get in close?"

"I can, but the resolution on the hotel's cameras is bloody shite. I doubt I'll be able to read what's in the envelope."

"I don't think you need to," Alex said. "I'm guessing it's an invitation."

"To what?" Cooper asked.

"There's a party tomorrow night at Leonard Latham's estate. Very exclusive. And since Valac is a guest at the house, I figure that's where the exchange will take place."

"And you know this how?"

"The locals on the island are more tuned into what goes on around here than we'll ever be, and some of them are very chatty."

She was lying, of course, and hoped she wouldn't regret it.

Cooper said, "Then why am I only hearing about it now?"

"I didn't think it was relevant until Favreau got that phone call."

"Alex, if you're holding anything back on us—"

Warlock cut him off. "Don't start, you two, this is neither the time nor place."

Deuce laughed. "Nice one, dude."

"Thanks, mate. The good news is, if this party is tomorrow night, that gives us another full day to find those ever elusive codes."

"We won't find them," Alex said.

"I love your optimism, but I'd like to keep trying, if you don't mind."

"Think about it. What's the one way Favreau can guarantee that those codes can't be cloned or stolen and maximizes his safety at the same time?"

"I await your answer with bated breath."

"You just heard what he told me about his memory. He doesn't need an SD card because the codes are in his brain."

They all fell silent. Then Cooper said, "You know, I think Alex may be right."

"Works for me," Deuce said.

Warlock scoffed. "You really think he *memorized* them?"

"What better way to guarantee his safety?" Alex said. "If Valac kills him, the codes are gone."

"Then why go to all the trouble to set up jammers? Why put that note in his safe?"

"Because if his privacy is breached, he knows he can't trust Valac and he either bails or insists on a higher price."

"So where does this leave us?" Deuce asked. "We've got no way to switch the codes before he delivers them."

"That only makes our job easier."

"How do you figure?"

"It leaves us with one less headache to worry about," she said. "Once our main target is in play, we can neutralize Favreau and the codes along with him, then make the grab."

"Neutralize?"

"Another one of those pills should do the trick. And that party tomorrow night gives us a way to get to Valac without resorting to an all-out tactical assault. All I have to do is convince Favreau to take me along with him."

"And how do you plan to do that?" Cooper asked.

"By embracing my femininity," she said. "With some help, of course. How sure are you about your secret weapon?"

"I asked again and was told it wasn't a problem."

"Then I don't see how we have a choice."

When Favreau came back to the table, there was a bit of swagger to his gait.

Alex said, "You look like the cat who swallowed the canary. That must've been good news."

Favreau grinned and sank into his chair. "Ten-million-dollars good, baby."

"Divorce settlement?"

He laughed. "Like I told you, I'm here on business." He waggled his ring finger. "And for the record, I'm unattached."

She reached across the table and took his hands. They felt like pastry dough. "You never did tell me what business that is."

"I guess you could call me a commodities trader."

"Nice," she said.

"It is when you make a deal like this one. And all of a sudden I'm in the mood to celebrate."

"Ten million dollars is a very good reason to."

"You bet your cute little ass it is. How hungry are you?"

She shrugged. "I could eat, but it's not an emergency."

"What do you say we blow off dinner, go up to my suite, and relax for a while? We can order room service later."

Alex released him, grabbed her purse, and tucked it under

her arm. "I think that's a wonderful idea. There's just one thing."

"Yeah?"

"No drinks for you."

He laughed again and got to his feet. "Drinking isn't what I had in mind."

TWENTY-NINE

FAVREAU WAS ON her the moment he got her through the doorway.

Expecting this, Alex mentally gritted her teeth and let the moment flow as he pressed her against the foyer wall and went for broke, his mouth—and every foul smell it harbored—leading the way.

She gave him about thirty grueling seconds before slipping out of his grasp. "Slow down, Casanova. You're getting ahead of yourself."

He looked stunned. "I thought that's what we came up here for."

She headed into the living room, kicking off her heels as she went. "A girl likes a little romance. I know you're not drinking, but I wouldn't mind one. I hope you have vodka."

Favreau tried to pull himself together. He obviously hadn't been expecting this turn of events. "The minibar's in the corner."

"You're going to make me pour?"

"Oh, yeah, sorry." He crossed to the cabinet and found a bottle and glass.

As he fixed her drink, Alex strolled around the room, touching the furniture.

Anything was better than touching him.

"They really don't spare any expense here, do they?"

"You want to attract the rich," he said, "you gotta spend money to do it." He gestured. "Or wear a dress like that."

"And here I thought you'd rather I wasn't wearing it."

"Jesus, baby, you are killing me. Come over here."

She playfully wagged an index finger. "Not so fast, mister.

You have to seduce me first."

"How's ten million bucks for a start?"

"You think that's all I care about?"

"I don't think it hurts."

He crossed to her, handed her the drink, and reached out for her, but she again slipped away.

"You're really gonna drag this out, aren't you?"

"The longer you wait, the more you'll appreciate the reward," she said.

"Baby, I already appreciate everything about you. You're just about driving me nuts. And come on, it's not like we haven't done this before."

That's what you think, Alex wanted to say, but sipped her drink and circled behind the sofa.

She patted it. "Why don't you sit down and let me give you a massage."

"You're talking shoulders, right?"

"Don't be crude, Frederic. Women don't like crude."

"You're lecturing me now?" He shook his head. "You're just about the ballsiest girl I've ever come across, and I'll be damned if I don't love it. I'm used to women dropping to their knees at the thought of making a few hundred bucks for the night."

"You're not winning any points. Take a seat before I change my mind."

He grinned. "We wouldn't want that to happen."

As he sat down, she set her drink on the end table, then leaned forward and put her hands on his shoulders. She rubbed them for a moment, then paused.

"Why are you stopping? That felt good."

"I can't get any traction," she said. "Take off your jacket."

He leaned forward a bit, and as he slipped off his sport coat, she spotted exactly what she'd expected to see tucked in an inner pocket—an invitation to Leonard Latham's party. She took the jacket from him and feigned discovery.

"What's this?"

He turned. "What's what?"

She pulled the invitation free, read it, and frowned. "I thought you said you never heard of Pappy Leo? But it looks to me like you've been invited to his party tomorrow night."

"Oh, yeah, the guy who called me left that at the front desk. He couldn't get away tonight, so we figured we'd meet up there."

"At Pappy Leo's party."

"Yeah, what's the big deal?"

"Have you ever *been* to one of his parties?"

"No, I told you, I've never even heard of him before."

"They're legendary," she said. "We were hoping to get an invite for the show, but apparently we weren't worthy. And Latham's some kind of privacy nut. Personally handpicks all the guests."

"Well, if it makes you feel any better, I'll only be popping in and out. Take care of my business and be gone."

She leaned farther forward and slipped her arms around him, rubbing his chest, her lips close to his ear. "Will you be going alone?"

"That was the plan, yeah."

"Now why would you do that when you've got someone warm and willing to decorate your arm, at no charge whatsoever?"

He turned again. "Are you saying *you* want to go?"

Christ, how thick was this guy? "Only if you want me to."

"I don't know, baby. I don't think the people I'm meeting would appreciate that. They aren't very user friendly."

She kissed his earlobe. "I promise not to get in the way."

"You want to go that bad, huh?"

"I'm told these parties are a once-in-a-lifetime kind of thing."

"All right," he said, "I'll think about it. On one condition."

"Yes?"

"You've gotta seduce me, first."

She laughed and stood up, and gently whacked the top of his head. "It's not polite to beat a girl at her own game."

"Impolite, crude—you're trying to rob me of all my best

traits."

"We could throw in making love to a woman and forgetting all about it, too."

"Ouch," he said. "You don't fight fair."

"If you're not careful, I might start getting physical."

"It's about damn time," he said and got to his feet.

It took everything Alex had to wrangle Favreau into the bedroom without him ripping her dress off.

She pushed him across the bed, pulled off his shoes, and told him to get out of his clothes.

"I forgot my drink," she said and headed back toward the living room.

"Drink?" Favreau groaned. "Forget the damn drink and come here."

"And let that expensive vodka go to waste? You get comfortable. I'll be back in a sec."

The moment she stepped through the doorway, she cut straight to the foyer and opened the door. Cooper was waiting in the hallway with an attractive European Bahamian woman of about twenty-five who was only a hair shorter than Alex, with a similar build and bone structure.

His secret weapon.

He had found her through a contact he'd made at the strip bar where Favreau and Hopcroft had their rendezvous. Alex had been nearly as troubled by the suggestion to use a surrogate as Cooper had sounded, and now that the woman was standing in front of her, she was beginning to think they should try the knockout drug again.

But she knew that wouldn't work a second time.

"Did Shane explain to you exactly what we need you to do?" she asked.

"She knows," Cooper said.

Alex kept her gaze on the woman. "And you're okay with it?"

A shrug. "It's what I do every day. And you're paying me enough to take a couple weeks off."

"Hey, baby!" Favreau called. "You get lost out there?"

Alex rolled her eyes and looked toward the bedroom. "Just refreshing my drink!" She turned back to the woman and studied her for a moment. "Okay. Come with me."

She ushered her inside and closed the door.

"What's your name?" she whispered.

"Lita."

"Did you bring the scarves?"

Lita took them from her back pocket and held them up. Three of them, red silk.

"Remember, you don't say a word. Even if he speaks to you."

Lita smiled. "He won't be able to catch his breath long enough to speak."

Favreau was down to his underwear when Alexandra came back into the bedroom, still wearing that dress that looked like a million bucks but needed to be stripped from her athletic little body as soon as humanly possible.

A man could only take so much before the beast came out to play.

He noticed her hand was empty and said, "Where's your drink?"

She brought the other hand out from behind her back and held up some red silk scarves. "I brought these instead."

"Where'd those come from?"

"You'd be surprised how much my little purse can hold."

"Okay, but what are they for?"

She looked at him as if he should know the answer, and then it dawned on him. "You're not planning to use those on *me*, are you?"

"You didn't mind last night. Aren't we trying to recreate a memory?"

"Yeah, but…"

"You just lie back and relax. You won't regret a minute of it."

Favreau liked the sound of that, but he wasn't sure about

getting tied up. Kinkiness had never been his thing. But then a woman this hot had never spent time with him voluntarily, so he didn't put up a fuss when she crossed to the bed, wound one of the scarves around his left wrist, and tied it to the headboard.

She repeated the ritual with his right hand, and damn if he didn't feel like a fool lying there in his BVDs with his arms splayed.

She noticed his discomfort and said, "Go with the flow, Frederic. Go with the flow."

At this point, he didn't have much choice.

But then she got up on the bed with the third scarf and brought it toward his eyes.

"Wait a minute—wait," he said. "You're gonna blindfold me?"

"It's all part of the game, baby."

This was the first time she'd called him that, and the way her tongue wrapped around the word, coupled with the shot of cleavage she was giving him, was enough to kick his motor into high gear. He could feel his body starting to react.

"Aww, fuck it," he said. "Do whatever you want. I'm yours."

She smiled and kissed him, then slipped the scarf over his eyes and tied it behind his head. He was relieved to see the fabric was thin enough that it didn't completely obscure his vision. He couldn't see much, but figured it was better than nothing.

She climbed off the bed and he heard her moving around, then the lamp on the nightstand clicked and the room went dark. The only light came from the open bedroom doorway.

A moment later he saw her standing there, little more than a shapely silhouette.

"I think I really do need that drink," she said.

"Oh, don't you dare."

"You said to do whatever I want."

She was teasing him and was damn good at it.

"Then get it already and get your ass back in here."

When she disappeared from the doorway, Favreau felt a momentary spike of panic. What if this had all been some elaborate ruse? What if she really *was* working for Valac, and this was his way of making old Freddy look like a fool?

But then half a minute later she was standing in the doorway again, drink in hand. He could barely see her, but it was enough. She knocked the drink back, tossed the empty glass to the carpet, then took half a step forward and began peeling the dress off her body like it was a second skin.

What she was doing to him right now should not have been legal. Not here. Not in the US. Not even in his adopted home of France.

He couldn't remember the last time he'd been this turned on. He was breathing too fast, almost hyperventilating, afraid he might lose it before she got any closer.

Or have a heart attack.

She stepped out of the dress, turning slightly, showing him her profile, and he could see her breasts bouncing. She paused a moment to stroke them, then she turned again, and he lost her in the darkness. But that didn't matter, because a second later he felt the bed move as she climbed on, grabbed hold of the elastic waistband of his underwear and pulled, exposing him in all his glory.

Then he felt her skin against his and something warm and wet and wonderful happened and he tried to hold back but he couldn't help himself, losing it in record time.

But that didn't matter, either, because she kept on going until he was ready again, and no matter how much he begged her to untie him and take off the blindfold, she didn't listen, didn't say a word, just did things with her teeth and her tongue and her fingers and her body, and before he knew it they had gone three rounds—*three glorious rounds*—and he was exhausted, used up, spent, worn out, and slowly drifting off to sleep.

When he was halfway to dreamland he felt her untying his wrists, felt her hot breath against his face, but he couldn't move, his entire being drained of energy. Weightless. Drifting.

Then she whispered in his ear, "I told you you wouldn't regret it."

And he fell asleep smiling.

THIRTY

WHEN FAVREAU OPENED his eyes, there was sunlight in the room.

Had he had another blackout?

But no, he knew he hadn't, because he remembered every moment, every exquisite detail of what had happened during the night. His world had been challenged, conquered, rocked by a woman he was now convinced could get him to do anything she asked.

And do it gladly.

That's how good it had been.

He remembered the feel of her body against his and felt himself stirring again. And then there she was, standing in the doorway, wearing that slinky dress and holding her shoes in her hand.

"I'm late," she said. "The guys are gonna be mad."

"Send them over here and I'll kick their asses."

"Somebody needs to."

"Did I happen to mention how amazing you were last night?"

"You may have said it in your sleep a couple times. But maybe you were dreaming about someone else."

He laughed. "Not likely. Why don't you forget about work today? We'll go outside, get sunburned. Have breakfast on the beach."

"Listen to you. I thought you liked to stay indoors?"

"What can I say, I'm a transformed man. Tell your roommates to buzz off. You don't need them anyway."

"I made a commitment," she said, "and I'd like to stick to it. But there's always tonight, remember?"

"Tonight?"

"The party? At Pappy Leo's house?"

"Gee, I don't know, baby. Like I said, that could be tricky."

She frowned. "Why? Are you afraid of these people?"

He thought about Valac's thugs and lied. "No, I just don't want to chance blowing the deal."

"And I'm some kind of deal breaker?"

He grinned. "You're a heartbreaker, I know that much."

"I'm serious, Frederic. Are you ashamed of me?"

He sat up. "Now, come on, I never said that. But these are touchy guys and—"

"Okay, I see what this is. You got what you wanted and now you're done with me. Thanks for a great time."

She turned in a huff and disappeared from view. Favreau heard the door slamming as he scrambled out of bed and snatched up his pants. He yanked them on and nearly stumbled as he zipped up and ran into the foyer.

He pulled the door open, saw her moving down the hall toward her suite and said, "Alexandra, wait!"

She stopped. Turned.

"Screw it, all right? You can come. I want you to come."

"I don't want to blow your deal."

"No, no, no, I'm an idiot. Forget those guys. Hell, they may even show me a little more respect if I've got you hanging on my arm."

She softened. "Really?"

"Really."

"You're sure?"

"Absolutely, baby. I wouldn't have it any other way."

Alex had neglected to get a new room key, so Deuce had to let her in.

"I feel guilty," she said.

Cooper stood near the computer cart, watching as Warlock ran a 3D simulation module based on blueprints and satellite images of the Latham estate.

"Guilty?" Deuce said. "About Favreau? The guy's murderous scum."

"No, about Lita, the girl Cooper hired. I can barely stand touching the creep and she got the full treatment." She took a breath. "At least he passed out. That was a blessing for both of us."

Cooper looked up from the screen. "That wasn't an accident. I had her slip him just enough of the Stonewell cocktail to persuade him to sleep."

"Really? But how did she—"

Cooper held up a hand. "You don't want to know."

Alex nodded. "Yeah, you're right. Sorry I asked."

"If it makes you feel any better, I gave her an extra thousand. She left with a smile on her face."

For the next few minutes, Cooper brought Alex up to speed, mapping out their strategy and filling in the details he and the others had worked out.

Alex listened carefully, but part of her mind was drifting, thinking first about Favreau and Lita, but soon moving on to Thomas Gérard and Eric Hopcroft and the text message she had received from her father.

If it's too much to ask, I'll understand.

Was it too much?

She wouldn't know until tonight.

THIRTY-ONE

ALEX AND FAVREAU were picked up by a limousine.

There was a whole line of limos in front of the hotel that evening, where several of the guests—dressed to the nines and babbling happily—waited to be whisked away to Latham's wonderland. The secret was now out. The party of the year was about to begin, and many of those who had been left in the cold were confronting the hotel's concierge, wondering how they, too, could join the anointed.

Alex felt as if she was headed to the prom from hell, saddled with an escort who would never have made even her D-list in the real world. She wore a dress that was a bit less revealing than the previous ones—and allowed for more flexibility—but the look of rapture on Favreau's face the moment he saw her only increased her sense of dread.

Thankfully, the look faded by the time they climbed into the limo. Alex knew he must have been thinking about dangerous and shady business associates and double crosses and all the things that could go wrong tonight.

So was she, for that matter. But there was only one thought that held the uppermost spot in her mind.

Her promise to her father.

Consider it done.

As the limo made the turn out of the driveway, Favreau put a hand on her knee and squeezed. "So what do you say, baby? You happy now? Is this what you wanted?"

What she wanted was his hand off her knee. Unfortunately, breaking his fingers wasn't an option. "Like I told you, these parties are legendary."

"If they're so legendary, why haven't I ever heard of

them?"

"Because you're a guy who likes to spend his entire day in his room, remember?" She gave him a sly smile. "Unless you've got business to attend to."

He slid his hand upward and caressed her thigh. "I'd much rather attend to you."

Resisting the urge to elbow his kidney, she placed her hand over his. "All in due time, darling. All in due time."

Cooper, Deuce and Warlock hijacked the catering van about a block from the company parking lot.

Thanks to Warlock's scouring of Leonard Latham's recent credit transactions, they were able to target Gold Coast Kitchens, the catering service hired to handle ancillary food preparation and additional staffing for Latham's overworked kitchen help. The driver was running late, the last of several trips to the estate, and an impromptu roadblock using the rented Buick had encouraged him to pull over.

The sight of their weapons sealed the deal.

He raised his hands without argument and Cooper hit him with a tranq dart, knocking him cold in ten seconds flat.

"Nice," Deuce said. "Another Stonewell cocktail?"

Cooper nodded. "He's good for a few hours."

"Poor guy's just trying to make a living. Probably never hurt a soul."

"He could be a wife beater for all you know."

Deuce thought about this. "I think I'll go with that scenario."

After dragging the driver out of the vehicle, they checked the ID in his wallet and threw him onto the backseat of the Buick as Warlock waited behind the wheel.

Deuce moved around to the van's cargo hold, opened the doors, and found a tall metal food rack that carried a couple dozen pies of various persuasions in pink windowed boxes stamped GCK BAKERY. The smell that wafted from inside was a little slice of heaven. He was sure he detected cherry-raisin, one of his favorites.

Now if only he had some ice cream.

Cooper was already dressed in an outfit similar to the uniform worn by the Gold Coast catering staff—black pants, white shirt, and black vest. His outfit might not have been an exact match, but they doubted anyone would take much notice.

He checked his watch and climbed onto the driver's seat of the van. "Alex should be there any minute now. We'd better get moving."

Deuce nodded, then crossed to the Buick, and got in next to Warlock.

"Let's put some wheels on this wagon and ride," he said.

Without a word, Warlock popped the car into gear and punched the gas.

When Alex saw the dark and shuttered fruit stand less than a block ahead, her gut tensed.

They were almost there.

She always got this way right before an op kicked into high gear, like a performer about to go on stage not knowing what kind of an audience to expect.

But tonight was on a whole other level. Tonight she was about to walk into a situation with so many variables—not the least of which was her own internal conflict—that she couldn't be sure she'd walk out again. It was almost like running a raid on a Baghdad bunker with an unknown number of armed insurgents inside.

She had gone over the blueprints of the estate and Warlock's 3D simulations, but diagrams and software models couldn't tell her anything about the human factor.

It didn't help that she was currently weaponless. They had a plan to remedy this once she was inside, but there were no guarantees the plan would work.

It also didn't help that Favreau had spent the last twenty minutes trying to paw her at every opportunity. Fending him off without *pissing* him off was a skill she'd had to develop on the fly.

As they got closer to the fruit stand, their car slowed to a crawl and fell in line behind three more limos in the midst of making the turn onto the Latham estate. She craned her neck to see what lay ahead, but the long driveway was bordered by the same jungle of trees that populated the rear of the property.

Following a route lit by a string of solar lamps, the car twisted and turned through the jungle until she saw the house in the distance, dramatically lit by floodlights.

"Holy shit," Favreau said. "What is this place, the Taj Mahal?"

It wasn't quite that massive, but it looked a lot larger in person than it had on Warlock's computer screen. Unlike the hotel, there was nothing Art Deco about this place. As Deuce had mentioned, it looked like an old Southern plantation house, with columns and balconies and large shuttered windows. It was almost offensive in its size, especially when Alex considered the ramshackle houses that surrounded the estate.

The line of limousines rolled through a raised security gate, two armed guards carefully assessing each vehicle as it passed. Not far beyond, they reached the end of the road and turned slightly, circling toward the front of the house, where a phalanx of white-gloved housemen waited with smiles on their faces.

As their vehicle came to a stop, one of the housemen opened their door and Alex and Favreau climbed out.

"I think I'm starting to get it now," Favreau said, his demeanor having clearly switched from skeptic to true believer. "We might just have to stay for a while."

THIRTY-TWO

As HE NEARED the end of the service road, Cooper said, "I'm almost to the rear gate. Are you guys in position?"

"We will be by the time you get to the house," Deuce told him.

"All right, wish me luck."

Taking a deep breath, he drove the catering van over the rise and headed toward the guard shack. One of the two guards stationed there stepped out and held up a hand as Cooper neared. Beyond the lowered security arm, the Latham house and grounds were lit up like a parade float, and Cooper could hear the *thump, thump, thump* of a bass beat playing.

He eased on the brake and rolled down his window, painfully aware he didn't look remotely Bahamian, but hoping St. Cajetan was enough of a melting pot that it didn't matter.

The guard came up to the window with a clipboard in hand. "Purpose of your visit?"

Cooper stared at him. "Seriously? Read the side of the van."

The guard nodded and made a note on the clipboard. "Name?"

Cooper used the one he'd found on the driver. "Winston Laroda."

He was taking the calculated risk that with the constant stream of catering trucks going in and out today, the faces and names of the drivers had become a blur to these guys.

As the guard checked his clipboard, the second guard—who had the demeanor of a man in charge—approached them. "He's all right, I remember the van. Go open the gate." He looked at Cooper. "I'll still need to see what you've got in back."

Cooper gestured. "It's unlocked. Do whatever you have to."

The second guard went around, opened the doors, and stared in at the metal rack full of pie boxes.

"Rich or poor, everyone loves pie," he said, then closed the doors and patted the side of the truck.

As the security arm raised, Cooper rolled up his window, let out a breath, and hit the accelerator, following the road past the rear of the house and around to a delivery ramp at the side. As he backed down the ramp toward a loading dock, the van beeped a warning.

"I'm almost in," he said. "Warlock, are you in range yet?"

"I believe I am. It's all up to you now."

The plan was for Deuce and Warlock to park the Buick in the adjacent neighborhood, make their way toward the estate on foot, then split up—Warlock looking for a place to perch with his laptop while Deuce positioned himself as close to the house as possible with a sniper rifle, just in case they needed a diversion.

Or backup firepower.

"What about you, Deuce?"

"I'm looking at you as we speak."

"See you on the other side," Cooper said, then came to a stop and cut the engine. He reached down and retrieved a black plastic packet from under the seat, and carried it into the back of the van.

He chose one of the pie boxes on the center shelf, pulled it open, and removed the pie—French apple from the looks of it. He laid the packet inside, put the pie on top of it, and closed the windowed lid. It was a tight fit, the crust pressing up against the plastic, and he knew it wouldn't fool anyone who took too close a look, but the casual observer might not notice anything amiss.

He returned to the front of the van, opened the driver's

door, and climbed out, then went around to the back doors and pulled them open.

Most of the deliveries had been made during the day so the loading area was empty. Cooper unlocked the rack's wheels and pulled it out onto the dock. He got behind it and rolled the rack through the service doors toward the hallway on his left.

Latham's mansion may have carried the facade of a Southern plantation house, but according to the blueprints, its three stories and basement were a labyrinth of hallways and interconnected rooms more akin to a medieval castle, and easy to get lost in. The second and third floors held the living quarters, the main floor boasted a full-size ballroom and ancillary staff offices, and the janitorial and kitchen facilities were down in the basement with the loading dock.

As Cooper turned a corner, he found himself staring at a security checkpoint with a metal detection portal in the middle of the hall and once again hoped that the combination of repetition and his uniform would work to his advantage. Trying to look as casual and unconcerned as possible, he rolled the rack toward the portal.

One of the two guards manning it jumped in front of him, and gestured for him to pass the rack to the second guard.

"Those things set the machine off every time," he said. "Too much noise."

"Mmm, pie," the second one said as he rolled the rack around the metal detector to the other side. "This one looks like coconut cream. Do you think we'll get a slice after we finish our shift?"

The first guard directed Cooper to step through the portal. "You're a dreamer, Perry. Once the guests and those vultures in the kitchen are done with them, there won't be any left."

Cooper put his wallet and cell phone in a tray, stepped through the portal without making it beep, then retrieved his belongings and moved toward the rack.

"Wait," the second one said, producing a security wand. "I have to check it out."

The sight of the wand made Cooper's intestines clench. He stood there, still trying to look casual, as the guard—Perry— passed his wand over the boxes. Instantly, the thing started to squeal.

"I don't know why you bother," the first one said. "You know it's these metal racks that do it. Happens every time."

Perry flicked off the wand. "I bother because if I don't and something goes wrong, I lose my job." He turned to Cooper. "You don't have any explosives or weapons in here, do you?"

Cooper grinned at him. "If I did, they probably wouldn't taste very good."

Both guards laughed and the first one said to Perry, "Just check a few of the boxes and let him go. He has a job to do."

Perry studied the top row of the rack, peering through the plastic windows at the pies, then opened one up and breathed it in. "I was right. Coconut cream. I wish my wife could bake like this."

"You're lucky you *have* a wife," the first guard told him. "Now let the man go."

Perry held up a hand to silence him and crouched down to look at the center rack. Cooper glanced at the weapons holstered on their thighs and wondered how quick they would be to use them. From their looks and attitude, he pegged them as temp security staff, not part of Latham's regular crew.

Perry reached forward, opened another box, and again breathed in. "Sweet potato. Second only to coconut cream."

"Stop salivating and be done with it already. You're making me hungry."

But Perry suddenly froze, his gaze on the center row of pies. "What's this?"

Thinking he had just been busted, Cooper's gut tightened as Perry grabbed hold of a box, pulled it out, and opened the lid to reveal a decadent-looking chocolate chiffon pie.

"I would kill a man for a slice of this." He looked up at his partner. "Do you think anyone would miss it?"

"Put it back or you'll get us both in trouble."

"What's one pie out of so many?"

"Put it back, Perry. Now."

Looking disappointed, Perry closed the lid and returned the box to the rack.

"Go on with you," he said to Cooper as he backed away from the pies. "You're the devil in a black vest."

The guards laughed again and Cooper joined in this time, trying not to look relieved as he grabbed hold of the rack and rolled it toward the kitchen.

The music inside the mansion wasn't loud enough to be annoying, but the thump of the bass vibrated in Alex's bones. She had been expecting a more stately kind of party, with a string quartet and politely applauding guests, but instead she heard the peal of raucous laughter beneath the equally raucous music.

As guests entered the mansion's massive entryway, they were greeted by beautiful women carrying computer tablets and wearing tight, low-cut dresses. A tall and stunning black woman approached Alex and Favreau and said, "Invitation, please?"

Favreau produced his from his jacket pocket and handed it to her as he took her in appreciatively, not bothering to hide it from Alex.

If she had given a damn, she probably would have made a crack, but she had too many things on her mind at the moment to concentrate on her playacting. Favreau could pour this woman into a glass and drink her, for all she cared.

The woman touched the screen of her tablet, then held the invitation in front of the built-in camera lens so it could read the barcode at the bottom of the card.

The tablet beeped and she smiled. "Good evening, Mr. Favreau." She turned to Alex. "May I see your invitation, please?"

Uh-oh.

"Mine?" Alex said. "I don't have one. I'm with him."

The woman looked apologetic. "I'm so sorry. I'm afraid

Mr. Favreau doesn't have clearance for a guest. I can't let you in without an invitation."

"Didn't you hear the lady?" Favreau said. "She just told you she's with me."

"Yes, I understand that, sir, but—"

"What? I'm not allowed to bring a friend?"

"Did you request that she be included?"

"I'm requesting it now."

She smiled politely. "Just a moment, sir." She touched her screen, and tapped the headset clipped to her ear. After a beat or two, she said, "Yes, I have a Mr. Favreau here and he's insisting his guest be allowed in without prior clearance." She paused, then looked at Alex. "Name, please?"

"Alexandra Barnes."

She pointed. "Can I have you look up at that camera in the corner?"

"Why?" Favreau asked.

"You have to understand, sir, that we've had trouble in the past with people trying to crash Mr. Latham's parties. We need to check her face against our database and make sure she isn't one of them."

Favreau started to protest, but Alex stopped him. "It's okay. I don't want to cause any trouble."

She looked up at a camera mounted near the ceiling.

After a moment that felt as if it lasted forever, their greeter touched her earpiece and nodded. "All right," she said, and looked at Alex and Favreau. "I'm sorry for the delay. You may proceed to the security station."

Alex knew she may have passed the initial scan, but she was concerned security wouldn't stop with a search of the internal system, and sooner or later would get a hit on one of the international databases. She could only hope she'd be done here before that happened.

"And I thought *I* was paranoid," Favreau said, as they followed the crowd toward one of three security portals. "You'd think this guy Latham is the leader of the free world."

"He does make your ten million dollars look like pocket

change."

Favreau grinned. "You'd better be careful or I'll tell that African goddess to throw you out."

"And here I was about to suggest a threesome."

Favreau's eyes went wide and he looked as if he was about to choke. Alex feigned a laugh and patted his back. "Easy, darling. Don't have a heart attack before the night's festivities begin."

"What festivities are we talking about?"

"Oh, do I have plans for you," she said.

They stepped up to the center security portal. Beyond it was a large ballroom, dimly lit and crowded with people. If Hopcroft was in there somewhere, and she certainly hoped he was, he might be impossible to find.

"Wallets, keys, and cell phones in the tray," the attending guard told them. "Purses on the conveyor belt."

As Alex put her purse on the ramp, she noted a hint of concern clouding Favreau's face.

"What do you need my wallet for?" he asked.

"It's part of the procedure, sir. When you step through the portal, we don't want you carrying anything that might set off the alarm."

"And how's my wallet supposed to do that?"

"I didn't set the rules, sir. Wallet in the tray."

Favreau's concern triggered Alex's curiosity. She furtively watched as he reached into his jacket pocket and fumbled around for a moment, before producing his wallet and cell phone and dropping them into a tray. The wallet fell open slightly and Alex was surprised by what she saw.

Or, rather, didn't see.

The hotel key cards that had occupied the uppermost slot were missing. There had been two of them in there—one of which she and Warlock had tried on Favreau's door with no success, and returned to his wallet while he slept in her bed.

So why would he remove them before putting the wallet in the tray?

She was almost sure that's what he'd done.

The answer came to her in a flash as she passed through the security portal.

Oh, crap.

She needed to get Warlock on comm as soon as humanly possible.

THIRTY-THREE

THE KITCHEN SUPERVISOR told Cooper to take the rack of pies to the staging room. Thankfully, the blueprints had given him a fairly good idea of where it was located.

By the time he reached the room, he had reactivated his transmitter and extricated the plastic packet from the pie box, stuffing it down the front of his pants. This was a bold move, considering the intermittent CCTV cams and how busy it was down here, but he'd been partially hidden by the rack and he doubted anyone had taken notice.

If they had, he'd know soon enough.

The staging room was bustling with kitchen staff frantically preparing trays of hors d'oeuvres to be taken upstairs to the ballroom. Several servers stood by, snatching up the trays as soon as they were ready. Cooper parked the rack of pies against an empty wall, then swept past them all and exited the room. He turned a corner and moved down a hallway, trying to get his bearings.

"Hey, Warlock," he said, "refresh my memory. I'm in the south hall headed west. Which hallway leads to the server room?"

"Second on your left," Warlock told him. "And it's bound to have a camera on it, so you'd better activate your jammer. I figure you've got a minute or less before they start to wonder if it's something more than a glitch.

Cooper looked up and saw the cameras covering the two halls. Reaching into his pocket, he pressed a button on his cell phone to activate the signal jammer. He quickly made the turn, and found himself in a short corridor that dead-ended at a windowed door marked IT STAFF ONLY. He tested the knob, found it locked, but was relieved to see it was old school and could easily be picked.

After pulling the plastic backing from his phone, he extracted his lock-pick set from the hidden compartment and was inside less than ten seconds later.

The IT room was small and packed with racks of wires and hard drives and an array of routers. He found the CCTV unit mounted on the wall in back, then reached into the cell phone compartment for a micro-wireless transmitter and a miniature pair of wire cutters. He went to work, splitting the main feed and routing it through the transmitter.

When he was done, he said to Warlock, "You should be getting a signal now. How's it look?"

"A thing of beauty, my friend, and in record time. I almost feel like God."

"Do you see Alex anywhere?"

"Hold on, I'm checking...and if I'm not mistaken, she's entering the ballroom with Freddy, who looks as if he's trying desperately to grab her bum."

"He's lucky she's in character, otherwise he'd be missing a hand." Cooper closed the CCTV box and pocketed his phone. "I'm headed upstairs to make the drop."

As they stepped into the ballroom, Alex still saw no sign of Eric Hopcroft or Reinhard Beck or even the night's host. Not surprising considering the dim lighting and the density of the crowd.

At the moment, though, finding them wasn't the first thing on her to-do list. That would come when they contacted Favreau. And while it might be nothing more than a distraction, a reason not to think about her real purpose here, her current number one priority was talking to Warlock.

She turned to her escort. "What time are you supposed to meet with your friends?"

"No idea," Favreau said. "These guys like to keep me in suspense."

She pointed at the bar. "Why don't you get us some wine?

I need to find the little girl's room."

"You're gonna leave me here all by my lonesome?"

She gestured to a buxom blonde dancing vigorously nearby. "You can sightsee while I'm gone."

Favreau smiled and rubbed Alex's butt. "You're something else, you know that? Don't trip and fall into any billionaires' beds. You're all mine."

Ugh. She really despised this guy.

She pulled away from him and threaded through the crowd, exiting into a hallway at the rear of the ballroom. It was less noisy here, but not by much. She reached into her purse and activated the transmitter in her cell phone, then put the phone to her ear, feigning a call, in case anyone was watching.

"Warlock, do you read me?"

"Well, hello," he said. "Glad you could join us."

"I owe you an apology. I think I may have been wrong about that whole memory thing."

"You?" he said. "How can that be possible?"

"Just tell me this—hotel key cards are encoded with data, right?"

"As anyone with a rudimentary understanding of technology should know, it's how they communicate with the lock on your door."

"You remember how Favreau had two key cards in his wallet?"

"Yes."

"Well, he seemed very skittish tonight about letting them pass through the X-ray machine, and I keep thinking about the one we tried in his—"

"Oh, bugger, it's a fake, isn't it? That's where he's storing the codes."

"That's what I was about to say, yeah. That's why it didn't work."

Warlock swore under his breath. "Why didn't I see it? I had that bloody card in my hand…"

"None of us saw it," Cooper chimed in. "So maybe he's

smarter than we think he is. Alex, you need to switch that thing out before he meets up with Valac."

"With what?" she said. "I don't have a duplicate. I left mine in my room. Besides, he has two of them. How would I know which one to switch?"

"Point taken. But you do have access to them, right?"

"More or less," she said.

"Then take them both and hope he doesn't notice until it's too late."

"And if he does?"

"We'll make it up as we go along."

"All right," she said, "I'll do what I can. Did you drop off the package?"

"Yes, and you'd better grab it while you have the chance. It's in the restroom in the northeast corner of the house. I'm leaving there as we speak."

"Good. I'm on my way."

Alex returned the cell phone to her purse, swept past a group of chattering guests, and headed toward the drop point. Cooper passed her along the way, giving her a subtle nod. As she approached the restroom in question, she spotted a woman in a blue gown about to reach for the doorknob.

With two quick steps, Alex cut in front of her, saying, "I'm sorry, I *really* need to get in there," then dodged inside and locked the door.

According to the blueprints, this was one of the smaller bathrooms in the house, yet it was bigger than her living room back home. She crossed to the toilet, removed the basket of potpourri on the tank, then lifted the lid and set it aside.

Right below the water line, wedged behind the flushing mechanism, was a black ziplock bag. She pulled it out, carried it to the sink, and opened it, removing a Kahr P380 micro compact pistol with a six-round magazine. It wasn't much bigger than her hand.

She lifted her dress and carefully repositioned the tactical thigh holster she wore on her right leg. After sliding the

P380 into place, she let the hem drop and inspected herself in the mirror.

No sign of any telltale bulges.

She dumped the plastic bag, returned the tank lid and potpourri basket, then flushed the toilet and headed for the door, bracing herself for what was to come.

THIRTY-FOUR

WHEN SHE GOT back to the ballroom, Favreau was gone.

She looked toward the bar, but didn't see him standing in line to order their drinks. She spun around and checked the dance floor, hoping she wouldn't be assaulted by the sight of Favreau dancing, but didn't see him there, either.

"Warlock, give me some help here." She hoped he could hear her over the din of the music. "I've lost Favreau."

"Not to worry, he's at your two o'clock, getting some food, and chatting up a bird who could stand to lose a few."

Alex turned and spotted Favreau standing by a caterer's table, drinking a glass of wine as he spoke to the buxom blonde they'd seen dancing earlier. The blonde was filling a small plate high with food as if she was afraid she might miss out on something.

Instead of moving toward them, Alex stood with her hand on her hip, a look of mild disapproval on her face as she waited for Favreau to notice she had returned.

He finally spotted her and grinned. He said something to the blonde, picked up a second glass of wine, and headed Alex's way. "I was starting to wonder if you'd ever come back."

She nodded toward the blonde. "So you figured you'd arrange for a backup? I told you to sightsee, not rent a room and move in."

He handed her the extra glass of wine. "Is that jealousy I'm hearing? That raises our relationship to a whole new level."

She took hold of his jacket lapel, rubbing her thumb along it. "Don't get ahead of yourself, Frederic. I haven't known you long enough to be jealous."

"Maybe we can do something about that."

"What do you mean?"

"After I'm done here, I'm headed back to Paris. You could come along. Spend some time."

"And what about my job?"

"Come on," he said. "You'll never get anywhere working for those idiots. You come back with me, maybe we can figure out a game plan to launch your career. I'll have the money to do it."

"Really?"

"I like you, baby. I like being around you."

"Gee, I wonder why."

He shook his head. "It's not just that. You're something special. I mean it."

Alex had the dreaded realization that there was only one way she could react to this. And as much as the thought repulsed her, she knew it might give her the opportunity to grab those key cards.

Setting her glass of wine on a nearby table, she said, "You're special, too," then leaned in and kissed him—a good solid kiss that tasted like Chablis and tobacco and breath mints. She was reminded of that moment on the sofa and wanted to run away in horror, but they were in the thick of it now and running wasn't an option.

She slipped her hands inside his jacket and caressed his ribcage, feeling more fat than bone, then carefully raised her right hand toward his left inner pocket, hoping the kiss was enough to keep him from noticing as she dipped the hand inside.

It was a difficult angle, and as she stretched her fingers past his wallet and cell phone, she had the sudden worry that maybe he'd put the cards back inside. But just as she thought his tongue couldn't get any farther down her throat, she touched one of the key cards, then the second, and quickly clipped them between her index and middle finger.

She was about to pull them free when the music abruptly

stopped, the lights went up and a brassy fanfare blasted over the speakers. Favreau broke away from the kiss and stepped back, startled, causing the cards to slip from Alex's fingers.

Shit.

They both turned to look across the ballroom in time to see a man step onto a small portable stage and throw his arms into the air, waving at the crowd.

Leonard Latham.

Cheers and applause erupted, and he basked in the adulation as only a narcissist could, the expression on his face suggesting that every clap of the hands, every cheer, every shout of "Pappy Leo!" was well deserved.

He finally made a motion for silence and said, "Hope you're all having a good time here in St. Cajetan."

The crowd erupted again and Latham soaked it up. When the applause died down for a second time, he launched into a story about the creation of this wonderland, about how hard he had worked to carve out a place where those who had made something of themselves had no reason to be ashamed for who they were and how much wealth they had accumulated.

But his words were nothing more than a buzz in Alex's brain. He could have recited the Gettysburg Address and she wouldn't have noticed, because her gaze wasn't on Latham at all, but on the man standing behind him, at the rear of the stage, looking out at the crowd. A tall man with curly gray hair whom Alex hadn't seen for many years.

The man she had come here to kill.

Uncle Eric.

If it's too much to ask, I'll understand.

But was it too much?

As she stared at Eric Hopcroft in the flesh, and thought of the horror of her mother's death, thought of that poem and of family and friendship and betrayal, the fury returned, this time with a colder, harder edge.

No, it wasn't too much at all.

She wanted him dead.

Consider it done.

Then the speech was over and the crowd was roaring as the lights dimmed and the music began to *thump thump thump* and Alex no longer cared about key cards and codes and anything else to do with this goddamn op.

Favreau grinned and said, "So where were we?"

But she ignored him and moved into the crowd of dancers, shoving them aside as she headed across the room. Favreau called out behind her and Warlock began chattering in her ear—

"Alex, what's wrong?"

And she ignored him, too, her gaze on Hopcroft and Latham and a small crew of muscle boys as they moved together in a group toward a side door.

"Alex," Warlock said again. "Where are you going?"

And now Cooper chimed in. "Warlock, what's going on?"

"I'm not sure, but she left Favreau and took off across the room, headed for the stage. Let me check another angle."

"No," Cooper told him. "Keep your eyes on Favreau. I think I know what she's up to."

Warlock answered in the affirmative and now Deuce spoke up. "Is Alex in trouble?"

"She's fine, Deuce. Keep watching the house."

"That's easy for you to say. I feel pretty useless out—"

Alex jabbed a button on her cell phone, cutting the transmission, and kept moving. Hopcroft and the others were stepping into a hallway now, but Latham looked as if he wasn't ready to leave. He said something to one of the muscle boys, and another one put a hand on his back and shoved him forward.

Alex picked up speed, trying to close the gap as they disappeared from view. She was less than three meters from the doorway, hiking up her dress as she moved, reaching for the P380 strapped to her thigh when Cooper stepped in front of her, blocking her passage.

"Alex, stop."

She let the hem drop. "Get out of my way, Shane."

He put his hands out. "Listen to me. I know there's something going on that you're not telling me about, and I know it has something to do with—"

"Move, or I swear to God I'll hurt you."

"No, you won't, because that's not who you are."

"You don't know anything."

"I know *you*, all right? When I gave you those car keys yesterday, I knew where you were going, and I knew that it could jeopardize the mission, but I also knew you would calm down and come to your senses before you did anything foolish."

"Good for you. Now *move.*"

"Hopcroft isn't going anywhere. So calm down and think about what you're doing, because going off half-cocked won't—"

"He killed my mother, Shane. Do you get it now?" She felt tears in her eyes. "He was one of my father's best friends and he killed her and I want to know why. I want to know why before I kill *him.*"

Cooper stared at her, stunned.

She stepped toward him. "Did you hear what I said?"

To her surprise, he stepped out of her way.

"Go on," he said. "But I hope you've got some kind of plan, because you're about to set off your own explosion and there's no telling who may get caught in it."

He was right and she knew it, but she couldn't help herself.

She swept past him and reached for the pistol again, getting it in her hand as she moved into the hallway. She heard voices ahead and when she turned the next corner, she saw Latham and the muscle boys at the far end of the next hall, heading up a flight of stairs—

—but Hopcroft wasn't with them.

Alex spun around to look behind her, but saw no one. The guests were all inside the ballroom and Hopcroft was nowhere to be—

"Hello, Allie Cat. Long time no see."

She spun again and found Hopcroft standing in the middle of the hallway, smiling at her, with two of the muscle boys at his side.

"I think you and your friends need to come with us," he said, nodding past her.

When she turned, she saw Cooper and Frederic Favreau being marched toward her down the hall, three more muscle boys holding them at gunpoint.

Looking as if he was about to piss his pants, Favreau's eyes widened when he saw Alex. "What the hell *is* this, baby?"

One of the muscle boys slapped his head.

When she looked again at Hopcroft, he gestured to the pistol in her hand.

"You might want to drop that," he said. "I wouldn't want you get hurt before we've had a chance to catch up on old times."

THIRTY-FIVE

"ALEX?"

No answer.

"Shane?"

Again, no answer.

"For Christ's sake—Warlock, are *you* there?"

"I'm here, mate. Just trying to wrap my arse around what just happened. Both Alex and Shane are off comm."

"Why? What the hell is going on?"

"We've got a situation on our hands."

"What kind of situation?"

"The kind that involves half our bloody crew being taken hostage, along with Freddy boy."

Silence.

"Deuce, did you read me?"

"We've gotta get in there."

"That's a lovely sentiment, but you may as well commit suicide. If these CCTV feeds are any indication, the guards are all on alert. It's only a matter of time before they check to see if there are any more of us lurking about."

"So we get proactive."

"Would you mind telling me how?"

"I'm working on it. Do you know where they've taken them?"

"The second floor's best I can tell you. That's the private residence, but there aren't any cameras up there, so I don't have eyes."

Deuce thought for a moment. "You *can* loop the feeds on the cameras you're hooked into, right? Replace them with a static image?"

"I can, but these people are trained and that will only fool them for so long."

"I just need it long enough for you to clear me a path."

"A path?"

"To get me down this hill and inside that house without being seen."

"That might work for the guards manning surveillance, but what about the ones standing post? You start shooting, you'll be announcing your intentions to the entire estate."

"Not if I use Cooper's tranq gun."

"You must be joking."

"Hey, it worked on the delivery guy, didn't it?"

"I like you, mate, but you're certifiable."

"You won't get an argument from me. Now start making those loops."

It's called a clusterfuck.

A military term for an operation that's so fouled up that it's nearly impossible to repair. The irony being that the culprits are usually the personnel involved, making bad decisions at all the wrong times.

Alex knew there was nobody to blame for this particular clusterfuck but her. She had let emotion get the better of her, causing her to make the wrong moves from the very beginning, starting with her decision to sell the house in Key Largo.

The guards put cuffs on her, Cooper, and Favreau, then marched them upstairs and separated them.

They took Alex into an unoccupied bedroom and sat her in a chair. One of the men waited with her until the door opened and Eric Hopcroft stepped inside.

He told the man to get out, and waited until they were alone before sitting on the edge of the bed.

He said, "Look at you, Allie Cat. All grown up."

"Don't you call me that."

"Would you prefer Ms. Barnes?"

She said nothing.

"You know, it's only by chance that I saw you on the monitor in the security office. They were running a facial scan and I couldn't quite believe my eyes. So I checked out the name you had given the hostess and what do I find? Some cheap travel website you supposedly work for."

"Maybe I do."

He pulled her Kahr P380 out his pocket and showed it to her. "I suppose this is a fringe benefit? We found one exactly like it on your boyfriend."

She said nothing.

"And then there's the question of Frederic Favreau. I have a hard time believing you're in any kind of relationship with him. The man's a toad, and look at you. You've grown into quite a beautiful young woman."

"He hired us to protect him," she said.

"Oh?"

"He told us he had a business transaction, but didn't trust the people involved. I can see why."

Hopcroft smiled. "Nice try, but why the ruse with the website? That makes no sense. And judging by the look on Favreau's face in the hallway, he had no idea who you really are or what you're up to." He paused. "Who are you working for, Alex?"

She said nothing.

"Mr. Gray?"

She had heard the name before. From Thomas Gérard. The man he'd said had initiated this operation and requested her involvement.

She hesitated only slightly. "Never heard of him."

"Maybe you know him by his real name. Richard Munro. He's got a very cushy job there in Washington, working for the Department of Homeland Security." He leaned forward and whispered, "I don't think they know he's a duplicitous, backstabbing bastard. Then again, maybe they do."

She said nothing.

"Munro is an old friend of your father's and mine. We were all at the Company together."

"The CIA?"

Hopcroft nodded.

Alex wasn't buying it. "My father was never CIA."

"Really? Think back to your childhood, Alex. All the trips he took, and the little knickknacks and toys he brought you and Danny from other countries. Every one of those countries was a political hotspot, and there was your father, right in the thick of it."

"I don't believe you."

"I don't expect you to," he said. "I don't expect you to believe a word I say. But I have a feeling that Munro or *some*body has filled your head with lies. Because I know you didn't come here to help Frederick Favreau." He paused. "You came here to kill me."

She said nothing but her eyes must have given her away.

He smiled. "What did they tell you about me?"

"Not 'they.' My father."

His eyebrows raised. "You've been in touch with Frank?"

"He's been in touch with me," she said. "And you're right, I *don't* believe a word you say. But I believe him. And he says you killed my mother."

Hopcroft studied her, then closed his eyes, lowered his head, and said nothing for a long moment. Then he sat upright again, set the P380 on the mattress, and slipped a hand into his pocket.

He brought out a square gold coin. A Bahamian fifteen-cent piece.

"You remember when you were about eleven years old and I showed you a little vanishing trick called the French drop?"

She remembered, vaguely, but said nothing.

He demonstrated by holding the coin between the index finger and thumb of his left hand, then closed his right fingers over the coin and carried it away.

When he opened his hand again, the coin was gone.

He showed her his left hand and the coin was sitting on his palm.

"It's an illusion," he said. "A trick of the eye."

"I'm afraid your tricks don't impress me anymore."

"No, but apparently Richard Munro's do. He's the master of the French drop and many other illusions. Like the illusion that your father is a traitor. That's one of his finest maneuvers. And now he seems to have gone to great lengths to convince you of something else that isn't true." He paused. "Frank didn't tell you I killed Mitra, because he knows better. He knows I would never have hurt her or allowed any kind of harm to come to her. Not if I could help it."

"And why is that?"

"Because I was in love with her."

THIRTY-SIX

"YOU'RE FULL OF crap," Alex said. "You didn't love her. That's just another one of your tricks."

Hopcroft shook his head. "There's so much you don't know about our past, Alex. Things we could never talk about."

"You mean like my mother's first marriage?"

He stiffened. "You know about that?"

"I've seen the video," she said. "And you're in it."

"Did Munro show it to you?"

"I told you, I don't know this Munro person. The video came to me anonymously. Talk about shattered illusions. I feel as if I was lied to my entire childhood."

Hopcroft lowered his head again. "I'm so sorry about that. But they were all necessary lies."

"Necessary? Why?"

He hesitated. "That's something your father needs to tell you."

"Fuck you," she said. "You sit there and pretend to have sympathy for me, but you can't even tell me the truth? Who's the man my mother was marrying? Where is he now?"

"It's not my place to say."

"Of course not. Why would you even want to? You're consorting with a known terrorist. A guy who's wanted in six different countries."

"Maybe that's another illusion."

She balked. "Which part?"

"The part about me."

"Right," she said. "Yet there you are with my gun, and here I sit cuffed in a chair."

"What do you want from me, Alex? You want me to prove it to you?"

"Yes. That's exactly what I want. You're very good at showing me coin tricks, but all I see is a guy hanging around with thugs and facilitating the transfer of some very dangerous information."

He paused. Looked at her. "You want the codes, don't you? That's what this was originally about."

"I don't really give a damn anymore."

"You would if you knew what they are."

"All right, then. Illuminate me."

He was silent, but she could see by his eyes he was considering the pros and cons of telling her.

He said, "They're the key to a little secret your friend Munro would just as soon keep to himself. But your father knows, and so do I. I'm guessing that's why Munro sent you to kill me. It's exactly the kind of thing he'd do. There's a certain symmetry to it."

"You still haven't told me what they are."

"GPS coordinates."

"To what?"

"To seven different strategic locations around the world. All highly classified. What Munro calls the Seven Wonders."

"Locations for what?"

"Chemical storage facilities, containing an organophosphorus compound that makes sarin gas look like a household disinfectant. The US government thinks the inventory has been destroyed, but Munro knows better. And with those coordinates in the wild, he has quite a problem on his hands."

"Yet you're about to help Frederic Favreau sell them to Valac."

"I'm telling you, I'm not what you think I am. It's all illusion."

"And I still don't believe you."

"Then maybe this will help."

He got to his feet, took a key from his pocket, then walked

around behind her and unlocked her cuffs.

Alex looked at the P380 on the bed but remained where she was.

"Go ahead," he said. "I'm unarmed."

She still didn't move.

He went to the bed and picked up the pistol, released the magazine, and showed her it was full. After slapping it back into place, he offered the weapon to her, grip first.

"It's what you came here to do, isn't it? If you don't trust me, if you believe the lies that Munro has filled your head with and you think I would kill the woman I loved, the woman my best friend married, then by all means, take it. Pull the trigger."

Alex stood up, took the pistol from his hand, then kicked the chair aside and stepped back, pointing the muzzle at his chest.

"Tell me the truth," she said.

Her hands were trembling.

"I've told you all I'm willing to, Alex. Everything else has to come from Frank."

"And when is that supposed to happen? I haven't seen him since I was a teenager."

"He'll come to you when he thinks you're ready."

"When he thinks I'm *ready*? You're lying," she said. "*You* killed her. He *told* me you killed her."

"Did he? Did he really?"

She almost said, "Yes, he did!" but that would have been a lie. The accusation had come from Thomas Gérard. And while that poem and the story surrounding it had been a powerful convincer, how could she be sure others didn't know about them? The people she was dealing with, the people she worked for, were all very good at extracting information by whatever means necessary. She knew for a fact that Thomas Gérard was a liar. No speculation there. He'd lied to her from the very beginning.

Had what he told her about her father been a lie, too?

Had the text message?

If it's too much to ask, I'll understand.

Her certainty crumbled as she realized that of course it was a lie. Her initial instincts had been right. Her father would never have asked her to kill Hopcroft even if the man had killed her mother. He would have never asked her to kill *anyone.*

"Make your choice, Alex. But think about one last thing before you do."

"What?"

"Why would I be standing here if none of this were true?"

And that was the clincher, wasn't it? Why would he bother to come here? For old times' sake? That seemed unlikely. Why not have her shot and been done with it?

Yet here he was, trusting her with a loaded weapon in her hand.

She lowered the pistol.

"You're your mother's daughter, Allie Cat. I can't tell you how much you remind me of her." He gestured. "You even have her ring. She got that from her grandmother."

"Stop, Uncle Eric. I don't want to hear any more right now."

"Then you'd better put that weapon in that holster strapped to your leg. It's time for you to meet the man I work for."

"But why?" she said. "Why do you work for him?"

"Because I want the truth, too. And the people *he* works for have it. The closer I get to him, the closer I get to them."

She didn't bother asking him what he meant by all that. He wouldn't tell her anyway.

She said, "You know I didn't come here just for you, or those codes. I came for Valac. That's what I do. I'm supposed to take him back with me."

Hopcroft nodded. "Then let's try to make that happen."

THIRTY-SEVEN

Deuce emerged from the jungle and made his way under cover of darkness down a shallow incline. The loading dock was several hundred meters away, a CCTV camera mounted on the roof above it.

"Warlock, are you ready with that first loop?"

"Give me a mo. Almost there."

"Hurry it up, will you?"

"Contrary to popular belief, I can't work miracles, so hold on. In the meantime, watch yourself. There are two guards coming 'round from the left, headed for the dock."

Deuce stepped back and crouched, wishing he had something more than shadows to hide in. He heard voices a moment before he saw the guards round the corner. Holding himself very still, he followed their progress as they moved parallel to the dock and headed to the far right side of the house.

When they were gone, he said, "Come on, dude. Give me that loop."

"It's done. Go."

Deuce lit out, running at a full clip across the yard until he reached the Gold Coast catering van that Cooper had arrived in. He looked past it toward a set of steps and an open door that led into a basement hallway. He knew there was another camera in there. It was next on the list.

"Tell me when," he said.

"Now. Go."

He scrambled up the steps, keeping the tranq gun at his side, and ran through the doorway into the hall. Up ahead the corridor angled to the right, where the security stop, manned by two guards, would be located. Another camera, mounted high on the wall, was pointed in their direction.

"Do your thing, dude."

"Done."

Deuce may have been a big guy, but he knew how to travel quietly and quickly. He made a beeline down the hall and turned the corner, raising the tranq gun as he moved.

The two guards looked up in surprise and he fired two darts—*thock thock*—dropping them to the floor. As rapidly as he could, he dragged one, then the other, out of sight behind the machine.

"Tell me where I'm going," he said to Warlock.

"Down the hall and to your left, past the kitchen. But be careful, there are people milling about. Put the gun away and act as if you belong."

"This should be fun."

"I told you it was suicide."

"Yeah," Deuce said, "but who do I have to go home to? My goldfish is probably dead."

They took Favreau to a room about half the size of a barn, that may have been the most luxurious office he'd ever seen. The chairs, the sofa, the desk, the paintings on the wall all oozed money. The kind of money he'd like to have.

He still wasn't sure what had happened out there. One minute Alexandra was running away from him, the next he was being grabbed by a couple of goons. He didn't understand why they'd made such a fuss about Alexandra, although the pistol in her hand had been a pretty good indication that *something* was up.

Where had it come from? And why did she have it?

Had she only made a move on him to get to that party? Was she trying to horn in on his deal and snatch the merchandise? Or was she what he'd first suspected—a spy for Valac?

But if the last were true, why would they grab her like they had?

Whatever she was, Favreau realized he had meant nothing to her. He was merely a stepping stone. All the attention she'd given him had been a con, and he'd fallen for her like a chump.

And that made him both sad and angry.

The two hard cases escorting him took off his cuffs and sat him on the sofa. One of them was the guy from the bar the other day. The one who hadn't said anything.

To Favreau's right, in a big red armchair, was the guy who had made the speech tonight. Leonard whatshisname. Pappy Leo. And for a man who supposedly had more money than God, he didn't look all that happy. Like he didn't want to be here, now or ever.

Behind the big desk was a man with a ponytail.

Jesus. Fifty-something years old and he wore his hair like a schoolgirl. What was that all about?

Favreau had never seen the guy before, but he assumed it was Valac. Reinhard Beck. Nobody got a face with all that wear and tear without going through some heavy-duty shit. He reminded Favreau of the guy from those beer commercials. The most interesting man in the world. Only this one had that ponytail, and a look in his eyes that said he'd happily squash you like a cockroach if you got in his way.

Favreau didn't intend to get squashed. Not if he could help it. He just wanted to make this deal and get out of here.

Assuming there was still a deal to be made.

He was about to say something to that effect when the door burst open and the tall gray-haired man from the bar came in, pushing the whore in front of him. That's what Alexandra was, wasn't she? Another opportunistic tart whose only real interest was taking a guy for everything he had, even if it meant screwing with his head and heart.

Favreau wondered what they'd done with her partner. Coop. Hopefully, they tied him to a chair and beat the shit out of him.

The gray-haired man shoved Alexandra toward the sofa and told her to sit her ass down. She looked as if she wanted to strangle the guy, but did as she was told, not bothering to give Favreau even a single glance as she sat. They weren't two feet apart and she acted as if he didn't exist.

Bitch.

Instead, her eyes focused on Valac, still sitting behind that big desk as if *he* were the true king of St. Cajetan. Maybe he was, meaning the guy in the red chair was an impostor. A sock puppet. Someone so used to being controlled and manipulated and dragged out of his hole to perform for the crowd that he could barely look anyone in the eye when he wasn't on stage.

That was exactly what was going on, Favreau realized.

When had the coup taken place?

Months ago? Years?

Favreau didn't have much sympathy for guys like him. All that money and what did it get him? Anyone who was weak enough to let someone muscle in on his territory deserved whatever blew his way.

It took awhile, but Valac finally spoke. "Mr. Favreau, I think you owe us an explanation."

"Me?"

Valac wagged a finger toward Alexandra. "You *are* the one who introduced this unpleasantness into what should have been a simple business transaction."

Favreau sat forward. "Hey, she's got nothing to do with me."

"No?"

Valac picked up a remote from his desk and flicked a button. Behind him a large-screen TV came to life, displaying surveillance footage of Favreau and Alexandra going at it in the ballroom.

Valac froze the image. "Would you like to retract that statement?"

Favreau glanced at Alexandra and saw she had turned away from the monitor. He waited a moment, thinking if only she would look his way, then maybe...

But no. She wouldn't give him the time of day.

"I'm just a patsy here," he said. "I don't know what she's up to or who she's working for and I don't *want* to know. I came here to make a deal with you and that's it. As far I'm concerned, we could've handled all this over the Internet, but it was your idea to turn it into a vacation getaway. Not mine."

He was talking too much, sounding too desperate, and he knew it. But he couldn't help himself. It was all true, wasn't it?

"I would like to believe you, Frederic."

"Then believe me. I'll give you the codes, you give me my money and let me off this goddamn island."

"You have them with you now?"

"I probably shouldn't, but yeah. They haven't left me since I got to St. Cajetan."

"Show me."

Favreau started to reach into his jacket pocket, but Valac signaled to the hard case from the bar, who grabbed Favreau's wrist.

He winced. "What the hell?" The guy's grip was like the bite of a pit bull. "You people already searched me. I've been through a metal detector. You know I'm not carrying any weapons."

"Neither was she when she arrived," Valac said.

"Yeah, well, I don't know anything about that."

With a nod from Valac, the thug released Favreau.

Favreau rubbed his wrist, then stuck his hand into his jacket pocket and pulled out the two key cards he'd removed from his wallet earlier. He handed them to the thug, who in turn took them to Valac.

Valac studied them. "Very clever, Frederic. I must admit I would not have given these a second thought."

"That's kinda the idea," he said.

"Which of them holds the codes?"

"The one with the tiny nick on the corner."

Valac inspected them. "I don't see any nicks."

"Look closer. It's there. I made it myself."

"That may be true, but I still don't see it."

"What're you, blind?" Favreau started to rise, but the second hard case stepped forward and shoved him back down.

"Do that again," Valac said, "and I will have him break your legs."

Favreau swallowed. This wasn't going the way he hoped it would.

Valac held out the two cards to the thug who had brought them to him. "Karl, check these with the reader."

The thug took them and headed for a computer station to Valac's left. Favreau noticed Alexandra was tracking the guy with her gaze, looking at the cards. He couldn't help staring at that face and body of hers, wishing she hadn't turned out to be such a bitch.

Why couldn't he catch a break when it came to women?

Valac said to him, "I assume you put some type of protection on the card?"

Favreau snorted. "You think I'm stupid enough to hand those things over to you without an insurance policy? You transfer the money to my bank account, let me verify the transaction, and I'll give you the password when I'm safely back home."

The gray-haired guy laughed. "That's a bit one sided, wouldn't you say?"

"How so?"

"How are we supposed to check the authenticity of the codes if we don't know the password?"

Favreau shrugged. "I guess you'll just have to trust somebody for once in your life."

Valac nodded. "Trust. Yes. As you trusted the young lady."

"Hey, I told you, I'm not responsible for—"

"What type of encryption did you use?"

"What do you mean?"

"On the key card. AES? Blowfish?"

"I used an MD5 hashing algorithm, and believe me, you can try all you want but you'll never crack that password."

He tapped his temple. "It's all right here in my head."

"So you have me beat, do you?"

Favreau grinned. "You bet your ass I do. And I gotta tell you, it feels pretty good to pull one over on the great Reinhard—"

Valac raised a pistol and fired.

Favreau felt the impact, felt his chest go numb and saw a neat round red hole there.

Then he toppled forward and hit the carpet.

THIRTY-EIGHT

LEONARD LATHAM YELPED and pushed back in his chair as if he wanted to disappear into the cushion. "Jesus Christ, you just shot that guy!"

Valac narrowed his eyes at him. "Thank you for stating the obvious, Leonard."

At the sound of the shot, Alex had jumped to her feet and was backing away from the body. Favreau lay facedown on the floor, a pool of blood spreading beneath him. The guy had repulsed her and probably deserved to die for a multitude of reasons, but she wasn't thrilled about being a witness to it.

Hopcroft frowned at Valac. "Was that really necessary, Reinhard?"

"I didn't like him much."

"I get that impression."

"He was an amateur. I do not have time for amateurs." He waved his pistol at the muscle boy, Karl. "Are you going to check those cards or not?"

Karl gestured to the body. "You just shot the password."

"Were you not listening to him? The MD5 hashtag algorithm has been considered unsafe for over a year now, and our software will break it with ease. So scan both cards, see which one asks for a password, and we'll know we have our codes."

As Karl went back to work, Valac turned his reptilian gaze on Alex. "Don't think I have forgotten about you, Ms. Barnes. You treated my friend Frederic there quite poorly and look at him now."

Alex didn't respond. What could she say to a sociopath? It

took all of her will to resist shooting a glance at Hopcroft.

"Jesus Christ," Latham said again. "How could you just shoot the guy?"

Valac trained the pistol on him. "It's quite simple, Leonard. I point the gun and pull the trigger. Any more questions?"

Latham hastily shook his head.

Valac signaled to his other man. "Salvadore, take our host up to his room and give him his pill. He looks as if he could use it."

Salvadore gestured with his fingers and Latham rose from his chair, trying not to stare at the corpse as they stepped past it and crossed the room to the door.

When they were gone, Alex said, "How long has he been like that?"

"Who? Leonard?"

"From what I've seen of him on TV, he always struck me as such an egotistical bastard."

"He gave us trouble at first, but now he's a good boy. But what about you? How do you fit into all of this? Who is it you're working for?"

He obviously hadn't done much research on her yet, and she knew Hopcroft wasn't about to share. But before she could come up with a suitable answer, the one named Karl said, "Reinhard, we have a problem."

Valac sighed. "I'm speaking to the young lady. I don't appreciate interruptions."

"I think you'll appreciate this one."

Valac turned. "All right, what is it?"

Karl showed him the cards. "I didn't get any requests for a password. According to the reader, they're both legitimate room keys."

Valac frowned. "Check again."

"I've already checked twice."

Valac shot up from his chair. "*Check again*!"

Karl immediately turned back to the computer.

Hopcroft crossed to the desk. "Take it easy, Reinhard. It's

probably a glitch."

"Or our friend Favreau was playing a confidence game all along. And very poorly at that. I should never have agreed to do business with him." He pointed to the corpse. "Look what a mess he's making."

Karl said, "I hate to tell you this, sir, but I've tried three more times and got the same result. One of them is registered to Favreau, and the other to a company called Travel Planet Lifestyles."

Alex flinched. How could Favreau have gotten his hands on one of their…

And then it hit her.

When she returned his room key to his wallet, she must have mistakenly given him the one to her suite. That was why hers hadn't worked.

Her shock must have shown on her face, because Valac was now eyeing her with suspicion.

"What do you know of this?"

"Nothing," she said quickly.

"You lie. I can see it in your eyes. You don't survive in this business if you can't read people's eyes. What do you know?"

She backed away. "I don't know anything."

He looked up at the frozen image on the screen of her and Favreau with their lips locked. "You switched the cards, didn't you? When you were kissing him."

"No, I swear to you."

He raised his pistol, pointed it at her. "Give it to me."

"I'm telling you, I don't have it."

As he came around the desk, she wondered how quickly she could get to her own pistol. "I know you took it from him. Give it to me."

Hopcroft stepped toward him now and said, "Easy, Reinhard. Take it easy."

"She has the card. I know she does."

"Fine," Hopcroft said. "So I'll search her. We don't need any more bloodshed tonight."

Valac looked at him, softened. Lowered the gun. "You're right, my friend. Why am I arguing with some useless whore?"

Then, without warning, he raised the pistol again. As he fired at Alex, Hopcroft grabbed his arm, sending the shot into the carpet.

Alex dove to the floor, ripping at her dress, wrapping her fingers around the grip of the P380 as Karl launched himself from the computer station and pulled out his pistol. Bullets gouged the carpet only inches from Alex's torso as she rolled and came up firing. Her first shot punched the wall but her second hit center mass, slamming Karl against the computer desk, the monitor crashing to the floor.

Hopcroft and Valac tumbled to the carpet, struggling for control of Valac's weapon. The pistol went off and Hopcroft grunted, released his grip and fell away.

Before Valac could get to his feet again, Alex fired at him. He rolled to the side, barely escaping the hit. She adjusted her aim for a second shot, but when she pulled the trigger, the little gun jammed.

Valac thrust himself back to his feet and swung his pistol around, pointing it at her.

She sprang forward without thinking, hitting him in the chest and shoulders as his gun went off, the bullet barely missing her ribs. Before he could shoot again, she began punching him over and over and over, using all her strength, battering his head and bloodying his nose.

Fighting through her blows, Valac reached up and grabbed hold of her neck, throwing her off him as if she were a rag doll. She thudded into the carpet, the wind flying out of her. As she struggled to catch her breath, Valac dragged himself to his feet, staggered slightly, then picked up the pistol and pointed it at her head.

"Shlampe," he said.

Slut.

A moment before Valac's finger could find the trigger, Alex heard the door burst open, then Valac grunted and grabbed at his neck, clutching at the feathered tail of a tranq dart protruding from his jugular.

He dropped the pistol, fell to his knees, and pitched forward, out cold.

Still trying to catch her breath, Alex turned and saw Deuce —beautiful, beautiful Deuce—standing in the doorway.

He grinned. "And Warlock said I was crazy."

"We need to check on Hopcroft," Alex said as Deuce helped her up. "He's over by the desk."

"Hopcroft? Who gives a damn about—"

"Just do it, Deuce. I can't explain right now, but he's one of ours."

When they reached Uncle Eric, he'd already pulled himself upright and was sitting against the desk, the side of his shirt stained crimson. "I'm okay...the slug didn't penetrate..."

Alex checked his side. "You need help."

"Believe me, I've been through a lot worse than this...and help'll be along soon enough. That's why you need to grab Reinhard and go."

"I can't leave you like this."

"You can and you will. The key to the cuffs is in my shirt pocket. ...Your friend is in the third room down the hall." He tilted his head toward Valac. "Do you have a way to get him off the island?"

"We've got a floatplane and pilot waiting for us on the leeward side."

"Good. But you'd better...make it fast. The music downstairs probably masked the gunshots, but the guy who took Latham to his room will be returning any minute now."

"What will they do to you when they find you?"

"Nothing. With Reinhard gone, I'm in command. And getting shot...will actually work in my favor."

Deuce said, "I know I'm coming in late on this, but if you're in command, can't you call security off?"

"Not without blowing my cover. The group I've infiltrated

has to believe I'd never betray them...and I've worked too hard to get this far. So go. Now."

Deuce nodded, then went to Karl's corpse, relieved it of its gun, and stuffed the weapon in his belt. "How much resistance are we talking?"

"I don't think the rent-a-cops or Latham's guards will be much of a problem. They're mostly here for show. But Valac's got about a dozen loyal kamikazes...like Karl...and they'll want to get him back."

After crossing toward Valac, Deuce kicked Valac's piece over to Alex, then grabbed hold of him and hefted him up and over his shoulders like he was a prize deer.

Deuce was big, but it didn't look like fun.

"Can you manage him like that?" Alex asked.

"Do I have a choice? But don't worry, he's not as heavy as he looks."

She turned to Hopcroft. "I wish you could come with us."

"You know I can't..."

"Then at least tell me what's going on. Why are you doing this?"

"You father will tell you soon enough. Now, take your prize...and go. But when you get back home, don't trust any of them. Especially Richard Munro. He'll smile at you and tell you...whatever you want to hear, and you won't feel the dagger slipping into your back until it's too late."

Alex nodded solemnly, not wanting to leave him there.

Deuce said, "Come *on*, Alex, this asshole isn't getting any lighter."

She nodded, then threw her arms around Hopcroft's neck and hugged him, trying not to cause him too much pain. He laughed and winced and said, "I love you, Allie Cat, and so does your father. Always remember that. *Live* by that."

"I will," she told him. "I will."

THIRTY-NINE

VALAC'S MAN WAS on them before they got to Cooper, shouting as he raced down the hall, pistol blazing. Deuce dove for safety, sending Valac flying off his shoulders as Alex returned fire, cutting down the thug with a shot to the neck.

"You hurt?" she said to Deuce.

Already on his feet, he shook his head and began hefting Valac again. "Get Cooper. There's a service elevator in the south hall. I'll meet you there."

He grunted and took off down the hall like a lumbering Cyclops. Heading the other way, Alex found the room Cooper was in and threw the door open. He was on the floor, cuffed to a bed frame he had already half torn apart, trying to get loose.

"Thank God," he said. "I heard gunshots and thought the worst."

She took the key from her pocket and unlocked the cuffs. "I think I've used about six of my nine lives in the last ten minutes, but it isn't over yet. Deuce has Valac and is headed for the service elevator."

"Nice. Sounds like I missed a lot."

"We can play catch-up later."

As soon as Cooper was on his feet, she handed him Valac's pistol and they raced out of the room.

"This way," she said.

She led him down the hall toward the corridor that would take them to the service elevator. Rounding the corner, they surprised another of Valac's thugs, who had apparently been running toward the sound of the gunfire. His eyes went wide as he fumbled for the gun at the small of his back. Before he could get it free, Cooper buried a shot in his chest and sent him sprawling.

"That's three down," Alex said.

She grabbed Cooper's arm and pulled him down the hall and through a doorway, hoping she was taking them in the right direction. She'd done her best to memorize the basic layout of the house, but dodging fire had a way of shattering your concentration.

Hearing shouts behind them, they crossed through a bedroom and exited into yet another hallway. Alex was beginning to think whoever had designed this place had a fondness for M.C. Escher. They traveled the length of the new corridor then burst through a doorway, relieved to find Deuce holding the elevator open for them, Valac in a heap at his feet.

"Come on, come on," Deuce urged, waving them forward as if it would somehow speed their progress. "Took you damn long enough." As they got on board, he let the doors close and said, "Warlock, do you read me?"

"I'm here, mate. Did you find them?"

"All present and accounted for, with Valac in tow."

"Really? I'm impressed."

"Don't be until we've blown this pop stand. We're headed for the loading dock. I need you to put some blinders on Valac's men. Cut all the feeds to the CCTV."

"Copy that, but you might want to look for a different way out. They've found the van and the guards you tranked, so they're crawling all over the back of the house. I don't think they've quite figured out what's going on yet, but they know something's up."

"Shit," Deuce said. "What about out front?"

"Looks like a parking lot for limos. But most of the guards are either inside or out back, so they must be thinking you'll come out the way you went in."

"All right. Once you cut the feeds, get your ass back to the Buick and meet us at the rendezvous point. We'll be there as soon as we can."

"With pleasure, my friend, but do me a favor."

"What's that?"

"Tell Alex she still owes me a pack of snouts."

They got off the elevator at the first floor, Deuce once again hefting Valac over his shoulders. They tried to move quickly and quietly down the hallway past the ballroom, but as soon as they came around the corner, they discovered half a dozen of Valac's men heading in their direction.

Guns came up and bullets began to fly.

Deuce cut through a doorway into the ballroom with Alex and Cooper at his heels, returning fire. Putting his head down, he plowed through the crowd of dancers, showing no mercy as he knocked them aside and headed across the room. More than once, he thought he heard the jangling of jewelry as they stumbled out of his way.

Guests started shouting and pushing at him, but he didn't falter or slow down, determined to get to the front of the house before the weight of Valac's body made it impossible to keep moving. He was running on pure adrenaline at this point, and he knew if they got out of this alive, he'd have one hell of a backache tomorrow.

Nearing the far side, they saw another of Valac's men, a rodent-faced punk holding a FAMAS Infanterie assault rifle. Deuce tried to duck as the man scanned the crowd, but at his height and with Valac on his back, it was an impossible task. The punk spotted them and opened fire, shooting indiscriminately into the crowd. Around them, guests began to fall to the floor.

Holy shit, Deuce thought. *This guy is out of his mind.*

With bullets dancing at his feet, Deuce dodged left and nearly plowed into Cooper as his friend raised his pistol and put a hole in the punk's forehead.

Screaming in horror, the guests stampeded toward the exits, shoving at each other as they stumbled their way toward the front doors. Deuce, Alex, and Cooper used the pandemonium for cover, flowing with the crowd as Valac's remaining men tried to fight their way toward them.

When they got outside, Cooper sprinted to the nearest limousine, threw the driver's door open, dragged out the terrified driver, then leaned in and popped the trunk.

Deuce moved toward it as it swung open, and was only a few feet away when one of his legs finally gave out. With a groan, he buckled and fell onto the gravel driveway. His cargo tumbled across the grass, landing against one of the limo's tires. If Deuce didn't know Valac was tranked, he'd swear the guy was dead.

"Are you hit?" Alex said, dropping beside him.

"No. I'm okay. Help me up."

Alex helped Deuce to his feet, and together they tossed Valac into the trunk and slammed it shut.

More shots rang out as the thugs broke free of the exiting crowd, bullets gouging the grass around Deuce and Alex's feet. Alex raised her gun to return fire, but there were too many guests behind Valac's men. She couldn't risk a shot.

"Get in!" Cooper shouted as he started the engine.

The moment Alex and Deuce scrambled inside, Cooper hit the gas, the acceleration slamming their doors shut.

A cluster of shots punched the limo's exterior and shattered the rear window as the car headed straight for the security gate. Hopefully, Valac hadn't taken any of those hits, but if he had, Deuce wouldn't lose much sleep over it.

Two rent-a-cops came flying out of the guard shack, waving their arms for Cooper to slow down, and Deuce felt the car pick up speed. The guards hurled themselves from Cooper's path only seconds before the limo slammed through the security bar, shearing it right off its hinges.

The hit sent Alex flying sideways into Deuce.

She righted herself as Deuce shouted, "Dude, you want *me* to drive?"

But Alex knew Cooper couldn't hear him. He was lost in the zone, the bulk of his brain matter focused on getting them the hell out of there. She'd seen him like this a hundred times in combat, a relentless blood-and-bone machine that would not rest until the job was done.

As Cooper rocketed down the winding drive, Alex checked their six and spotted two vehicles racing after them. Unfortunately, they weren't limousines, or the usual fifty-year-old sedans St. Cajetan seemed to love so much. These were two black Jeep Patriots—an ironic name when you considered who was driving them.

One of Valac's thugs leaned out a window of the first Jeep, gun in hand.

Alex shouted, "Down!" and pushed Deuce toward the floor as shots strafed the side of the limo.

She wondered if these idiots even knew they were putting Valac's life in danger. If any of those bullets managed to pierce the trunk, that floatplane might wind up taking a corpse back to the US.

Another round of shots kept them pinned down as Cooper reached the end of the drive. As he jerked the wheel to make the wide turn onto the main highway, they were met with a long angry blast of the horn from a slow-moving '52 Cadillac heading straight at them. Cooper swerved to the side, missing the other car by inches, then righted them back onto the road and took off.

Seconds later, the first of the two Patriots came flying out of the driveway, whiffed the turn, and sank its nose into the rear flank of the Cadillac. Both cars went spinning, then the Patriot's driver lost complete control and the Jeep went into a roll, two of its occupants flying out the windows and slamming against the blacktop in a burst of blood.

The driver of the second Patriot played it smarter, easing off the accelerator as the car went into the turn. Within seconds he was on their tail, close enough that Alex could see his pockmarked face and the grinning salamander on the seat next to him.

"These guys are going down," Deuce said, and pointed his SIG Sauer out the rear window. But before he could get off a shot, the Jeep picked up speed and slammed into the rear of the limo, knocking him off balance.

Did these morons not know who was in the trunk?

As Deuce struggled to right himself, the Patriot glided into the oncoming lane and picked up speed again, pulling alongside them. With a whip of the wheel, the Jeep smashed into the side of the limo, causing it to veer toward the edge of the road as Cooper momentarily lost control.

"Oh, you are so gonna regret that move," Alex said.

She brought her pistol up, shattered the passenger window with a bullet, then leaned out and emptied what was left of her magazine into the right front tire of the Jeep.

The tire exploded and sparks flew as the rim scraped blacktop and the Jeep swerved out of control.

Cooper hit the brakes, allowing the Jeep to career past them, and the driver struggling to keep it steady, but it was no use. Less than a hundred feet ahead, the Jeep barreled off the highway and slammed into a ditch at the side of the road —an impact so brutal the Jeep seemed to fold in on itself, taking its passengers with it.

As Cooper once again sped up, Alex looked out the rear window, bracing herself for another round.

But to her relief, no one else appeared.

FORTY

WARLOCK WAS WAITING for them at the rendezvous point, a small secluded cove about a mile off the highway.

The floatplane sat on the glassy, moonlit surface of the water, its pilot standing on the dock, smoking a cigarette. He wasn't a Stonewell employee, but a freelancer who was paid enough to know when to shut up and do his job.

Warlock emerged from the Buick as Cooper brought the limo to a stop. Cooper popped the trunk, and Deuce and Alex climbed out, and immediately went to check on Valac.

As they had expected, he was still out cold, and fortunately—or perhaps unfortunately—the only sign of physical damage was the bloody nose Alex had given him, which had started to crust up around his nostrils. He'd have trouble breathing through it for a while.

Deuce reached in and groaned as he lifted Valac by the shoulders.

"You wanna give me a hand?" he said to Warlock. "My back feels like somebody stuck a screwdriver in it."

"Anything to hurry it up. Our pilot's getting a bit antsy."

Together, they pulled Valac the rest of the way out and dropped him to the ground. The asshole's head cracked against it pretty hard, but none of them could muster up much sympathy.

Especially Alex.

After they dragged Valac onto the floatplane, she turned to Warlock and said, "Give me the keys to the Buick."

"What?"

"The keys," she said. "I need the keys."

"Why?" Cooper asked.

She hesitated a moment. "I'm going back to the hotel."

"*What*?"

"You heard me."

"What the hell for?" Deuce said. "We can't be waiting around while you take a joyride."

"Deuce is right," Cooper told her.

"Then go back to Key West without me. It's only a short flight, so give the pilot a few extra bucks after you've landed and send him back for me. I should be done by then."

"Done doing what?"

"Going to the hotel."

Cooper sighed. "Alex, will you quit being so damn cryptic and tell us what you're up to?"

"I'll explain later."

"Why do I doubt that?"

"Why does it matter?" she said. "There's something I need to do. You remember when you told me you're here whenever I need you?"

"Yes."

"Well, right now, I need the keys to the car you rented."

They all stared at her for a long moment, then Cooper said, "Warlock, give her what she wants."

Warlock pulled out the keys and handed them to her, having sense enough not to make any cracks.

She turned to Deuce. "I'll need a room key, too."

He frowned. "I don't know what you're up to, but if you're going back to that hotel right after we almost got our asses shot off, you're gonna need company. I'm going with you."

"No," she told him. "I have to do this alone."

"Alex…"

"I mean it, Deuce. I know you're only trying to protect me, and God knows you had my back tonight, but if you try to tag along, I'll have to hurt you."

Deuce blew out a breath. "You've gotta be the most stubborn woman I've ever met." He dug in his pocket and handed her his room card. "If you somehow manage to get yourself killed, I'm gonna have to track down your ghost and kill you all over again."

"And I'll help him," Cooper said.

"Don't worry. That won't be necessary. This won't take long."

She started for the Buick, but Deuce stopped her. "Wait."

She turned.

"You emptied that pop gun you're carrying, right?"

She nodded.

He brought out his SIG, ejected the magazine, and replaced it with a fresh one. "Take this with you, just in case, and don't tell me no."

She took it from him without protest, crossed to the Buick, and got behind the wheel.

A few seconds later, she was on the road and gone.

FORTY-ONE

THERE WAS NO sign of any hostiles at the hotel. The drama that had unfolded at Pappy Leo's mansion apparently hadn't reached this part of the city yet. And even though Valac's security men knew Alex's face and name, she didn't think she'd be running into them anytime soon.

One way or another, Uncle Eric would see to that.

As she rode the elevator to her floor, the other passengers kept staring at her. It annoyed her at first, until she realized she must look like hell. Her dress was torn, her hair was a mess, and after rolling around on Latham's office floor trying to keep from being killed, she was pretty sure she had rug burns on her face, not to mention Favreau's blood on her clothes.

When she got to her suite and stepped inside, it seemed as if a decade had passed since she'd last been there. She was tired. More tired than she could ever remember.

She looked in the living room and saw Warlock's cart with three abandoned monitors sitting atop it. All other evidence of their planning had been cleared away and destroyed shortly before they'd left for the party.

But Alex didn't want to waste time thinking about that. The job was done, Valac had been caught, and once she was finished here, she could leave this island forever. First, though, she needed to change her clothes, grab what she came for, and get back to the rendezvous point.

She pulled off her dress and dropped it to the floor as she crossed to the bedroom and flicked on the light. She ripped at the Velcro holding the tactical holster to her right thigh and tossed the rig onto the bed, along with her P380 and

Deuce's SIG.

Her underwear was a sweaty mess, so she stepped out of it, too, then looked over at the dresser for the item she'd come to retrieve:

Her hotel key card, or, more accurately, Favreau's counterfeit card that contained the GPS coordinates.

There was only one problem.

It wasn't there.

Alex could have sworn she had tossed it there once she realized it didn't work. She moved to the dresser for a closer look, lifting up one of the hotel's tourist maps and a room service menu, but the key card was nowhere in sight.

She opened the top drawer and rifled though the pairs of shorts Stonewell had sent to her, but still no card.

An uneasy feeling started to grow in her gut. And just as she was convinced she was either crazy or it had been stolen, she saw it lying on the carpet next to the dresser.

She let out a breath, then picked it up and carefully inspected the corners for the tiny nick Favreau had made.

Bingo.

Right where he said it would be.

After stepping into a fresh pair of panties, she took some jeans from the closet and pulled them on, then slipped the card into her right front pocket.

As she started back toward the dresser to find a bra, she heard a sound, spun around, and froze.

Thomas Gérard was standing in the bedroom doorway.

And he was holding a gun.

"What are you doing here, Thomas?"

She didn't bother trying to cover up. There wasn't anything here he hadn't seen before.

"I was wondering the same thing about you," he said. "When I heard you left the rendezvous point, I thought I'd better come here and find out why."

She frowned. "How do you know about that?"

"Your pilot's an associate of mine."

Sudden dread washed over her.

"Oh, not to worry, your friends are safe. I couldn't care less about what happens to Valac. He was always a fringe benefit. I think spending the rest of his life in a supermax prison is probably better than he deserves."

"I don't get it," she said. "What's your angle? Who do you really work for? Because I know it isn't my father."

"You figured that out, did you?"

"With some help."

"Then I take it Eric Hopcroft is still alive?"

"He is," she said.

He looked disappointed. "That's unfortunate, Alex. The man I work for won't be happy to hear that, and he'll probably take it out on me."

"You mean Mr. Gray? Or should I say Richard Munro?"

He spread his hands. "Guilty as charged."

"So all that stuff you told me about my father was complete nonsense, wasn't it?"

"Not all, I don't think. But I had nothing to do with that. I was merely acting as an intermediary."

"Why did Munro want me to kill Hopcroft?"

"To be honest, I don't really know. I don't ask him too many questions. I just cash his checks." He paused. "Let's get back to why you came here."

"Does it matter?"

He shrugged. "Probably not in the scheme of things, but it's a loose end and I don't like loose ends. And I can't think of a good reason why you'd leave your friends to come back."

"Maybe I like the clothes."

He laughed softly and waved the gun at her. "I have to admit I agree. Especially what you're wearing right now."

"Oh, don't spoil it, Thomas. Here you were so smooth and professional and then you go and ruin it with some juvenile remark."

He smirked. "Let me clarify. It's your nice new jeans I admire. When I came in here I noticed that you put something in your pocket. Care to tell me what it was?"

She stiffened slightly.

Did he know about the key cards?

"Well?"

"I'm afraid you're going to be disappointed," she said, then pulled Favreau's card from her pocket and showed it to him. "It's just my room key."

He looked at it for a second and shrugged. "Oh, well. It was worth a try."

Relieved, she stuck the card back into her pocket and said, "Since we're all about curiosity tonight, why don't you answer a question I've had ever since you stepped into that doorway?"

"Which is?"

"Why are you pointing that weapon at me?"

Before he could answer, she dove for the bed. By the time he pulled the trigger, she had Deuce's pistol in her hands.

Gérard fired three quick, wild shots as Alex raised the SIG and returned fire, answering with a larger number—

—*one two three four five*—

—all of which hit him in the chest and stomach and sent him flying backward into the living room, where he hit the floor and went still.

She got to her feet, keeping the SIG in her hand as she walked out to inspect the damage. With relief, she saw that Thomas Gérard—or whoever he was—would never be getting up again.

And then the pain came, spreading through her chest and side like white hot fire.

She looked down at her naked torso and saw blood.

How the hell…?

Gérard's shots, she realized. They hadn't been wild after all. All three had found their mark.

Suddenly the SIG felt very heavy in her hands, and the world around her began to tilt and spin and the fire in her chest grew hotter and hotter as her legs began to buckle and she fell to floor.

She stared up at the lights in the ceiling, which must have

been put on a dimmer, because they were fading, getting darker and darker...

And a moment later she was gone.

FORTY-TWO

IMAGES. FLEETING IMAGES.

And voices, too.

That's what Alex remembered.

Voices she recognized. Shouts. Deuce and Cooper, both frantically calling her name as the images flickered through her mind…some real, some imagined, some dreamed.

Then hands on her body. Rough hands. Men's hands.

And she began to float through the air, taking a magic carpet ride into the darkness, and back into the light.

Then the rough hands were gone, replaced by something smooth, like plastic or latex, and the lights were blinding, making her squint as the burning sensation in her torso sank deeper, seeping its way into her bones…and then the lights again began to fade.

She felt a pressure on her chest and someone shouted, "Clean!" or "Clear!" or maybe it was "Claire!" but she didn't know what that meant or who that might be.

Were they talking to *her*?

Then the darkness came again. A black, empty darkness that seemed to wipe away her pain. Not just the pain in her chest and side, but the pain in her head as well. In her mind. Her heart.

It enveloped her like a mother's loving arms—

—and she felt herself falling into nowhere…

She woke in a bed to find Deuce fast asleep in a nearby chair, and Cooper standing next to a meal tray, pouring himself a glass of water.

Feeling pain in her chest and side, she groaned. Cooper

put the glass down and came to her, taking her hand.

He looked as if he hadn't slept since Christmas.

"Welcome back," he said. "We thought we'd lost you a couple times there."

She blinked and glanced around the room. "A hospital?"

Cooper nodded.

"How did I get here?"

He raised a brow. "Did you really believe Deuce and I would let you go back to that hotel alone? We left Warlock to escort Valac to Key West and had McElroy meet him there with a team."

"I guess it's a good thing you're as stubborn as I am," she said. "When I saw these wounds, I was pretty sure it was over for me." She eyed the room again. "What hospital is this?"

"St. Cajetan General, believe it or not."

She tried to sit up. "What?"

"It's okay," he said, and gently urged her back down. "You're here courtesy of Pappy Leo himself. All expenses paid."

"You're kidding me."

"The police are saying you were attacked in your hotel by a stalker. Some guy you'd met in a Key Largo bar who became obsessed with you and followed you to St. Cajetan. They couldn't find any identification on him, so they're still trying to work that out, but you've been cleared for shooting him. They figure it was well deserved."

"At least they got that part right. But why would Leonard Latham care about me?"

"After we left his estate, Hopcroft gathered the rest of Valac's troops and fled. Latham played it all off as a band of thugs looking to rob his guests. There were a few people wounded, but fortunately none of the partygoers were killed."

"Unbelievable."

Cooper shrugged. "Works out for everyone, the way I see it. When he was briefed by Stonewell, Latham told them that

Valac had barged into his life seven months ago and was slowly draining his funds. He was a virtual prisoner in that house, while everyone chalked it up to his eccentricity. The way he sees it, you're one of the people who helped give him back his freedom."

"Well, good for me."

Cooper smiled. "McElroy and his bosses are very happy about the Valac acquisition. We told them your theory about Favreau's head for numbers, and everyone agrees that the codes must have died with him. At least that's what they want to believe."

Suddenly remembering, Alex sat up again. "Shit. Where are my jeans?"

"What?"

"My jeans? Where are my jeans?"

"In a bag under your bed, I think. Why?"

"Get them for me."

Her gave her a funny look, then bent down and retrieved the bag. She pulled it open and reached inside, squeezing the pockets of her bloodstained jeans until she felt the stiff plastic of Favreau's key card. Then she fell back against the pillows and let out a long breath.

He looked at her. "Is that what I think it is?"

She nodded, deciding it was about time she was honest with him. "I know it was the main focus of the op, but I don't want to give it McElroy. And I don't want you telling him about it, either." She gestured. "Or Warlock, or even Deuce."

He didn't even think about it. "Your secret's safe with me," he said. "All of them are, if you ever decide you want to share."

"Thank you, Shane. It's just that Hopcroft told me what's on this thing, and I don't think McElroy or anyone else at Stonewell can be trusted with the information. I'm not sure if I should destroy it, or hang on to it for a rainy day. Use it for leverage."

"It rains a lot in our world."

She offered him a wan smile. "I don't deserve you."
Then she squeezed his hand.

FORTY-THREE

MR. GRAY LIVED in a very tidy brownstone apartment in Georgetown.

Every evening at six o'clock, his wife of thirty years greeted him when he came home from work, and brought him a glass of Pinot and the day's mail.

Two days after the operation in the Bahamas was completed, although not quite to Mr. Gray's satisfaction, he found a postcard waiting for him.

The photo on the front was an oversaturated shot of the St. Cajetan hotel, with all those ridiculous old cars parked in front of it.

Curious.

When Gray turned the card over and saw there was no stamp or mailing address, he frowned.

Had this been dropped directly into their box?

As his gaze drifted to the handwriting that formed the short message, a small chill ran through him.

He knew that handwriting.

No one else made Ss like that.

And if there was any doubt, the initials at the end of the note made the identity of the sender quite clear.

The message itself was innocuous, but the implied threat was evident to Mr. Gray. He knew that from here on out, he would have to stagger his routine. Not be so predictable. Because you never knew who might be watching...

The card said:

> *Sorry I missed you.*
>
> *EH*

EPILOGUE

Key Largo, Florida

ALEX SPENT THE bulk of her recovery at the Shimmy Shack.

Cooper and Deuce joined her there for a few days and helped her clean up the place, and as they worked, she decided she must have been possessed by demons when she had agreed to sell it. Spruced up, the place was a gem, and most of her memories here were good ones.

Thank God, the agreement had turned out to be bogus.

Cooper brought Danny out for a week, and they spent a lot of time laughing and making new memories. She could tell that Cooper was starting to get very comfortable being around her during the off hours, and she knew what he wanted from her. But she wasn't ready to go there yet.

Wasn't sure she ever would be.

One night, when she was alone and had fallen asleep on the front sofa, she was awakened by a noise coming from the back of the house. She reached for her pistol and carefully worked her way toward the den, noting that the patio door, which she had closed, was now ajar.

She stepped into the room and froze. There, on the floor, was the sleeping bag she had tossed over the rail when she had first returned to Key Largo. She had forgotten all about it.

Angry now, she stepped over the bag and slipped out onto the patio. Once she was sure no one was lurking there, she looked over the rail into the moonlit darkness but saw no sign of anyone. Heard only the gentle lapping of the water below.

Intending to toss the bag over the side again, she marched back into the house, snatched it up, and something fluttered out from inside it and landed on the floor.

Another photograph.

Alex's skin prickled as she picked up the photo and stared at it. It was a shot from the same era as the wedding video, her mother standing near the steps of a mosque.

And it was clear by the bump in her belly that she was pregnant.

Pregnant.

Alex turned the photo over, saw another Google link, and her heart started to pound.

She ran to her bedroom and grabbed her tablet, then dropped to the bed and typed in the URL.

The file waiting for her was called *FEP.mp4*.

Her father's initials.

Her heart really pounding now, she clicked the download button, entered the same passcode she had used for the wedding video, and waited as the file was retrieved.

After tapping the link, she watched as the screen filled with the face of her father, and she couldn't quite believe it.

But it was him.

It was really him.

He was sitting in a dark room, only the light of a laptop screen illuminating him. He looked so much older than she remembered. Tired. Worn. But with eyes that had that same fire she had known as a child.

He said, "Hello, Alex. I know this has been a long time coming—*too* long—and I know what you must think of me and the way I left things with you and Danny. If I could have done it any other way, believe me, I would have."

Alex couldn't hold back. Tears were already streaming down her cheeks.

"But now that you're involved with some of the very people who forced me to run—people I believe are responsible for Mitra's death—I think it's time I answered some of the questions I know you must have."

He paused, his gaze focusing on nothing for a moment, as if lost in a very distant past.

Then he looked at her and said, "I think it's time I told you the truth about what happened to your mother."

Alexandra Poe Will Be Back

ACKNOWLEDGEMENTS

The authors would like to thank Elyse Dinh for her copy-editing prowess, and Pam Stack of *Authors on the Air* for sharing her detailed knowledge of the Florida Keys.

Thanks also go out to our families and friends for their continued support.

ABOUT THE AUTHORS

BRETT BATTLES

Brett Battles is the author of over sixteen novels and several short stories. His first novel, *The Cleaner*, was nominated for a Barry Award for Best Thriller, and a Shamus Award for Best Debut Novel. His second, *The Deceived*, won the Barry Award for Best Thriller.

He is one of the founding members of Killer Year, and a member of International Thriller Writers and Mystery Writers of America. He lives and writes in Los Angeles.

More info available at: brettbattles.com

ROBERT GREGORY BROWNE

Robert Gregory Browne is an AMPAS Nicholl Fellowship-winning screenwriter and ITW Thriller Award-nominated novelist.

He has written several thrillers published in the US and around the world, including the Amazon bestsellers *Trial Junkies, Trial Junkies 2: Negligence* and *Kiss her Goodbye*.

Rob lives in California with his wife, dog, two cats, and his beloved moka pot.

More info available at: robertgregorybrowne.com

Made in the USA
Las Vegas, NV
15 October 2024

96895964R00166